3.00

Welcome to Lightning Creek Ranch, nestled in the foothills of Montana's majestic Bitterroot Mountains, home to the strong-willed Brody family. Life isn't always easy on the Lightning Creek, but challenges are nothing new to the men and women who live and work here.

And there's something about the ranch, something in the beauty and solitude that works a kind of magic on those in need of a second shot at life...

Dear Reader,

I just love a good enemies-to-lovers story, so when I wrote the second book of The Brodys of Lightning Creek, I decided to have Jolie Brody meet up with Dylan Culver, a guy she drove crazy in high school—and not in a good way. Jolie is the youngest of the four Brody sisters and the most carefree, but beneath her easygoing exterior she is dealing with issues stemming from her father's untimely death—issues she doesn't fully acknowledge until she starts to fall for Dylan.

When police officer Dylan Culver returns to Montana to run the family ranch supply store while he heals from a duty-related accident, he is stunned to find his former nemesis, Jolie Brody, managing the store. He's even more stunned to find himself attracted to her. Jolie soon makes it clear that she will never ever get involved with someone who has a dangerous job, and that's a problem, because Dylan loves his job and he just might be falling in love with Jolie, too.

I hope you enjoy reading *To Kiss a Cowgirl*. I certainly enjoyed writing it. For more information about my books, including more The Brodys of Lightning Creek reads, please check out my website, www.jeanniewatt.com.

Happy reading!

Jeannie Watt

JEANNIE WATT

To Kiss a Cowgirl

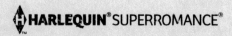

HARLEQUIN® SUPERROMANCE®

Recycling programs
for this product may
not exist in your area.

ISBN-13: 978-0-373-60937-6

To Kiss a Cowgirl

Copyright © 2015 by Jeannie Steinman

Printed in U.S.A.

Jeannie Watt lives in the heart of rural Nevada in a historic ranching community. When she's not at the computer writing, she collects and sews vintage clothing patterns and makes mosaic mirrors. Every now and again she and her husband slip away to San Francisco to run a 10K and soak up the city, but for the most part she enjoys living in her quiet desert setting, thinking up new ways to torture her characters before they reach their happily-ever-after.

Books by Jeannie Watt

HARLEQUIN SUPERROMANCE

The Brodys of Lightning Creek

To Tempt a Cowgirl

The Montana Way

Once a Champion
Cowgirl in High Heels
All for a Cowboy

Too Many Cooks?

The Baby Truce
Undercover Cook
Just Desserts

A Difficult Woman
The Horseman's Secret
The Brother Returns
Cop On Loan
A Cowboy's Redemption
Cowboy Comes Back
Always a Temp
Once and for All
Maddie Inherits a Cowboy
Crossing Nevada

Visit the Author Profile page
at Harlequin.com for more titles.

CHAPTER ONE

DYLAN CULVER MANEUVERED his beat-up Chevy truck between the stacks of hay and straw behind the family feed store and parked in his old spot next to the grain shed. He'd never in a million years thought he'd be back in Montana, back at the store. Back at the place his dad had worked so hard to keep him away from.

At least it was temporary. Four months until his cousin Finn returned from his National Guard deployment. Four months to focus on something other than the aftermath of his failed marriage or the accident that had put him on desk duty. By the time Finn took over the reins again, Dylan would be fully healed and ready to get the hell out of Dodge.

Okay…he was ready now, but he'd promised Finn he'd take care of Mike, their grandfather, and the store and that was exactly what he was going to do. The unsettled business he'd left in Washington State could wait.

Grabbing his granddad's dented metal lunch pail from the seat beside him, he opened the door and stepped out into the driving rain. Unlike the grain shed siding, which was now flapping in the wind, the tarps covering the hay seemed to be secure. Good, because he couldn't afford having hay returned due to mold.

In fact, after looking over the profit-and-loss sheets Finn had left with Mike, he was glad he'd become used to living frugally over the past couple months. Not that Finn hadn't done a decent job running the place, but with two chain ranch stores opening up within easy driving distance, they'd lost clientele—and employees. Their long-time cashier had left to go to work for Western World, and their bookkeeper had recently retired. Now with Finn deployed and his grandfather recovering from hip surgery and about to move into a smaller house, Dylan and the new bookkeeper had some challenges ahead of them.

Bowing his head against the rain, he started to jog as he rounded the corner to the main entrance, gritting his teeth against the residual pain in his injured leg. The lights were on inside the old building but the door held fast when he pulled on the handle. He reached into his pocket for his keys, but the door swung open before his fingers touched metal. "Thanks," he said, stepping inside and shaking the rain off before glancing at the woman who stood there.

"Jolie?" He had the odd sensation of his blood

freezing. Perhaps one of the warning signs of a heart attack?

"Hi, Dylan." Her voice was still husky, her hair still long and reddish blond, her eyes the greenest he'd ever seen. "Long time."

Not long enough.

When Finn had said he'd hired an assistant to help with the store, Dylan had somehow assumed he'd hired someone Dylan could work with. Well, now he knew why his cousin had been shifty about the new hire. What in the hell had Finn been thinking? And, yes, he definitely felt a strong squeezing sensation in the middle of his chest.

"You're dripping," Jolie said, interrupting his heart attack.

Dylan glanced down. There was water falling from the brim of his ball cap onto the floor near his boots. He pulled off the hat, gave it a shake. When he looked up, she was regarding him with an ironic half smile.

"You didn't know I worked for you, did you?"

"No." Dylan moved forward to set the lunch pail on the counter, trying not to notice that she looked even better than she had back in high school when she'd made his life miserable by not taking anything seriously. That wouldn't have bothered him if she hadn't been his chemistry partner for the year and if he hadn't needed a strong A to sew up some much-needed scholarships.

"I moved back to the Lightning Creek about six weeks ago." She leaned an elbow on the tall counter next to him, looking relaxed, as she always had during situations that'd sent his blood pressure skyrocketing. After nearly a decade of being a patrol cop, his blood pressure rarely triggered anymore…except, obviously, when he discovered that his nemesis was his employee. "This was the only job I could get close to home," she continued.

He noticed that while she'd sounded cool and confident, she was watching him carefully.

"Imagine that," Dylan said.

"It isn't because I'm unemployable," she said smoothly. "It's because it's the end of winter and no one is hiring."

"Except Finn." Bless his black heart.

"I might have reeled in a favor," Jolie said, and even though she spoke matter-of-factly, Dylan didn't want to know what kind of favor. "I needed the job and, frankly, I think this place needs someone like me."

"This place needs you?" She looked about as out of place there—with her form-fitting, blinged-out white shirt tied at the waist and short denim skirt—as a rosebush in a hay field. Easy on the eyes, but somehow didn't belong.

"Look at it," Jolie said, making a sweeping gesture. "Dark, depressing." She ran a finger over the counter next to her. "Dusty."

"It's a feed and seed store," he said as if she were dense, which he knew she wasn't.

"A depressing feed store. Why would anyone come here—"

"To buy feed?"

"—when they could go to a more modern place and get the same thing and a whole lot more?"

"Because we're a local institution."

"That would be the only reason as far as I can see. Your prices are barely competitive."

"Well, maybe if you took a job elsewhere you wouldn't have to be stuck in this dark, depressing..." He paused, trying to recall the third D she'd mentioned in her unsolicited critique.

"Dusty," she supplied. "And at the moment, I don't want a job elsewhere."

"Why not? Surely your talents could be better used in a less dusty environment."

"The employee discount. I buy a lot of feed."

"*And* you can't get a job anywhere else?"

"I could if I wanted to travel. I don't." She sauntered a step closer, her full lips curving into a half smile that didn't reach her eyes. "I can get something else when the market opens up. I have experience." She said the word in a way that sent his imagination shooting into areas it probably shouldn't travel, even if that hadn't been her intention. He yanked it back to where it was supposed to be. When had he ever reacted like that to Jolie Brody?

"However, the market is tight. I now have a job close to home and I'm sticking with it." Her smile became a touch warmer. "I promised Finn."

He and Finn were going to have a talk as soon as he could get him on the phone.

The bell rang over the front door and Morley Ames walked in, kind of. The old guy, a close friend of his grandfather's, was stooped over and skinnier than the last time he'd seen him, but his voice was just as booming as ever as he hailed Dylan.

Jolie smiled at Dylan and went behind the counter where she'd apparently been cleaning, since she quickly moved a bottle of spray cleaner out of sight.

"Morley," Dylan said, moving forward to shake the man's hand. "Good to see you."

"So it's true—you've given up law enforcement and moved home. I didn't believe it when Gina told me at the café."

"I'm just on leave," Dylan said, noting that Jolie gave him a quick, curious glance before settling herself in front of the computer. "I thought I'd come here to escape all the rain," he said with a smile, indicating the puddle that was forming around Morley's feet as water dripped off his black hat and raincoat.

The old man looked up at him with an appreciative smile. "We all need a change sometimes," he said.

"Can I help you with something?" Dylan asked before Morley launched into personal questions he'd have to deflect.

Morley pulled a piece of paper out of his pocket and unfolded it, squinting through his fogged glasses as he read, "Hen scratch. Rolled oats—two bags. Salt block—"

"Do you want minerals in that?" Jolie asked as she came to stand next to the old man, cocking her head to see his list. He beamed and handed it to her. She took it gently and squinted a little herself at the light-penciled script on the sheet of pale blue paper. "Lillian wrote this, didn't she?"

"Woman can't put pressure on a pencil," Morley muttered. "Arthritis."

"I have something for her," Jolie said. "A special cream that just came in. I'll see if I can find a sample while Dylan loads your truck." She handed Dylan the paper.

Way to give orders, Jolie.

Dylan frowned as he took the list, suddenly understanding why they were both squinting. It was as if Morley's wife had written in faint code. "Do you need this to write the ticket?" he asked Jolie, hoping she would decode it for him.

"Nope. I got it. Hen scratch, twenty-five pounds. Two fifty-pound bags of rolled oats. One salt block—"

"No minerals," Morley added.

"No minerals," she repeated with a smile. "Three ivermectin, bag balm and a fly spray." Jolie reached out to gently take Morley's hand in hers, examining it. "Are you using bag balm for your hands?"

"Yeah." Chapped and cracked hands were a mainstay of ranching life, particularly in winter. The ointment used to heal milk cows' chapped utters was the go-to remedy.

"It works," Jolie said. "But I have something else you could try…if you wanted."

"Will it make me smell like a whorehouse?"

"Unscented," Jolie said. "And it doesn't stay greasy like bag balm, so the hay and dirt won't stick to your hands."

"Throw it in. Maybe Lillian will like it."

Dylan loaded the truck and then came back inside the store as Morley drove away. "Are you in some kind of hand cream business?"

"What if I am?"

"I guess my question is more along the lines of should you be hawking your wares in my store?"

"I'm not selling the stuff," Jolie said. "I gave him samples."

"Am I selling the stuff?"

"You could be."

"I don't think so."

Jolie gave him a long look and he had the impression that he'd reacted exactly as she'd expected him to.

"If you diversify a little, or try some new sales gimmicks, you might bring in more customers."

"Our customers come here to buy feed, and I'm not into gimmicks." Thinking that he needed to get out of there, Dylan grabbed his lunch pail and headed for his cousin's—now his—private office. His father, uncle and grandfather had always subscribed to the theory that you stocked what the majority of your customers needed. Money spent on inventory that took forever to sell was money that could be in the bank, drawing interest. He may not have anticipated a future in business, but he did recall that particular facet of the sales game being discussed often and at length as the brothers debated what merchandise to carry beyond feed and seed.

Mike had even repeated his business theory a few times that morning before Dylan left for work, as if Dylan were going to start ordering useless items as soon as he got close to a computer.

He closed the door and stood for a moment, shoving thoughts of Jolie aside as he took in the familiar cluttered space that was now his center of operations. The desk was clean and the computer was almost new, but the counter and the top of the file cabinet were stacked high with old catalogs and an assortment of junk, as they had always been.

Piles had also accumulated along the wall under the old calendar, which featured a woman in Daisy Duke shorts kneeling on a tractor seat while holding a big wrench and wearing a come-hither smile. It'd been there for as long as Dylan could remember. As a boy, he'd been perplexed by the idea of a scantily clad woman kneeling on the tractor. Every woman he'd ever seen on a tractor had worn jeans and a T-shirt and sat in the seat so that she could drive the thing. And what was with the wrench?

He smiled a little as he put the lunch pail down next to the desk, remembering when he'd come to appreciate those Daisy Dukes and realized that the woman had no interest in plowing fields. He'd barely booted up the computer when the old-fashioned intercom buzzed and Jolie said, "Could you load up this customer?"

He went out into the rain to squeeze three bags of grain into the rear of a Subaru Forester, then decided to shift a pallet of grain for easier access. A few minutes later he came back into the store, shaking water off his hair, his leg giving a little as he turned to close the door.

"Who usually loads?" he asked Jolie, who glanced up from her computer screen.

"Finn."

"Who loaded customers during the past week?" The transition time between his arrival and Finn's departure. He knew it wasn't his grandfather, who'd had a hip replacement a month ago.

"I did."

"Was the forklift having problems?"

"The engine has been missing, and I had a hard time starting it." She tilted her head. "Why?"

"It won't start at all now."

"I had a feeling this day was coming." She reached for the phone. "Do you want me to call Bobeck's? See if they can send someone over to take a look?"

"I'll do it." It'd been a while since he'd ripped into an engine, but it'd be cheaper than paying Bobeck's mechanics rate. He took a few steps toward the counter and Jolie frowned.

"Did you hurt yourself?"

He'd figured the question would come up since his limp was still noticeable when his leg got tired and he'd made the mistake of overdoing his physical therapy that morning. "Banged up my leg in an accident."

Go ahead, Jolie. Ask what kind of accident. She'd always been brimming with questions about his personal life and comments about his lack of social life. But this time she said only, "Nothing permanent, I hope."

"No. It's almost healed." In a few weeks' time

he'd head back to his doctor in Lanesburg, Washington, to get the release he needed to go back to work once Finn returned home, which was why he'd overdone his PT. He had to get that release to continue his career.

"So you can still load the feed? Because if not I'll do it."

"I'm capable." And, besides, there was no way he was going to stand back and let Jolie do it.

"The offer stands," Jolie said, running her gaze over him as if assessing his capabilities.

She was enjoying this. He told himself to walk away, to let it be for now, but instead he said, "We need to talk about working together."

She looked surprised. "In what way? You're the boss, and I'm the employee."

Her matter of fact words felt like a trap.

"In the way that this is not going to be a replay of chem class." She had never understood how important it had been for him to do well in that class, in all his classes. To get those scholarships for his dad, even though it hadn't really mattered in the long run. His dad had passed away before he'd completed his schooling and he'd ended up being a patrol cop instead of a forensic specialist.

She stared at him for a long moment. "That's kind of insulting."

He flattened both palms on the counter in front of him. "I just want us to understand each other."

"Then understand that I'm insulted."

"That wasn't my intention."

"What *was* your intention?"

He felt his blood pressure ratchet up again. It was like a Pavlovian response when she was around—one that he hadn't felt in…oh, ten years. "My intention was to point out that this is not chem class."

"You're repeating yourself, so I'll repeat myself. I'm insulted." Jolie rose to her feet and walked out from behind the counter to take a stance in front of him, arms folded over her chest.

"When I took this job, the last thing I expected was for you to take over, but I can live with it. Finn hired me because I'm good with people and I can keep books. It isn't like it was a mercy hiring." She curled her lips slightly. "And I'm well aware it's not chemistry class…although if you think about it, it's not that much different—you being the supreme boss and me expected to do whatever you say." She pushed her reddish-blond braid over her shoulder with a quick flip of her fingers. "Now, if there's nothing else, I have work to do."

"No," Dylan said, realizing that he'd just been dismissed in his own store. "No. Nothing for now."

ONCE THE OFFICE door closed behind Dylan, Jolie planted an elbow next to the keyboard on the crowded desk and lowered her forehead into her palm. Dylan was not the only one who didn't want

to relive chem class, but damned if she was going
to tell him that.

When Finn had gotten the call to duty a few
weeks ago, he'd said nothing about Dylan coming
back. He'd sat on that bit of news until the day before he'd left; springing it on her at the going-away
lunch they'd shared with his grandfather. She'd assured him it didn't matter; told herself it didn't
matter. But it did.

How could it not, when Dylan was still holding
on to a ten-year-old grudge? As if it had all been
her fault. From day one, he'd made it clear that she
couldn't do anything right, so she'd simply quit trying and, toward the end, she'd moved into sabo-
tage...just a little. Enough to make him scramble
and to piss him off. A girl could only take being
made to feel stupid for so long.

She'd gotten a C in the class. Dylan had gotten
an A- and had acted as though the world had ended.
Her friends had loved watching the interplay between them and had deemed him hot, because who
wouldn't be intrigued by an ultraserious, totally
gorgeous guy?

His put-upon lab partner, that's who. Wasn't intrigued then; wasn't intrigued now.

Just...insulted.

Jolie stretched the kinks out of her back and
went to stand at the window to look out over the
empty parking lot. Finn hadn't been big on change

and obviously Dylan was even less so—especially if the suggestions for change came from her. Not that she had any huge ideas, but if someone asked her to come up with suggestions, she'd put her mind to it. Regardless of what the stubborn Culver men believed, they *could* have more customers, if customers had more reasons to come to the place except for feed and seed. Flowers, trees, hand cream. Anything.

Oh, crap. She whirled to face the closed office door. *The box.*

She was halfway to the door, ready to knock and ask for it, when it swung open. Jolie knew it was too late. Way too late.

Dylan walked out carrying the box, an expression on his face that would have made her laugh under any other circumstance. He placed the box on the counter and stepped back, nodding at it.

"Yours?"

Jolie peeked inside, even though she knew exactly what was in it—garter belts, skimpy bikini panties, get-the-girls-up-there bras, lacy stockings. "Yes."

"And this stuff is in my office why?"

"I needed a temporary place to store it between parties. I'm a distributer." Or rather, she had been. She'd quit a few weeks ago when she'd gone to work part-time at McElroy's. There were only so many things a person could work into a schedule…

Besides, she'd discovered that in a small community, one could only sell so much lingerie. Missoula and Idaho Falls had been much better markets. "I had a couple back-to-back parties."

"Please don't tell me the parties are one of your ideas to bring in new clients."

"It would work."

"I'll take that as a no." He pushed the box a few inches toward her. "Maybe you could store this at your own place."

She took the box and placed it under the counter. "Will do," she said on a sigh.

He gave her an unsmiling look and headed back to his office, his shoulders held even more stiffly than when they'd been in school. Maybe it was due to his profession. He'd never gone on to solve crimes in a lab or whatever it was he'd planned to do with all that chemistry knowledge, but he had become a cop. And that was all she needed to make her life complete—Dylan Culver with an even bigger authority complex.

The office door remained firmly closed until the clock ticked past 5:30 p.m. At that point, Dylan was no longer her boss, so Jolie turned off her computer, put on her raincoat, grabbed her box of lingerie samples and left the building without saying goodbye. Unprofessional? She had no idea. She didn't want to tap on that office door and appear to be asking permission to leave.

Her sister Dani was practically climbing the walls by the time she got home.

"I'm losing training time with all this rain," she said as she emerged from the kitchen wearing a cherry-print apron. When her fiancé traveled, she ate all her meals with Jolie. "I need my arena. Damned surveyor."

She and her fiancé and Jolie had each put up one third of the money for the training facility, but the company that was supposed to set up the canvas-covered training arena had yet to have the area surveyed and leveled. Until they did, there was no covered arena and thus no training during inclement weather.

"But we're growing hay as we speak," Jolie reminded her. She felt like doing a little happy dance. If this continued, there'd be meadow hay in the barn for the first time in years. One item checked off the very long list she'd made in a loose-leaf notebook. When the last item was checked off, Lightning Creek would once again be a bona fide working ranch. Her working ranch...well, hers and her sister's, but she'd be the one living there, managing it once Dani got married next summer.

"I'll give you that," Dani agreed as she returned to the kitchen while Jolie hung her damp coat on a hook near the front door. "But my arena should have been up by now and it's ticking me off. And it's not doing your practice schedule any good."

Jolie's barrel racing season started in a matter of weeks at the Glennan Memorial Day Rodeo and she and her mare still had some serious work to do to get up to speed. Unfortunately, the soggy conditions made practicing in the outdoor arena impossible, which in turn made it difficult to reestablish herself as a barrel racing contender—which she needed to do if she hoped to eventually establish a business.

She'd moved back to Lightning Creek Ranch with the idea of conducting barrel racing clinics while her sister continued to develop her successful horse training business. Between the two of them, they'd figured they could keep the ranch afloat and make enough to live comfortably—as long as one of them, aka Jolie, worked a steady job to help pay the land taxes and other incidental expenses.

But once she'd moved home, Jolie had found that she hated seeing the ranch lie fallow. All five cows had been bred the previous spring and all had successfully calved. But the fields were a wreck, the buildings needed re-roofing and the irrigation system needed revamping.

The ranch was in even worse shape than it had been during her teen years when it had slowly been slipping away from them as hay and cattle prices tanked. They'd hung on until the prices rebounded, but only by cutting back to bare bones while their mother worked at a full-time job.

So one late night, over a bottle of wine—or had it been two?—Jolie and Dani had come to an agreement. They would put the Lightning Creek right again. It wouldn't be a big operation, but they would increase the herd, lease out the fields, mow and bale the meadow hay instead of letting it go to waste. With careful management, they should be able to glean enough profit for Jolie to quit her job in a couple of years and until then they'd build the training business.

That had been the plan, anyway. Then Dani had become engaged to Gabe Matthews, the landscape architect who lived in the mansion next door. Even though Dani still used the ranch as her base of operations, revitalizing the Lightning Creek had become more Jolie's project.

Jolie had no problem with that. Finally she could put a bit of her animal science degree to work in a meaningful way instead of preg-checking cattle on a mega ranch. She also didn't mind being the decision-maker. As the youngest of four, she'd been bossed around more than the average kid, and enough was enough.

And speaking of being bossed around...

"Guess who my new supervisor is?" Jolie said, following her sister into the kitchen. At the stove, she sipped a little sauce off a teaspoon and reached for the salt.

"Mike?"

"Still laid up from his hip surgery. No. It's Dylan."

Dani turned back from where she was taking plates out of the cupboard. "Dylan?" Her mouth twitched.

"It's not funny, Dan."

"Is he as hot as ever?"

"I never found him hot."

"Liar."

"I could appreciate his attractiveness but it's difficult to classify someone who is ordering you around and generally pissing you off as *hot*."

Dani shrugged. "Hot is hot."

Jolie rolled her eyes and went for the wine-glasses. Pasta cried out for wine. So did her rather trying day.

Dani waited until they were seated with the bowl of pasta between them before she said, "I assume you'll be able to work together?"

"I have little choice. I like my job and once Finn gets back it'll be back to normal. All I have to do is hang on until then."

"You'll play nice with Dylan?"

Jolie smiled with mock sweetness. "Of course, Dani. He's my employer."

CHAPTER TWO

DYLAN CLOSED HIS laptop and pushed it aside. Finn wasn't answering his emails. It was probable that he wasn't available to answer, given his circumstances, or he might not be opening the mail from his cousin, knowing full well that said cousin had a few choice things to say about the help Finn had hired.

Dylan reached for the bottle on the sideboard next to Mike's kitchen table—his makeshift desk—and poured a shot of bourbon. The deed was done and now he had to live with it.

He lifted his glass in a salute to his absent cousin. "Up yours, Finn."

He sipped and leaned back in his chair. Hell, this might all be for the best. Having Jolie around could distract him from the other issues in his life. The box of lingerie had definitely distracted him. Steamy images of Jolie in a garter belt didn't mesh well with him trying to keep her on task in the store.

Was she still as easily sidetracked as she'd been a decade ago? Did she still head off on those wild tangents when she was supposed to be focused on the matter at hand? Her flippant attitude indicated a possible yes to those questions.

All he needed was to have to do two jobs instead of one. But again, maybe being that busy would keep him from fixating on getting the doctor's release he needed to go back on patrol and stop riding the desk. Law enforcement might not have been the career he and his father had plotted for him, but he loved it.

He didn't know if he could handle a desk job for the rest of his career—not unless he was wearing a detective's badge while doing so. He was scheduled to sit for the exam in a matter of weeks, but it was a crap shoot. He knew better guys than him that had failed it the first go, so he needed a contingency plan to ensure he didn't end up in Logistics until he did pass the exam. And that plan involved getting a doctor's release and going out on patrol.

"Hey, Dylan?" His grandfather's gravelly voice came from the back bedroom where he was sorting through belongings in preparation for his move to a smaller, more manageable house on the edge of town, closer to the store.

"Yeah?" Dylan pushed his chair back and got to his feet, putting the bottle on the sideboard before heading down the hall.

Mike was standing between two cardboard boxes

with neatly folded tops. "Can you haul these out to the living room so I have room to maneuver?"

"You bet." Dylan knew it killed Mike to have to ask for help, but at least he was asking. His recovery from the hip replacement had taken longer than expected because he'd tried to do too much too soon. Apparently he'd learned a lesson.

"Marjorie can't take the goats."

Dylan stopped in the doorway. "That's too bad."

"Yeah." Mike shook his head. "I don't want Maisy and Daisy to become *cabrito* dinner, but I have to be realistic here."

"I'll find them homes," Dylan promised before heading out to the living room with the first box. By the time he got back, Mike had the second box on the bed.

"This one goes to donation."

"Got it."

Mike nodded and turned back to the closet. He pulled out a garment bag; the one that Dylan knew held his father's wool WWII uniform. "Can't let that go," Dylan said.

"Don't have a lot of room in the smaller place." Mike had been all for moving. Taking care of his menagerie had become too much for him when his hips had started to go, and a house with two stories had been difficult to navigate. Unfortunately, moving to a one-story house meant parting with some of the stuff he'd hung on to for most of his life.

"We'll find room." Mike had been close to his own dad, just as Dylan had been close to his. He couldn't imagine letting go of the few keepsakes he had and didn't want Mike to have to do that, either.

"You know," Mike said, "I've had about enough of packing. Damned depressing business."

Dylan wasn't going to argue. He'd packed everything he'd owned almost exactly a year ago and moved out of his house. His marriage was over, but he still owned half a house he didn't live in—or he would until it sold. Every month he sent his payment to the bank and every month he contacted the real-estate agent to make certain she was doing her best to move the place. Not that he didn't trust Lindsey…but he didn't trust Lindsey. Not since she'd cheated on him, anyway.

"I just poured a shot," he said to his grandfather. "You want one?"

"In the worst way." Mike jerked his head toward the door. "Come on. I'll beat you in a game of cribbage."

ON HIS SECOND day of work Dylan arrived at the store just after 7:00 a.m., hoping he could figure out what the problem was with the forklift. He stopped inside the doorway and snapped on the lights.

A bulb popped and went out, leaving the place even dimmer than before.

He hated to admit it, but Jolie had a point about the store being dark and depressing.

He traced a finger over the nearest surface, very much as she had done the day before. It was dusty, too. Mike had hired a cheap fly-by-night janitorial service that came in once a week according to Finn. He'd have a talk with the owner the next time he had a few minutes, which, given the volume of customers they'd had the day before, would probably be right after he got the forklift running.

In the meantime…the light.

He set down his lunch pail and went into the supply closet. There were plenty of replacement lightbulbs but no ladder. He could go out to the warehouse and grab the big ladder there, which was covered with grain dust, or he could stand on top of the sturdy wooden shelves his grandfather had built. An elephant could dance on those shelves and they wouldn't budge, so that option seemed reasonable—and a lot easier than dragging the ladder in through the rain.

Lightbulb in hand, he pulled a chair to the shelves and stood on it to push aside the boxes of horseshoe nails, raising a cloud of dust. Yes, he'd talk to the janitors. Today.

He stepped from the chair onto the shelving, searching for a handhold on the top shelf. He took hold of the narrow metal electrical conduit running up the wall and eased himself up, getting a knee onto the second-to-the-top shelf. He could just reach the light fixture from—

His knee slipped and he barely missed clipping his chin as his feet once again hit the chair, which toppled sideways. Wildly, he clutched for something, anything, and then hit the ground next to the chair as horseshoe nails rained down on him.

Shit.

For a moment Dylan sat staring up at the light fixture, the base of the broken bulb held in one hand. At least Jolie hadn't been there to share the moment, although he wouldn't have tried something that stupid if she'd been there to witness it. No, he'd have made the trip to the warehouse and hauled in the dirty ladder.

He pushed himself to his feet, grimacing at the pain that shot through his hip. Gingerly he flexed his bad leg, glad that he hadn't injured it further. He could only imagine the humiliation of having Jolie find him lying on the floor with a compound fracture or something. As it was, he was bruised but not broken, and he had time to clean up the evidence before anyone got there.

Or in theory he should have had time. He'd just retrieved a broom and dustpan when he heard the very unwelcome sound of the key sliding into the front lock. A few seconds later the door opened, the bell jingled and Jolie stopped dead in her tracks just inside the doorway. Slowly her green eyes moved up from the sea of nails to his face.

"I don't want to talk about it," he said gruffly, shoving aside an empty nail box with his boot.

"Oh, but I do," she said.

She pointed from the broken bulb he'd set on the shelving unit to the burned-out light above him. "Did we break some safety rules?"

"Enough," Dylan said in a clipped tone as he started to sweep nails. Flat nails didn't sweep well.

"After all the grief you gave me about following rules? Enough?" She walked forward, stopping a few feet from him. "Wear your goggles, put on your apron, no elbows on the table."

"I didn't want to lose points for stupid stuff," he said, finally bending to brush the nails into the dustpan with his hand.

"You were crazed."

"I had to do the work of two."

"No. You never gave me a chance."

"You were never serious enough to focus."

Her jaw shifted sideways. "Maybe I acted like that because of the way you treated me."

"Well, that was a crappy thing to do."

"So was treating me like I was stupid," she said, turning and walking around the counter to start up her computer.

"If it walks like a duck…"

"This duck was never given a chance."

"The duck never stopped quacking. And, for the record, I never thought you were stupid."

He glanced over in time to see Jolie's chin come up in an expression that he knew well—in fact, it surprised him how well he remembered.

"I can barely see in here," she said, surprising him by changing the subject instead of launching into an argument. "Do you think you can change that lightbulb without killing yourself?"

He didn't answer as he scooped nails out from under the shelving unit. A second later feet in metallic sandals that showcased intricately painted toenails came into view. He looked up as she dropped a box to the floor.

"For your nails." She cocked her head. "I hope you didn't reinjure your leg."

"No."

"Thank goodness for small blessings, eh?" She turned and walked away.

"Hey," he said, stopping her. "Shouldn't you be wearing shoes with toes?"

"Really?" she asked flatly. "You're going to go there?"

"I get the irony," he said, gesturing to the mess he'd made by breaking the rules himself.

"Worried I'd file a workman's comp claim?"

"Maybe I just don't want you to get hurt."

"Maybe I could wear goggles and a rubber apron, too."

"Damn it, Jolie." Suddenly he was seventeen again, fighting the tide that was Jolie.

"Fine," she said before he could come up with anything better. "I'll wear shoes with toes from now on. But…if I find you lying in a heap somewhere, all I'm doing is calling 9-1-1. No first aid. No mouth-to-mouth."

There was no reason in the world for the term "mouth-to-mouth" to catch his attention, so Dylan pretended it didn't. But damn if it hadn't gotten him thinking. And once again those garter belts flitted into his mind, which kind of pissed him off. "If I croak, you may not have a job."

"As things are now, I may not have a job. Your store is slowly dying, Dylan."

His mouth tightened as she took her seat behind the counter and shook her mouse, bringing up a screen as she pointedly ignored him.

Given he had no response to her assertion, since he knew she was right, he put his head down and started gathering the remaining nails and dumping them into the box.

WHO DID HE think he was, lecturing her on safety when he'd attempted to kill himself that morning?

The boss.

Jolie propped her elbows on her desk and pressed her fingertips against her temples.

There was no arguing that point, even though

she had. He was the boss. She was the employee. If push came to shove, and if she wanted her paycheck, then she needed to abide by the rules of the game.

Boss. Employee.

So reminiscent of their chemistry class relationship where he'd been the self-appointed boss. She hadn't been the employee, but she definitely hadn't called the shots and had resented being ordered around. The curse of being the youngest in the family.

Dylan had finished cleaning up the nails and disappeared out the front door to get the big ladder from the warehouse, so Jolie went to the supply closet and found another lightbulb. She set it on the counter and went to hold the door as Dylan began awkwardly dragging the long stepladder through the entryway.

She waited until he set it up and had a foot on the first rung before she said, "I was out of line earlier."

He paused, his hands gripping the sides of the ladder, waiting, as if for a punch line.

She didn't have one.

"Thank you," he said gruffly before starting to climb. He shot her a quick look after he took out the dead lightbulb, as if still waiting for her to say something else.

Jolie had nothing.

She stood silently with one hand on the ladder, steadying it until he'd climbed most of the way down, then she headed for her side of the counter. She had accounts to mail out today, which meant it would be one of their busier days—that was the way it'd happened the only other time she'd mailed accounts, four weeks ago. It was as if people wanted to get in and charge things quick before they knew how much they owed. But more than 90 percent of their accounts were years old and the people all paid, eventually, according to Finn. Jolie didn't want to alienate the paying public, so she put a happy face next to the words *past due*, which she wrote in pink ink instead of using the official red-ink stamp.

A couple happy faces later she put down the pen and headed for Dylan's lair, where she knocked on the half-closed door. He looked up from the file he'd been staring at with a frown.

Dragging in a breath, Jolie took his silence as permission to enter.

"Here to take back your apology?"

"No. Just to say one more thing."

"I'm all ears." No. He was all long, lean muscle, but she wasn't going to allow her mind to drift in that direction.

"Chem class ended ten years ago. Obviously it had a big effect on both of us since we're sniping at each other like we're still seventeen."

"So…?"

"So." She came forward to lean her palms on his desk. "We say whatever else we want to say on the matter here and now. Get it out and over with, then we bury it. As we should have the instant we knew we had to work together."

"All right."

"You go first."

"I, uh, think I've said everything I need to say." He really couldn't think of anything that hadn't been said.

"As have I."

"Then I guess we move forward."

She smiled grimly as she pushed off from the desk. "Yes. In closed-toe shoes."

THE WOMAN PUT him on edge and then, to confuse the issue, she'd been utterly reasonable just now, suggesting that they bury the past and even apologizing to him.

Had she ever apologized to him before?

What could she have said? "Sorry, Dylan, for my attempts to destroy your 4.0 grade point average and thus affect your scholarship eligibility"?

He hadn't told anyone back then how important going to college had been to him, and he was kind of glad of that after he'd quit school following his father's death.

Mike had insisted that he go back and finish his

biochemistry degree, but long study sessions and grieving didn't jibe so he'd quit school and by a fluke had gotten the opportunity to attend police officer training school.

Action had felt good, had helped him get his head together, and after a few weeks on the job he'd realized that he'd accidentally found a profession he could happily make a career of. He might not be a college graduate, but he was doing something that mattered.

Dylan's lip curled as he massaged the shoulder he'd hit on the shelf on his way down to the floor that morning. He'd trusted Lindsey. And now he felt like a chump, but he wasn't giving up a career he loved.

"Customer needs loading up." Jolie's voice came loud and clear through the intercom. Rather than answer, he headed for the door, limping the first few steps before the knee he'd banged loosened up. He gritted his teeth and kept his stride normal as he walked to the counter where Jolie handed him a ticket. "Red Dodge."

No doubt, since it was the only vehicle in the lot. "Thanks," he muttered.

The customer—a good-looking blonde in her early thirties—stood just outside the door. "Hi," he said as he came out the door before glancing at the ticket. Eighteen bags of alfalfa pellets.

"Would you mind backing your truck up to the warehouse door?"

She smiled, her warm brown eyes crinkling attractively at the corners, and held up the keys. "Would you please do it?" she asked. Over her head he saw Jolie raise her eyebrows in an amused way, then look back down at her computer screen.

"Not at all," Dylan replied, taking the keys.

He was a little surprised when she got into the truck with him rather than wait inside. as he'd thought she'd do.

"You're new here," she said, flashing a smile his way.

"I'm Dylan Culver," he said, pointing to the Culver Ranch and Feed sign on front of the building before putting her truck in gear and swinging it in a reverse arc.

"Related to Finn, then?"

"Cousin."

"Ah," she said as if he'd said something profound. "I'm Codie James."

"Nice to meet you," Dylan said with a quick nod. He maneuvered the truck to the loading area, put it in Park and opened the door, leaving it running. Eighteen trips later, he patted the rear of her truck, giving Codie the signal to drive on. She waved at him in the mirror and pulled away.

Jolie didn't look up when Dylan came back

in—in fact, it was almost as if she were purposely not looking at him.

"What?"

"Nothing."

He came over to lean on the counter. "Nothing my ass."

Jolie's fingers stilled on the keys and then she settled her hands in her lap before explaining. "Codie and Finn had a...thing...going on for a while, and I couldn't help but notice that she was looking at you as if you're next on the menu."

"Thanks for the warning." Dylan was not surprised to find out the two had been involved. Codie looked as if she enjoyed men and Finn enjoyed being enjoyed.

Jolie shrugged one shoulder. "It wasn't a warning. A guy like you should be adept at reading the signs and making a decision as to whether you want to engage or not."

"A guy like me?" The question came out before he thought and he instantly regretted it.

"A guy with a hotness factor."

She spoke so matter-of-factly that for a second he thought he'd misunderstood her. But there really wasn't any way to misunderstand her meaning.

"Don't look so stunned. You're physically fit, good-looking." She let out a sigh. "Sorry. I thought you knew."

"I, uh…" He slapped the counter. "I've got to go see what the deal is with the forklift."

"Don't break any safety rules," she called as he headed for the door.

He didn't answer.

JOLIE WAS STILL smiling when she looked back at the computer. She'd made Dylan Culver blush. Ha.

She finished the accounts, helped a couple of customers buy small items that didn't require her to roust Dylan from the warehouse where he was either avoiding her or actually fixing the forklift. She'd never known Dylan to back down from anything, so she assumed he was fixing the forklift… but she rather liked the idea of him avoiding her— even if it meant that she was all alone in this depressing store.

At least they'd had a decent number of customers today, which gave Jolie hope that perhaps the past month had been a fluke, and that perhaps once the weather turned nice, people would start coming in…although in her gut she knew that they would go to the bigger stores where they could not only pick up feed but also plants and maybe some better tack.

It was almost five o'clock when Jolie gave up and went out to the warehouse to make certain Dylan wasn't pinned beneath the forklift or something.

She'd assumed he was fine, since she called orders out to the warehouse and no customers had come back in complaining that they hadn't been loaded. She had not, however, heard the roar of the small forklift and when she walked into the warehouse, the reason was fairly obvious.

Dylan was bent over the engine, muttering to himself and looking as though he was having the time of his life. When the door clicked shut behind her, he stepped away from the machine and Jolie wrinkled her nose as she took in his grease-stained shirt and jeans.

"Whoever does your laundry is going to be pissed," she said.

"I do my own laundry," he said, patting the crescent wrench he held into the palm of his hand.

Jolie leaned against the door but didn't say anything, wondering if he'd done the laundry when he'd been married not that long ago. Finn had mentioned the breakup in passing, but Jolie had asked no questions. It wasn't her business, although she wondered about the woman Dylan had married. Had she tired of his perfectionist ways? Although… now that she thought about it, perfectionists didn't climb shelves to change a lightbulb. They took the time to get the ladder and do the job correctly. It was possible that the Dylan she thought she knew was not the Dylan standing in front of her.

"I just wanted to check with you before I went home," she finally said when he started frowning at her, as if wondering the direction of her thoughts. He glanced at the dusty clock above the pallets of feed as if surprised at the time.

"See you tomorrow." He patted the wrench in his palm again as he spoke, showing all the signs of an impatient male that wanted to get back to work.

"We had a good day today."

"Yeah." He spoke on a note of caution as if sensing she was about to launch into something. So she did.

"A day with this many customers is unusual. Really unusual."

"I've seen the books." The words came out with enough of a clip to convince Jolie that he was aware of the reality of the situation, so the closed-off look on his face was all the more frustrating.

"I think we could bring in new customers if we're creative."

"And you have ideas." His openly dubious expression made her want to smack him.

"I do," she said evenly.

"Let's hear them."

She felt color starting to rise in her face. "I don't have anything formal put together."

He set the wrench down on the seat of the forklift. "I'm good with informal."

"All right. Well, I thought we might put in a small coffee bar for the regular patrons."

"Because people like to hang around a feed store."

"They might."

"I'm kind of interested in bringing in paying business."

"Well, I've thought about a theme day."

His dark eyebrows came together. "Such as?"

"Oh, I don't know. Western Day? Hawaiian Day?" Okay. That was a wild stab and a bad one, but she wasn't backing down, although she was very aware now that she should have prepared something before broaching this with Dylan the Detail Guy.

"Hawaiian Day?"

"Tiki lights? A luau?" She spoke as if she believed in what she said while knowing she was beat. It was time to back down, to get real, or he would never take any of her ideas seriously. "Okay. Feed store luau isn't such a great idea."

"Maybe we can give a kitten away with each purchase?" Dylan said.

"Like I said. I don't have anything formal, but we've got to do something."

"We?"

Jolie blew out a breath and pulled the keys to her trusty GMC pickup out of her pocket. "You are impossible to work for." And with that, she headed to the door.

DYLAN WIPED THE smears of oil and grease off his hands with a paper towel. What had started as a seeming quick fix had rapidly escalated into a full-blown overhaul. He hadn't finished because he needed parts, so hopefully no one would want a pallet of wood or anything like that tomorrow. He wadded up the towel and tossed it in the trash. He'd enjoyed his afternoon, which was something considering the way his day had started. Working on engines made him think of his dad—the happy times.

From outside the warehouse he heard Jolie's old GMC fire up. Even it sounded as if it was in a huff over him refusing to consider theme days at the store.

Theme days. Right.

Well, she had been correct about one thing— they'd had a decent day sales-wise, made even better by the fact that he'd been able to load everything by hand.

The business definitely wasn't as good as it had been when he'd been a teen, helping Mike out in every way he could since his dad had been too ill. Finn had brought him up to speed in that regard, but by cutting one full-time position and doing the loading himself, Finn had gotten the place to where it was making a marginal profit—enough to support himself and his grandfather.

Dylan intended to trim even more off the budget. He couldn't get rid of the only other full-time position—the counter person/bookkeeper, aka Jolie—but he was going to look at doing something different with the janitorial side and maybe cut some of the items that didn't turn over as rapidly as the feed. Stock that sat around without selling was money not earning interest.

He studied the forklift for a moment, then, decision made, he set down the wrench. Tomorrow he'd continue the battle. Right now he was tired and hungry.

After rolling down the warehouse door, he went to lock up the store. Jolie had already done that, so he let himself in, grabbed his coat and the lunch pail with his untouched lunch and headed out the door to his empty house. His grandfather had his weekly poker game at the lodge hall, so he'd be eating alone.

He got into his truck and leaned his head against the headrest before starting the engine. He didn't mind being alone, but he hated walking into an empty house. It reminded him too much of what home had been like right after his father died— what he'd been like after his father had died. Alone, more afraid than he'd wanted to let on. Not quite twenty and still in need of some serious guidance, it'd been a rough time to lose his only parent.

He'd rallied then and he'd rally now. You rode life or life rode you. Even though there'd been times over the past months when he'd felt as if he was barely in the saddle, he was going to ride life.

CHAPTER THREE

"DID YOU GIVE Dylan his prescribed dose of pain today?" Dani asked as she plopped down a basket of laundry fresh off the line.

"He was too busy causing his own pain," Jolie said, gathering up a sheet and burying her nose in it. She loved air dried sheets.

"How so?"

Jolie gave her a rundown of how Dylan had attempted to kill himself changing a lightbulb.

"Actually," she said in a musing voice after she'd finished, "it made me like him more—for about a minute." Until he'd shot down her impromptu ideas for attracting new business. "I never dreamed he was a cut-corners kind of guy."

"I don't think you know him very well."

"Are you kidding? We spent about two hundred hours together during our junior year."

"And talked about?"

"The many ways in which I was failing him?"

Dani shrugged and shook out a bed sheet. "You don't know him."

"I know how he made me feel." Jolie reached

out to take her side. And how he'd made her feel today, but she wasn't going into that with Dani, so she simply said, "But you're right. I never got past the surface. Something about his attitude toward me put me off." She brought two corners of a sheet together before glancing up at the clock. "Cripes. I gotta get going or I'll be late, and you know how Jim feels about that."

She ran upstairs, slipped into her cowboy boots and threw on a white Western shirt over a rose-pink camisole. The jeans, well worn and just a little on the tight side—thank you, Lycra—were perfect for a night pouring drinks. She pulled her hair into a ponytail, slapped on some lipstick and headed for the door.

Working two jobs and trying to make some headway putting the ranch back together put a crimp in her social life, but she had a dream and student loans. She couldn't pursue her dream and pay back loans without making a few sacrifices. Her social life had been the first thing she'd put on the chopping block.

"I'm out of here," she called to Dani as she passed the utility room.

"Try not to scare Gus when you come home."

The big dog lifted his head and Jolie leaned down to pet him as she passed by. "I think he's getting used to the idea of me coming home late a couple times a week. Last time he only barked a little."

Unfortunately one booming bark was enough to bring anyone up out of bed.

Jolie ran out to her truck, tossed her purse onto the seat and got inside. Thursday nights weren't bad. Tonight—Friday—the place was usually hopping, making her glad that Culver's was only open for half a day on Saturday. If people wanted feed, they needed to get there before noon, and sometimes after working until two in the morning, closing the bar and getting up at six o'clock to go to work, Jolie found it challenging to stay awake until noon.

But maybe tonight would be the rare quiet Friday night.

DYLAN DIDN'T OFTEN get the sense that the walls were closing in on him—or rather he hadn't until he'd moved back home. Even his grandfather had noticed. The poker game had been canceled, Dylan had done the PT for his leg before dinner and now the two of them were attempting to watch a basketball game.

"Look up old friends," Mike said.

Old friends. He'd been gone for a long time—more than a decade—and the majority of the people he'd gone to school with had moved on to careers in other areas of the state. And, frankly, he didn't feel like connecting with anyone from his past—not until he figured out his present and his future.

"Join my poker game next week," Mike suggested. "We need a few more players."

"You guys would fleece me," Dylan said. He was only half kidding. Mike and his friends pretended to play for pennies, but they were actually out for blood.

"Yeah, maybe," Mike allowed with a half smile.

"Maybe I'll head down to McElroy's Tavern, catch up with Jim and Mac." Everything in him wanted to stay holed up, to continue licking his wounds and avoiding company, but in the long run that wasn't going to work. He had to get out, start building a new life.

"Jim you can catch up with," Mike said. "Mac's working across the state at the oil patch. He only makes it home every few weeks."

"I guess I do have some catching up to do." He considered for a moment then said, "You want to come with me?"

"You want to go out with your grandfather?"

"Yep."

Mike scowled at him, as he had when Dylan had been younger and tried to get off work at the store early.

"Come on," Dylan said with a smile.

"I'll go for one beer."

"Agreed."

"Let me change my shirt," Mike said, pushing himself to his feet. "Although I don't think going out with your grandfather is the best way to get your social life up and running."

"It's a start," Dylan said. And about all he felt like dealing with at the moment.

They arrived early in the evening, but there was already a decent-size crowd filling the place. The bar area was crowded, so Dylan jerked his head toward one of the few empty tables near the door.

"Hold the table," Dylan said. "I'll get the round."

Mike pulled out a chair and Dylan started toward the bar, edging up as a space opened. Jim was busy filling orders and it was pretty obvious that Dylan wouldn't be doing much more than saying hello.

He scanned the crowd as he waited, recognized a few faces but not that many. Apparently most of the people his age were home doing family things. Once upon a time he'd been at home doing family things—when he hadn't been on shift.

He finally reached the bar, moving over as a server squeezed past him to slip behind the bar and set down a tray. He watched as she bent over in front of him, pulling bottles out of the cooler, took in a long, reddish ponytail and a nicely curved ass that seemed oddly familiar. Then she stood, met his eyes in the mirror behind the bar and he realized whose ass he'd been admiring.

"Let me know when you've seen enough," Jolie said without bothering to turn around.

How the hell did a guy respond to that?

Dylan's mouth tightened and she seemed to take that as an acknowledgment of her touché, turning toward him and meeting his eyes in an unsmiling way before bending to take clean glassware out of the rack beneath the bar.

"I didn't realize you worked here," he said.

"I do," she said, loading dirty glasses into the rack. She worked quickly, her movements precise, well practiced.

"Jolie," Jim called without turning his head, "get the limes going when you have a second."

"Sure thing." She finished the loading and then turned to pull some limes out of the small fridge.

"What can I get you?" she asked, looking up at Dylan once again, her expression all business—very much the way he'd like to see it at the store.

"Two Buds."

"Draft?"

"Whatever's easiest."

She pulled a couple of long-necks out of the cooler, set them on the bar, popped the tops and pushed them forward. "Tab?"

Dylan shook his head and slapped down a ten. "Keep the change."

He thought she was going to argue, but she took the bill and turned to the register. Dylan grabbed the bottles and headed back to his grandfather.

"Is that Jolie Brody?" Mike asked as he took the bottle.

Dylan sat with his back to the wall, telling himself to keep his eyes off Jolie although they kept drifting in her direction. "In the flesh."

Mike twisted his mouth thoughtfully. "Doesn't she work for us?"

"She does. Must be moonlighting."

"No law against that," Mike said. "But I can't help wondering how much sleep she gets."

"I guess it doesn't matter as long as she does a decent job for us."

"Finn liked her."

"Finn likes all women," Dylan replied dryly.

"Takes after me," Mike said with a grin. "But I don't think he liked her that way. I think he liked her like a friend."

Dylan tried to imagine he and Jolie being friends…the image wasn't gelling. And he also didn't seem to be able to stop watching her. Cop training kicking in, he told himself. He scanned crowds. He noticed things. He watched people. But he was watching Jolie more than was necessary under the circumstances.

And so were several other guys in the room. Even when he was talking to his grandfather, he was aware of just where she was in the room. Behind the bar, schlepping drinks to a table, disappearing outside for what was probably a brief break from the heat in the room.

"Making sure she doesn't get herself into trouble?" Mike asked on a wry note.

"Just…" Dylan shrugged. "I'm not sure."

"She's a good-looking gal," Mike said gently.

"And I'm still putting my life back together after the last good-looking gal. Besides, she works for us."

Mike took a drink of beer. Now he was following her with his eyes. "Finn said she's going into business with her sister eventually."

"Trying to set me up?" Dylan asked on a note of amusement, although the thought made him kind of nervous. His grandfather had a lot of friends, who probably had granddaughters…

"Nah," Mike said. "You can handle that part of your life." He smiled a little as he lifted his beer. "You're on your own."

Dylan almost believed him.

DYLAN LEFT EARLY. One drink with his grandpa and he was out the door. Jolie had to give him points for spending time with family, but it was Friday night. He'd hooked up with a couple of old high school friends, Jess Moody and Les D'Angelo, who were now county deputies—not that Jolie had been keeping track of him or eavesdropping as she cleared a nearby table or anything—and been invited to play pool.

Mike had looked game, but Dylan had shaken his head and not long after that had left. Jolie's first thought as she'd watched the heavy wooden door swing shut behind him was *Way to party hearty, Dylan.* The second was that he'd been through a divorce and probably still felt like crap. She needed to give the guy a break…pretty generous thought on her part considering the way he'd blown her off that day.

After he'd left the crowd picked up even more and the rest of the night passed in a blur as busy nights in a bar tended to do. She stayed late to help Jim close and suggested that next time one of the help called in sick on a weekend night, he try harder to find a sub.

"Sorry about that," he said as he counted out a stack of bills and slapped a rubber band around them. "Won't happen again. But, hey—" he grinned as he looked up at her "—you made a million in tips."

That she had.

"I'll happily split them tomorrow," she said.

"You keep them. And sorry I didn't get to Maddox sooner."

Maddox was a local bully/buffoon who loved to mess with the servers when he'd had a few too many. Jim usually nipped matters in the bud, but tonight he'd been too swamped to deal with the guy early on.

"Not a problem. I'm pretty adept at dodging him."

"I'll ban him if he doesn't stop. And if Dee is still sick, I'll get my sister to help."

"Thanks, Jim. See you."

Twenty minutes later she walked up to her door. Gus let out one mighty bark, no doubt waking Dani, then practically flattening her in his joy to see her again, home safe and sound. She crept through the house without turning on lights, but Dani was awake. She could hear her punching her pillow a few times to get into proper sleeping shape—a habit she'd had since they were little girls sharing a room.

"Sorry," Jolie called softly.

"Not a problem," Dani muttered as Jolie stepped into her own room and closed the door.

She dumped her tips on the dresser, shucked out of her clothes and tossed them into a heap—bar clothes never got worn more than once before seeing the washing machine—then slipped into her oversize Grizzlies T-shirt and climbed into bed. And there she lay awake. That last encounter with Dylan in the warehouse was still weighing heavily on her mind. Her ideas hadn't been the greatest, but he could have brainstormed with her instead of subtly mocking her.

Or had it been subtle?

Whatever, he'd mocked her instead of trying to get on board with ideas that were only meant to help. She needed to come up with a way to bring some customers into the store—and not only to provide herself a more secure future there. She wanted to show him that she wasn't the screw-up he seemed to think she was. And, damn it, she was going to do that.

A big, slurpy dog kiss awoke her a little after seven o'clock after she'd slept through her alarm and she groaned as she rolled over. Gus took that as an invitation to heave his big body up onto her bed. Since it was a twin bed, Jolie had little choice but to be engulfed with fur or get up.

Grudgingly she chose the latter. It was going to be a long morning at the feed store, but the one bright spot to having gotten next to no sleep was that she had finally come up with a way to bring in some business. An idea that should work.

No. An idea she was going to *make* work, because she wasn't going to spend the time until Finn returned being treated like some mindless bimbo who needed constant management.

JOLIE WAS LATE.

She'd been early every other day this week, but

today she was already fifteen minutes late. Dylan wondered if he was going to have to call when her truck roared into the parking lot, swung around the building and parked next to his.

She didn't notice him standing at the edge of the warehouse bay as she scrambled out, slammed the truck door and then started jogging toward the side entrance. Dylan stayed where he was, debating. Did he want to be a dick about this? No. Things happened. People ran late.

It was just that he had a good idea she was late because she was working her other job and the anal part of him said that his business shouldn't suffer because she needed another paycheck.

He turned and walked into the warehouse. They both knew why she was late and he assumed it wasn't a habit. Finn might have liked her as a friend, but he wouldn't put up with poor job performance.

He walked to the forklift and flipped the ignition. The machine chugged to life and kept running. Dylan climbed aboard and started shifting pallets, making room for a new shipment due later that morning.

A new shipment that he half wondered if they needed.

The store had had no customers so far this morning, with the exception of a woman who'd stopped by with a desperate look on her face, wondering if they had hoof glitter. She was on her way to a rodeo and needed it for her performance. Jolie had been in the back room, so Dylan had delivered the sad news that they didn't carry hoof glitter.

"Well, do you have hoof black?" she'd asked.

Again he'd shaken his head. "We specialize more in feed and general tack."

The lady had looked around at the grim interior, nodded, and said thanks just as Jolie came out of the backroom.

"We didn't have what she needed?"

"Hoof black?"

"Would it kill us to have a few bottles?" she asked.

"Yes," Dylan said bluntly.

"You're in a mood."

"Maybe I have my reasons."

She folded her arms over her chest. "If my being late is one of the—"

"No."

"Does your leg hurt? Because of the fall?"

"No."

She closed her mouth at his second abrupt answer, then when he didn't say anything else, turned and walked to her computer, her denim skirt accentuating the swing of her hips.

Wisely, given his dark mood, she gave him a wide berth during the few hours before closing, but as soon as he flipped the Open sign around to

Closed, he turned to find her standing a few feet behind him, arms folded over her chest, as if she'd been waiting for the perfect moment to attack.

"I've been thinking about the hoof black lady... and the slow day."

"And you want to know why I won't add a lot of miscellaneous stock?" She raised a shoulder, which he took to be a yes. "Because stock that doesn't move is money that could be earning interest in the bank."

"I get what you're saying. But, Dylan, adding a little more stock might help sales."

"What exactly do you think we should add?"

She looked as if she'd been waiting for him to say those exact words. "I want to add a few fun things to the inventory."

"Fun?"

"Well, maybe not as fun as hoof glitter, but things that people, women mostly, might buy on impulse."

"Like, say..."

"Jewelry."

He gave a scoffing laugh. "Jewelry."

"Yes." She tilted her chin sideways in that stubborn way he knew all too well. "And if we do it right, it won't cost you anything."

"How do we do it right?"

"By creating a Western-themed boutique—" she

held up a hand as Dylan started to interrupt her "—stocked with commission items. No initial outlay. If it fails, we lose nothing."

Dylan tried to come up with a reason this wasn't a good idea…and drew a blank.

"And before you get all negative—"

"You're pretty sure I'm going to do that?"

"History does tend to repeat itself."

"I'm not negative… I'm serious. A realist."

"Well, sometimes, Dylan, it feels good to believe that good things can happen."

"Where, if I won't be perceived as negative for asking, do these commissioned items come from?"

"Local artisans."

"I do not want a bunch of doilies in the store," he said adamantly.

"There's nothing wrong with doilies…but I was thinking along the lines of…other things."

"What kinds of things?"

"I can show you examples." She walked behind the counter and dug into her bag, coming up with her phone. She turned it on and started flipping through photos.

"Here—this wine rack looks cool. And there are these cow-themed photo frames. I thought some pottery might be nice…" Her voice trailed off as she took a long, hard look at him. "I'm talking to myself, aren't I?"

"Jolie, I have enough to do trying to run the part of the store that I know works."

"It doesn't work, Mr. Realist," Jolie said. "We need customers. This might bring people in—just like it does in the bigger ranch stores."

Dylan shook his head. "I don't—"

Jolie pointed a finger at him. "I know you don't. And you won't."

"This is my grandfather's business."

"And that means you're going to run it the way it's always been run come hell or high water?"

"I don't want a freaking boutique in my feed store."

"One month."

"What?"

"Give me one month. We'll see if the customer base increases." She folded her arms over her chest. "I'll do everything. All you have to do is allow me the space."

"You can get people—artisans—to sign on for one month?"

The corners of her mouth lifted in a slow smile. "I can do anything."

The way she said it made him believe her. "What happens after the trial period," Dylan asked, "if the customer base doesn't increase?"

"I send everything back to the artisans and

thank them for their time. However, I think the bigger question is what happens if it does increase."

"I have more money in the till?"

She stared at him as if waiting for the correct answer.

"You want a raise?"

She slowly shook her head. "No. If the customer base increases, you are going to admit to me that I was right."

"All right," he said slowly, sensing there was more.

"And you are taking me out on the town. Wherever I want to go. Whatever I want to do."

He frowned deeply even as something kicked inside him at the thought of going out with Jolie. "Why?"

"Maybe, for once, I'd like to call the shots." She smiled darkly. "And I need to warn you... I am not a cheap date."

CHAPTER FOUR

DYLAN LEANED AN elbow on the counter. "Why do I get the feeling that this is more about making me pay for past crimes than you getting to call the shots?"

She glanced at her fingernails. "Maybe they're one and the same."

"That's what I thought."

She looked up, her green eyes lit with…something. "But you know…" she said slowly, "this might be good for you."

"How so?"

"You need to loosen up. Stop analyzing every facet of your life."

"And you can help me with that?"

"Being loose is my forte." Dylan's lips automatically quirked and Jolie rolled her eyes. "Not what I meant."

"And there go my fantasies."

Where in the hell had that come from?

It was those damned garter belts. Even Jolie looked a little surprised at his unexpected words.

No, she looked a lot surprised. And she called him on it.

"Do you care to explain that comment?"

Scrambling for an answer, since he couldn't exactly say "garter belts," Dylan countered with, "Can you explain why you say half the things you say to me?"

"To put you off-kilter."

"That's why I said it." He hoped. He waited a beat then asked, "Did it work?"

"Yes. I was definitely thrown off my game for a few seconds."

"I'll have to do more of that."

"I'll have to do the same."

Back on safe ground.

"Could make for an interesting few months."

"Is that what you want, Dylan? An interesting couple of months?"

The question gave him pause. He'd come home to help out Finn and Mike, to plot out his future and to try to put the past behind him. Pretty much the last thing he'd been looking for was "interesting," but he wouldn't mind being distracted. For the first time in his life he didn't have an immediate goal and it made him edgy. Being loose was not his forte.

"I don't know what I want," he said honestly.

"I know what I want. I want to class this place up and I want to start by putting in a gift store."

Dylan gritted his teeth, wondering how she'd managed to circle around so smoothly while he was still trying to get a foothold. "One month." Her face brightened. "Increase our customer base in one month." And he'd figure out a way to let Mike know that change was afoot without having him come unglued.

Jolie cocked her head. "On second thought, that's not enough time."

Dylan fought with himself then decided it was easier to give in. She'd probably lose interest after a few weeks and he'd never have to break the news to his grandfather. Jolie had never had a lot of follow-through.

"Two months," he finally said. "Max."

"I can agree to two."

He smirked at her. "Generous, considering you asked for one."

"But the time doesn't start until I have a display area and the artisans are contracted. Right?"

"Depends on how long you take doing that," he said before he turned and headed for the door, making his escape while he could. He needed some quality time with the forklift.

Dylan blew out a breath as he crossed to the warehouse. He was all for more business, but it had to be business that meant something to him, not just people popping in to buy a trinket…not that he believed that anyone was going to be trinket shopping in a feed and seed store. And, truthfully? He didn't believe there would ever be a commissioned gift shop in Culver Ranch and Feed.

He rolled up the warehouse door instead of the main door and walked inside when Marcel, the big orange cat that patrolled the premises, shot past the forklift. Marcel was usually invisible, preferring to do his patrolling under the cover of darkness. The cat poked his head out from between two pallets then disappeared again.

That reminded Dylan. He had to call another of his grandfather's friends to try to find homes for most of Mike's livestock. If he couldn't find them homes, then he was going to have to come up with a solution as to what to do with a couple of goats, a dry milk cow and several barn cats. The chickens and ducks—the easy animals to give away—would go with Mike to his new house. The cats were too wild to move. The place wasn't zoned for goats and cows.

He reached into his pocket and pulled out the phone number he'd written on the sticky note and then crossed to the phone hanging on the warehouse wall. Maybe this nice lady would take at least one of the crew off his hands.

THAT EVENING A white crew-cab Ford with a logo on the side pulled out of the Lightning Creek driveway just as Jolie pulled in. She hadn't caught the lettering on the side of the truck, but it was obvious from the orange stakes in the field that the surveyor had finally showed up. Not only that... Gabe was back from his trip and he and Dani now stood near the surveyed plot, deep in conversation. Jolie parked her truck and, gathering her coat around her, headed over to where her sister and future brother-in-law stood.

"Wow," Jolie said. "Officially surveyed. The first big step toward training in the rain."

"Yup." Gabe looped an arm around Dani and Jolie instantly knew something was up. Dani had on her brave face and Gabe's expression was taut—neither looked as though they were celebrating a milestone.

Oh, great. "Hey, welcome back," Jolie said to Gabe as if nothing were amiss. "I thought you weren't due until Tuesday."

"Change of plans." He smiled at her, his tense expression relaxing a bit. He was a good-looking guy—dark-haired, blue-eyed—and wildly in love with her sister, which made their strange behavior after his early return all the more disturbing.

"What happens now with the arena?" she asked, playing along.

A gust of wind hit them as she spoke and Dani pulled her sweatshirt hood up over her hair. "As soon as the area is leveled, then the crew comes to put up the walls and stretch the canvas over the ribs."

Yeah. There definitely wasn't enough excitement, but after bouncing a quick look between Gabe and Dani, Jolie decided not to ask questions. Instead she smiled. "After I move the cows, maybe we should break open a bottle of wine, warm up some leftover pasta and celebrate in style."

"Sounds good," Gabe said.

"All right, Gus. Let's move the girls." The big dog had enough Border collie in him to be a decent cow dog and he dearly loved it when he got to help Jolie move the cattle from the area she had them grazing to the next. Dani had always been a strict horsewoman, but Jolie had an affinity with cattle, therefore as soon as she got home, she took over their care. Dani would move to the Staley property, where Gabe lived, once they married, so, all things considered, it made perfect sense for her to handle cattle matters.

Jolie marched out across the pasture. The cows, knowing the routine, fell in behind her, new calves trotting close to their mothers' sides. It was as if they all knew Jolie was going to open the electric fence that kept them from grazing the new growth. She allowed them into the knee-deep grass, shutting them off from the area they'd just eaten down.

In another day, she would open another gate and continue the process. It had taken her and Dani a couple of days to string the wire, creating what amounted to grazing cells, but the two days' work would pay off in more efficient grazing and less impact to the pasture through overgrazing.

The cows streamed into the area past her as she held the wire. As soon as the last one was in, she reconnected the wire. Gus gave a mighty bark, as if he'd just taught those bovines a thing or two then fell in beside Jolie as she headed back to the house. Gabe and Dani were on the porch, again in conversation.

Jolie bit her lip.

They'll tell you whatever it is when they're ready.

But she hated unfinished business and her stomach was working its way into a knot, so she did what she always did—smiled and pretended nothing in the world bothered her. She should have known better than to try that with the sister who knew her too well.

"It's nothing," Dani said as they followed Gabe into the house.

Jolie nodded and trotted upstairs to change into a sweatshirt and jeans. When she got back downstairs, Gabe had the wine open and Dani was reheating the pasta in the microwave.

"That little black heifer calf slipped under the wire again and her mama went nuts," Dani said conversationally.

"I take it she slipped back in?"

"After wandering around, exploring. I think she was just torturing her mom a little."

"Like we did," Jolie replied.

"I can't believe you two would do that," Gabe said on a wry note.

"We didn't mean to," Dani said. "It was just that Mel and Allie were so—"

"Anal."

"I was going to say perfect."

"Have it your way," Jolie said. She caught her sister's eye and they laughed. The four Brody sisters were tight, and had become tighter after their father had passed away, but it was no secret that Allie and Mel were the serious older sisters, who'd taken it upon themselves to help shoulder their mother's burden. Dani and Jolie had done what they could, but they'd been young.

"They were overly responsible," Dani said to Gabe.

Gabe handed them both a glass of wine. Dani raised her glass in a salute. "To the arena."

Glasses clinked and once again Dani and Gabe exchanged a glance.

Jolie set down her wine. "I was going to be polite and not pry, but…what's going on? Is one of you pregnant or something?"

"N-no," Dani sputtered, looking startled at the question.

Jolie shrugged one shoulder. "I wouldn't have really minded that."

"In good time," Gabe said, settling a possessive

hand on Dani's shoulder. He looked down at her and she nodded.

"It's no big secret—"

"It's more like a startling new development," Gabe said. "I just got offered an eighteen-month position filling in for a friend of mine."

"Where?" Jolie asked, lowering the wine she'd been about to sip.

"Pennsylvania."

"That's a long way from here."

"Yeah," Dani said. "But it's only eighteen months, great contacts for Gabe."

And no doubt a nice chunk of change. Gabe had invested almost everything he had in the Staley property next door to keep the Lightning Creek Ranch from becoming neighbors with a large resort and water park.

"So what does this mean?"

"We still have to decide." Dani spoke a little too brightly. And she'd yet to touch her wine.

"You know I'd hold down the fort while you're gone," Jolie said.

"I plan to stay here," Dani said.

"Why?"

"I'm building a business."

"You could take a hiatus. You started from scratch a year ago and look what you have now. A crammed schedule."

"We talked about that," Gabe said. And that was

all he said. The microwave bell dinged and they all glanced over at the machine, as if it had some answers.

"I had a startling development myself," Jolie said, sensing the need to change the topic. Dani and Gabe obviously still had some talking to do and she couldn't blame them. Eighteen months was a long time. "Dylan agreed to let me set up a commissioned Western gift shop at the store."

"I didn't know you wanted to do that."

"It seems a good way to attract people." Jolie took the bowl out of the microwave and carried it to the table. "It can't hurt. I'm working on expanding his stock, too, but he has this thing about not having stuff that doesn't move well."

"He has a point," Gabe said.

"The store is dying. I know a gift store isn't the big answer, but it might spark more business. We have to do something or I'll be looking for another job and I like working there. It pays okay and I'm pretty much my own boss for most of the day and it's close."

"It's hard to compete with chain stores," Gabe said.

"But Culver's is a local institution. You'd think people would—"

"Do what's convenient unless they have a reason to do otherwise." Gabe made a considering gesture with one hand. "The gift store isn't a bad start. Maybe some advertising."

"Yeah. I thought of that, too. Dylan's only here until Finn comes back, so on the one hand, I don't think he wants to make tons of changes, but on the other, I don't think he wants the store to die on his watch."

"He's not staying?"

Jolie shook her head. "He's only here until Finn gets back." Rather than talk about Dylan, a subject that made her feel oddly unsettled, she wanted to ask more questions about the arena—when the walls would be installed and the canvas cover arrive— but one look at her sister's strained expression and she didn't say a word on the subject.

Later that evening, though, as Dani was getting ready to walk to the Staley house with Gabe, Jolie cornered her upstairs in her old bedroom where she was digging through her coat closet.

"Have you seen my gray fleece?"

"I think you already took it over to Gabe's." Her sister was in the slow process of moving her belongings to the mansion, where she spent most of her off time.

Dani continued shuffling through the hangers with a slight air of desperation. "I can't find it over there."

"Are you okay?"

Dani leaned back out of the closet. "Of course."

Jolie nodded in a way that clearly stated her disbelief. Dani gave a small snort and went back to her search. "He needs to take this job. It'll be a boost to his consulting business."

"Is business bad now?"

"No. But there's a lot of competition out there and he isn't exactly in an urban environment. He depends a lot on word of mouth and this could really help."

"Eighteen months is a long time."

The hangers quit clacking together and Jolie heard her sister sigh. "It isn't like he'll be gone the entire time. Military wives put up with long separations."

"Yes, they do."

Dani poked her head out again. "I'm just a little taken aback. It never dawned on me that we might have a lengthy separation in our future."

"Why don't you go with him?" Even though Jolie hated the thought of running the ranch alone on top of everything else. But she could do it. For her sister.

"I might," she said. "But…what'll I do? Sit in an apartment and knit?"

Jolie raised an eyebrow. "Really, Dan? Worst-case scenario? That's not like you."

Dani came out of the closet, a fleece in each hand, neither of them remotely gray, and sat on the bed. "I know." Her shoulders sank. "I didn't expect this. The job offer or my reaction."

Jolie sat beside her and put an arm around her. "Yeah. Just when it looks like smooth sailing, a bump always appears."

"I need to man up."

"No one wants to spend time away from someone they love."

"I'm tougher than this. But…" She made a helpless gesture. "I have never felt so freaked out by a separation before. What is wrong with me?"

"You guys will figure this out."

"I guess. If you see my gray fleece, let me know." She gave Jolie a sharp look. "It's not in your closet?"

"I never wear gray if I can help it."

After Dani and Gabe said their goodbyes and headed off across the pasture to his place, Jolie poured herself a glass of wine.

Love, it appeared, could be a major inconvenience—not only to the happy couple, but also the ranch-tending sister.

JOLIE SPENT THE next day trying to shove Dani's dilemma out of her head—no easy task since the sisters had always had each other's back during times of trouble. She called artisans in the area she'd located through internet searches, asking if they had any stock they wouldn't mind displaying on commission. The majority seemed interested—until discovering that the person calling wanted to display their wares in a semi-rural ranch store.

She booked one potter and thanked the rest, asking if they knew of other people who might be interested. She'd planned to keep her list of contributing artisans small to begin with, never dreaming that she might have to really scrape to find *anyone* interested in displaying at the store.

She leaned back in her chair, refusing to allow herself to feel defeated. She could do this. She would do this—not only for the store, but because Dylan so obviously thought it was a bad idea.

There had to be local people who produced artisan items. Perhaps even an artist.

Jolie knew only one local artist who just happened to be a royal pain in the butt; but there had to be more. This artist, however, had the potential to actually send clients to Culver Ranch and Feed.

Jolie blew a breath that puffed out her cheeks, fought with herself for another minute and then called Marti Kendall to ask if she would like to display her watercolors.

And as she dialed, she wondered which Marti she'd be talking to. People who were merely acquainted with the horse trainer were invariably charmed. Those who'd grown up with her were more familiar with the feeling that you never knew whether Marti would be your friend that day or your foe. It all depended on what was in it for Marti. But they'd had several years of high school art together and Marti was one hell of a watercolor artist. More importantly, having her artwork in the store might bring in business from her horse ranch clients.

"In Culver Ranch and Feed?" Marti said on a note of disdain after Jolie explained that she was starting a commissioned boutique.

Jolie gritted her teeth and explained, "We're trying something new. I thought that your watercolors would bring people in and that would help the other artists." Nothing wrong with a stroke of the ego—especially when Marti's was so stroke-able—and no need to explain that at the moment there was only one other artisan.

"True," she said. "I could bring in a few of my smaller pieces."

"I'd love to feature them." Jolie held her breath.

"I'd need a decent display area. I don't want them stuck up over some dusty shelves with fly spray on them."

"I'm in the process of building a display area." Or she would be. Soon. All she needed to do was to figure out what was on hand to build it with.

"Will I be able to see the display area first?"

Jolie forced herself to smile to keep her voice light. "Sure. I should be done by Friday of next week." Which would give her twelve days to come up with something worthy of Marti's work.

"Great. I'll see you then."

Jolie hung up and pinched the bridge of her nose. Having Marti would be a good thing. Especially if they could talk her into buying her feed there, since her father owned one of the premier horse ranches in the area.

A thump at the window drew her attention and she turned to see the big orange cat sitting on the sill, studying her with his wide yellow eyes. After Finn left, the cat had started appearing at the window regularly and Jolie realized that there was no one there to feed the big feline except her. The cat put his paws up on the window once he realized he had her attention and batted at the glass, looking very much like a mime trying to get out of a glass box.

"Coming." She grabbed her jacket and made her way to the warehouse where she kept the food in a plastic container. The cat strutted in after her, keeping his distance then breaking into a trot when he heard the lid come off the food container.

"Oh, yes," Jolie said as she dished out the kibble. "You are a cool customer, aren't you?" The cat brushed past her. He didn't tolerate being touched, but when she fed him, he always managed to throw his body against her leg at least once in a fly-by show of gratitude.

Jolie replaced the container on the shelf, then stood there taking in the stillness of the warehouse. Whenever she had to venture out there during the day, Dylan had his radio playing, a local station with a mix of old rock-and-roll and country stand-bys. He never plugged in headphones, almost as if he wanted to be on the alert.

Well, he had been a cop. It was probably a survival thing.

Jolie strolled over to the forklift, giving the cat his space so that he could eat without worrying that she might try to touch him or something. How many times had Dylan dissembled the thing since he'd been back? At least twice. But the last time he'd used it she'd noticed that the nasty miss in the engine had been fixed.

After checking for grease, she eased up into the driver's seat and put her hands on the wheel. Finn had taught her to operate the thing, in case he was unavailable, but she'd only had to load a couple of times. Truth be told, she wasn't that anxious to drive the forklift on a regular basis. She was good with a tractor, had done her time on the swather and baler during her teens, but she had the oddest feeling that she and forklifts were not meant to be. Maybe something about the ability to skewer anything in her path.

The sound of a truck pulling in from the rear entrance brought her head up. Dylan.

Please don't ask how many artisans I've booked.

She got off the forklift and started for the door, but Dylan walked in before she got there. The cat took one look at the intruder and shot across the warehouse, disappearing behind some grain bags. Dylan looked down at the half-eaten bowl of cat kibble, then back up at Jolie.

"Marcel was eating while you were in here?"

Jolie frowned back at him. "Obviously."

"Huh."

"Huh what?"

"Marcel doesn't like people."

"He does if you feed him. A few days after Finn left, he came to tell me that his bowl hadn't been filled for a day or two. After I fed him, he decided I was okay." The phone rang, sounding over a loud-speaker. Dylan picked up the warehouse extension.

"Culver Ranch and Feed. Marti…of course I remember. What can I do for you?"

He listened for a moment then held the phone out to Jolie, watching her curiously as she said, "Hi, Marti."

"I can bring in eight pieces, but after giving the matter a bit of thought, I think I'd like an 80-20 split instead of 70-30."

Jolie shifted her gaze to the far side of the warehouse. She very much wanted to say, "No, that's not fair to the other artists." Except there was only one other artist, so instead she said, "How about 75-25?"

A long silence followed and Jolie wondered if she was going to have to do without watercolors. Then Marti said, "For the first month. After that, we can renegotiate."

"Sounds fair. I'll have the agreement ready when you stop by."

"A week from this Friday."

"That's right," Jolie said brightly.

"See you then."

Dylan hadn't moved during the conversation and when Jolie hung up the phone, she found herself standing a little closer to him than she'd expected. She didn't step back. Stepping back simply wasn't her way.

"Marti Kendall is one of your artists?"

"She does beautiful watercolors of horses." Jolie got the distinct feeling that Dylan was also very aware they were standing too close and he wasn't going to be the one to back off.

"Do you have anyone else interested besides Marti?"

"One potter."

"Only one other artist?"

"I've been kind of busy doing my job," Jolie said dryly.

"How many people did you ask?"

"Look," she said, forcing herself to focus on

coming up with an answer rather than the man standing too close to her because they were both too stubborn to back off. He smelled…good. "I just started this process and there was nothing in our agreement about reporting my progress to you."

"Let's make an addendum."

"I called nine people."

"And got one."

"It's a feed store, Dylan."

"That is exactly why this probably isn't going to work."

"Do you always give up this easily?" she blurted.

Dylan looked surprised. "I never give up easily."

"Then why do you expect me to?"

He opened his mouth and abruptly closed it again. The cat peeked out from behind a row of shovels and Dylan jerked his head toward the door. "Maybe we should get out of here so Marcel can finish eating."

"Sure." It was the perfect excuse to put some physical distance between them and she was glad that he'd been the one to suggest it. She also had the strong feeling that she would not have liked whatever he'd been about to say.

They'd just stepped outside when the phone rang. Jolie forced a smile. "Ah. Probably an artisan calling back." She gave him a smug nod then headed back into the warehouse to the extension phone.

DYLAN WATCHED JOLIE GO, fairly certain it was not an artist on the phone. Why would an artist display their stuff in a feed store? It made no sense. He had to admit, though, that Jolie wasn't rolling over in the face of adversity—not yet anyway—but he had a feeling it was because she knew he expected her to fail. He did, but he didn't need to harp on the matter.

So, in the interest of maintaining a peaceful work environment—and also because he seemed to be noticing a few too many things about his bookkeeper, like the way she wore her jeans—Dylan would keep their relationship briskly businesslike.

For the remaining days of the week, he did not mention the gift boutique and Jolie kept quiet on the matter, too, which made him believe that the project was indeed falling by the wayside.

At least she had given it a shot. And he had to admit that he kind of felt bad when he walked through the store and heard her talking earnestly on the phone to someone who was probably in the process of telling her no dice. He didn't say anything. Why rub salt into the wound?

That night after dinner, Dylan went for a slow jog around the neighborhood. His bone had mended—it was the injured muscles and ligaments that still had a way to go. But he was healing. He was running farther, faster, and he no longer limped when his leg got tired.

He'd thought about calling Pat Michaels, his ex-partner, to see how things were going at the precinct, but hadn't been able to bring himself to make the call. After the accident, he and Pat had naturally seen less of one another but he also had the strangest feeling that his partner was distancing himself from him and he didn't know why. He hadn't been culpable in the accident and he was unaware of being on the wrong side of any precinct politics, so he'd finally decided that something outside of the job was eating at Pat. It happened. It also made him hesitant to call.

Hell, his life in Montana was so far removed from his life in Lanesburg, maybe it was better to focus on the here and now instead of worrying about things he was no longer part of—at least for the time being. He'd bring himself up to speed once he got his medical clearance and sat for the detective exam. When he was back where he belonged.

DYLAN HAD KEPT HIMSELF busy in his office and the warehouse for several days after Marti's call. Not once did he mention Jolie's project, nor did she, even after booking two more artisans—a leather-worker and a woman who made picture frames. She was making progress, but she wanted to fill the front of the store with interesting items, make a statement, catch the eye as people came in and then keep them coming back when gift-giving occasions arose. No one was going to drive a few extra miles for a tiny selection of handcrafted goods. She needed more artisans.

When she walked into the bar that night, Jim raised a lazy hand to greet her and she could see that it had been a slow afternoon, which wasn't unusual for a Thursday. He poured them both seltzer water, as he usually did when they had downtime, and after putting her purse away, she perched on her stool near the edge of the bar.

"Probably not a big tip night," she said, nodding at the two patrons playing a game of pool.

"It'll be a sleeper," he agreed. He leaned his elbows on the bar opposite her. "So how's your big project coming?"

"I'm halfway there. I need just four more artists to have a respectable showing."

"I talked to Mac."

Jolie had her glass halfway to her lips then put it back down. She'd asked Jim about his brother's ironwork, but Jim hadn't been hopeful about Mac agreeing to participate. "And?"

"He said I can pull some of his stuff out of the garage and let you display it. I got you two wine racks and two towel bar sets."

"Oh, my gosh." Jolie practically jumped off the stool. Mac's wrought-iron work was gorgeous.

"And he's working with a guy whose brother just

got out of prison at Deer Lodge. He hitches horse-hair and has some belts he'd like to commission."

"Jim, you are a bona fide doll."

He went a little red. "I know."

Jolie's run of good luck continued for the next few days. On Saturday she heard back from a leatherworker who had spur straps and wallets to display and on Monday a silversmith finally returned her message and agreed to drop off twenty pieces of jewelry. She was so tempted to walk into Dylan's office and slap her list of artists on the desk in front of him, but she refrained. Partly because she was above that and partly because he'd been avoiding her, which made her believe he'd felt the same sense of tension building between them that she did.

During her lunch hour, Jolie walked the area near the front of the store where she wanted to build her display and debated about how best to squeeze in an attractive backdrop, *attractive* being the key word. The walls were painted flat white and the floor was half-century-old cracked tile. She didn't have a lot of time and her budget was very close to zero dollars. She would have to make do with what she could scrounge around the place.

She went back behind the counter, flipped open the notebook she used to jot down special orders and, after a moment, started sketching, trying to come up with a way to cover the walls, build shelving, disguise the floor—

The bell above the door rang and she jumped a mile. Dylan gave her an odd look as he crossed the room and she slowly closed the notebook.

"Did I interrupt something?" he asked curiously.

"No. I was just drawing."

"Drawing."

"Ideas for my display."

He stopped on the other side of the counter. "I take that to mean that you contracted your seven artisans?"

"I did. Now I'm going for ten."

"Can I see your plan?"

"I don't think so," Jolie said with an easy smile. It was beyond rough and she wasn't presenting any ideas to him until they were polished. She'd learned her lesson about that.

"Is it some big secret?"

"Maybe I don't want you taking over."

His eyebrows shot up as if he had no idea what she was talking about. "Why would I take over?"

Her lips twisted. *Really, Dylan?* "Because that's our history. You take over."

He raised his hands in a gesture of surrender. "This is your baby. I'm just curious in case Mike has questions."

There was something in his tone that caught her attention. "Will Mike have a problem with this?"

She liked the gruff old guy and wouldn't want to upset him.

"Mike doesn't like change."

"At all?" Was that why Finn had also dragged his feet when she'd discussed improvements during the few weeks they'd worked together?

Dylan gave his head a slow shake. "Not a fan. It's gotten worse over the past few years."

"Then moving has got to be killing him."

"If the house didn't have so many damned stairs, he'd never leave."

"Well…" she said slowly, "can you convince him this will be a change for the better? After you convince yourself, of course."

He didn't deny that he had to be convinced, but she hadn't expected him to.

"How are you going to display this stuff when it comes in?" He leaned an elbow on the counter as he cast a sweeping glance around the store and again she had that feeling of being too close to him, even though there was a good two feet of wood and glass between them.

"I'll have to rearrange, but all of your stock will be easily available."

"Just run any big changes by me, okay?"

"Sure." She caught the scent of his aftershave and it made her want to lean even closer…maybe even follow him when he retreated to his office. That had never happened in high school. Had they been so busy sniping at each other in the lab that she'd never noticed that the guy was jangling her nerves?

No. Something had changed. They were still sniping…but it felt different. And even though Dylan was technically her boss, it didn't feel the way it did with Finn.

Maybe because of that fantasy comment he'd made?

Even though she told herself it was only a quip, meant to throw her off balance, it had stuck with her. As had the realization that Dylan had lips that could take part in a fantasy—hers—and that was… disconcerting.

She cleared her throat, bringing his attention back to her, which had not been her intent. She smiled at him, hating the feeling that she was somehow at a disadvantage because his very presence was making her feel all edgy and unsettled.

"You were going to say something?" he finally asked.

Instead of saying no, as she should have, Jolie decided to take control. "I was wondering if you have some kind of time frame in which you have to get back to your other job."

He blinked at her as if she was not making sense. Or as if he didn't want to answer that particular question. "Counting the days until I'm out of your hair?"

"Actually, no. I was just curious."

"As soon as Finn gets back, I'm heading home."

"You're on leave?" She leaned on the counter. He was withdrawing. Fast.

"Yes."

"Your old job waiting for you?"

"Pretty much."

She waited a moment. "Not going to share any details, are you?"

"Don't really see any need to," he said, his eyelids dropping an iota. He regarded her for a few long seconds, as if challenging her to ask yet another question he wasn't going to answer.

She did love a challenge.

"What happened to your leg?"

"The windshield got shattered on my cruiser and I lost control and hit a power pole."

"Oh." She hadn't expected a real answer, but before she could ask about the windshield, he raised his index finger in a warning gesture.

"Don't ask, because I'm not answering."

"All right then," she finally said, pulling her papers closer and doing her best to ignore the sparks snapping between them. "I think it's time to heat up my lunch."

"Don't let me keep you." He gave a slight nod and headed for his lair.

Once he disappeared, Jolie shut her eyes and let out a short breath.

CHAPTER FIVE

DYLAN SHUT THE office door and tried to shake off the feeling that he'd just escaped. Ridiculous. He had work to do and he'd wasted too much time chitchatting with Jolie.

The office was a paper nightmare and he'd been slowly going through everything, one file at a time, deciding what was needed, what should be shredded and what could be simply trashed.

He hated paperwork—all cops hated paperwork except for the overachievers—but this seemed like a good time to make a few more inroads.

Over the course of the next hour, he filled two black garbage bags with stuff that shouldn't have been kept in the first place: old calendars, advertisements, magazines, catalogs. It was as if Mike hadn't thrown anything away in the past decade. Dylan couldn't figure out why until it struck him that most of the collected junk was dated after 2005—the year Grandma, the keeper of the office, had passed away. Maybe Mike had given up after that. Maybe going through the accumulation after he'd stopped grieving had been too much. It'd obviously been too much for Finn, since he hadn't tackled it.

Or maybe he hadn't felt the need to hide out from his associate.

The thought came creeping out of nowhere and Dylan disregarded it almost as soon as it registered. He wasn't hiding…he was just in his office, with the door closed and no intentions of coming out any time soon.

All right, he was hiding, but it wasn't from Jolie. He was avoiding questions that he didn't want to answer. Hell, he was avoiding questions he couldn't answer because he didn't *know* the answer. He'd never been one to run away from hard issues, but he didn't want to discuss them with Jolie, and he really didn't want to come right out and tell her to mind her own business. He sensed that, despite everything, she was honestly concerned about him on some level and it seemed cold, even for him, to tell her to back off.

And then there was the matter of the tension between them that they were both obviously aware of and both obviously ignoring. Something else he didn't care to think about. But it was a big part of the reason he was in the office doing something that Finn could do when he came back.

Avoiding uncomfortable situations was out of character for him and the fact that Dylan was doing just that, even if it did result in a cleaner more organized office, pissed him off.

"Customer needs loading up."

He dropped the file he'd been shuffling through and headed for the door, grabbing his gloves off the still-cluttered top of the file cabinet as he walked by.

Codie's red Dodge was parked outside the front windows. Praying for strength, he headed out the door.

CODIE JAMES WAS flirting hard and heavy with Dylan, who didn't seem to mind one little bit. In fact, he seemed to be into it. Not that Jolie was purposely spying, but it was hard to miss the action going on next to the bright red pickup parked not that far away from her window. Despite her intention to keep her eyes focused only on the screen in front of her, Jolie shot a quick look out the window in time to catch Codie pat Dylan's chest before she opened the truck door.

Dylan smiled widely in response to whatever the blonde had said and Jolie started typing again. She had nothing against Codie, hadn't minded one bit when she'd dated Finn, but she didn't like the way she was now aiming her sights at Dylan. It was as if she was picking off the Culver guys one by one.

She forced herself to keep typing. So what if when she looked back out the window the red truck driving away had two people in it instead of one? Dylan was the boss. If he wanted to head off with a flirtatious customer in the early afternoon...well, so be it. None of her affair.

Which meant that there was no reason for her jaw to be clamped so tightly shut that it ached.

At least it'd been unseasonably hot and sunny all day, which meant her practice arena behind the barn might finally be dry enough for her to finally work. It'd been days since she'd been able to practice her barrel runs and she was so ready to get on Jenabelle and lose herself in some speed work. Nothing helped her center more than practice and right now she felt a strong need for centering.

DYLAN GOT BACK to the store close to closing time. Codie dropped him off with a smile and a wave and he'd waved back. Nice woman. Sexy woman. Unfortunately she was not a woman who could use two goats.

When he'd first asked, she thought they might be perfect for her younger sister to use for goat tying practice, but after driving to Mike's and taking a look, she'd deemed them too stout.

Dylan had to admit that Maisy and Daisy were sturdy girls and, due to Mike's TLC, both were overweight. Perfect for eating, but Dylan would rather shoot himself in the foot than send the goats off to butcher. Mike might talk about being realistic but he loved his girls.

The store was empty when Dylan walked in. He stopped just inside the doorway and listened, trying to locate Jolie. His office door was open, the light off. The restroom was also dark. She hadn't left because her truck was still there, so that left the warehouse. Dylan reversed course and crossed the graveled area between store and warehouse. Nothing. And then he heard the clatter behind the grain shed. He followed the noise, rounding the corner in time to jump back as a cedar board landed at his feet.

"Oh. Sorry."

Dylan looked down at the board, one of several lying near his feet, then back up at Jolie. She wiped her oversize glove across her forehead, leaving a faint smear of dirt on her smooth skin.

"Dare I ask?"

"Materials to build the display." The shop had stacks of old metal and damaged fencing stored behind it because Mike had never been able to let it go. It might be useful someday and now it appeared that it was…but not in a way his grandfather had ever intended.

"Ah." He regarded her, noting that despite the gloves and the closed-toe shoes she'd worn every day since their dust-up about safety rules, she was not dressed for digging through the wood pile. She frowned a little then looked down, following his gaze as it traveled over her denim skirt and smooth, bare legs. What she wore was totally appropriate for work, but somehow when she was straddling the woodpile it looked about as congruous to the situation as Miss Daisy Duke Shorts did holding her wrench on the tractor calendar. And his response was edging in the Miss Daisy Duke direction.

"I'm wearing the proper shoes," she said dryly, easily following his thoughts.

"That won't keep you from getting a splinter in your knee."

"We all have to take chances, Dylan." She reached for another board. "I hope you don't mind me being out here. I can see any customers that come in and the outside phone ringer is on."

"I don't mind." He didn't totally understand Jolie, but after two weeks of working together, he didn't question her commitment to her job. If only she'd taken lab as seriously he wouldn't have felt old before his time.

"I'm done with everything I could do inside, plus I updated the web site, the Facebook page and designed next week's flyer."

"We have a Facebook page?"

She looked at him as if he'd asked if the world was round. "Of course. All businesses do." She leaned down to pick a board out of the stack, inspected it with a critical eye and then discarded it. "I didn't know if you were coming back," she said a little too casually.

"Sorry I didn't tell you I was leaving. Spur of the moment." The look she shot him was easy to read—she'd thought he'd headed off for a nooner. "I'd hoped to talk Codie into taking Mike's goats."

She slowly looked his way and he wondered if he'd seen an expression of relief chase across her face. Probably. No one wanted a scummy boss and heading off with a customer for a little midday play was definitely scummy. "Mike's giving away goats?"

"Trying. He's moving to a smaller place and we have to find homes for some of his farm animals. Codie thought her sister could take the goats."

"But she couldn't."

"They're too square for goat tying. Apparently they prefer a leggier lightweight goat for that."

"Ah." She started stacking the boards that were lying close to his feet. "What other animals does he have?"

"A milk cow that's been dry for years, but he doesn't have the heart to send it you-know-where. A bunch of wild cats."

"How are you going to give away wild cats?"

"Beats me. They'll probably stay with the place."

"Sounds like you have a problem, Dylan."

"Only one of many."

Jolie nodded but didn't answer. She also didn't say a word when Dylan picked up the eight cedar boards.

"You want these in the store?" he asked. "If I'm not taking over, that is."

She made a smirking face at him, feeling more comfortable now that he'd slung a barb. "I'd like them to dry."

"Is this enough?"

"It's a start. If I need more, I'll get them tomorrow."

"Fair enough." It was 5:45 p.m. when they got into the store, fifteen minutes after closing. Jolie carefully propped the boards up against a small stretch of empty wall space, then went behind the counter to turn off her computer.

"I didn't realize it was so late," she said. "I need to hurry if I'm going to have time to practice before dark."

"Practice?"

"Barrel racing."

"You still do that?" He remembered her being something of a rodeo star in high school. It had only hammered home how different they were. He'd ridden the occasional horse, but his life had centered more around motorcycles and good grades.

"I'm getting back into it. I have rodeos coming up and I need to get my horse tuned up. It's finally dry enough to work her a little." She came back around the counter with her purse in one hand and her coat in the other, stopping just before she got to the door. "I have to admit," she said with a slight smile, "I didn't know what to think when you drove off with Codie."

"I have an idea what you might have been thinking," he said.

She gave him a wry smile. "Never in my wildest imagination did it involve a goat."

THE ARENA WAS drier than Jolie had expected and she took advantage, setting up her barrels and then saddling Jenabelle.

They warmed up, doing a lazy canter, then a couple of slow runs around the barrels. Jenabelle tossed her head, wanting to do what she did so well, but Jolie hadn't used her in a while and kept her moving more slowly than the mare wanted. It was only the last two runs that she let Jenabelle do her thing. They had some work to do, but this first practice was promising and Jolie felt satisfied when she dismounted and led her mare out of the arena.

Dark clouds were gathering to the north and she was glad she managed to slip in a practice before the next set of storms showed up.

"More rain," Dani said as they met at the hitching rail. She sounded down again and Jolie wished she'd just freaking decide to go with Gabe. She'd never seen her sister so torn before and it bothered her. Was this what getting seriously involved did to a person? Dissolve them to jelly?

She watched Dani out of the corner of her eye as her sister expertly unsaddled the young horse she'd been riding. There was more going on than that. It seemed almost hormonal…damn. Her sister was pregnant. That would account for the moods. And why Gabe's job across the country seemed more traumatic than it needed to be. Dani had never been afraid to be alone before, but now…

Jolie huffed out a breath.

"What?"

She looked over to see Dani frowning at her. Not the time to ask about her hypothesis. "Just thinking about work."

"Any flare-ups today?"

"No. Codie James came by and hauled Dylan away during working hours. I thought the worst, of course, but came to find out Dylan was trying to give her a pair of goats."

"Goats, you say?" Dani eased the saddle off the horse and started toting it to the tack shed.

"Mike is moving to a smaller place. Dylan's trying to find forever homes for his livestock." Jolie followed Dani into the shed and set her saddle on its rack, then laid the pad out upside down to dry.

"How long until they end up here?"

Jolie gave a short laugh. "Why would they end up here?"

"We have the room and Dylan is going to think of that."

"I don't think he's going to ask me for any favors."

"And you're not going to offer?"

Jolie just stared at her sister. "I hadn't thought of it, no." Dani headed out of the tack shed and Jolie followed. "Why would I offer?"

Dani untied the horse's lead rope. "Because you're a soft touch when it comes to animals."

"We have enough mouths to feed."

Dani gave an approving nod. "I agree. Thank you." She headed off toward the pasture with the buckskin gelding, leaving Jolie staring after her, wondering if she'd been played.

"DID YOU KNOW we had a Facebook page?" Dylan looked up from his laptop as he spoke. He and Mike were sitting in their loungers on either side of the cluttered lamp table watching television—or pretending to watch television in Dylan's case. It was the way they spent most of their evenings when they weren't sorting through his grandfather's stuff. Mike liked the company and Dylan was doing his best not to be constantly looking for something to do… In other words he was working on forcing himself to relax.

Mike didn't take his eyes off the news when he said, "I'd heard a rumor. Finn said it was a good way to advertise."

"Have you seen the page?"

"Why would I go looking at Spacebook?"

"Facebook." Dylan wasn't surprised at his grandfather's answer. Mike used the internet to read the news. Other than that, computers were for playing long games of solitaire.

"Jolie made the page," Mike continued as he switched the channel again, his eyes never leaving the television. "She and Finn were talking about it one night when they were here for dinner."

"Jolie was here for dinner with Finn?"

"Mmm-hmm." Mike's little dog, Speck, jumped up on his lap and he automatically scooped her into the crook of his arm.

"The page isn't half bad."

The banner was a photo of Marcel sitting on the window sill next to a pot of red geraniums. The Culver Ranch and Feed sign that Mike had carved forty years ago curved over the top of the window. It was very charming and down home. And at least twice a week Jolie updated the status of the store, including little tidbits about nutritional values of the various feeds, little known facts about the origin of certain grains, factoids and the occasional true-false or multiple-choice trivia questions with ten-percent-off coupon codes to be emailed to winners. It seemed that Jolie knew more about his store—and little known feed and seed facts—than he did. It also seemed as if she and his cousin were closer than he'd realized.

They were just friends. Dylan knew that, but what he didn't know was why he didn't like the idea of Jolie and Finn being close. And what about that favor she'd called in? He still wondered about that occasionally.

Mike stayed focused on his show, idly rubbing Speck's ears.

"Jolie's putting a boutique into the store," Dylan said, figuring he may as well come clean since Mike seemed good with the Facebook page and coupons.

Mike turned his hawklike gaze toward Dylan. "A what?"

"Boo-teak," Dylan enunciated.

"What for?"

"To draw in customers. She's been itching to add stock. I told her we'd stay with the tried and true, so she came up with this idea to display artisan work on commission."

Mike's frown deepened, but he didn't immediately start telling Dylan how artisan items would distract from their stock.

"Helen had talked about doing that once."

Not the expected response. "It's only for a two-month trial period."

"Why the time limit?"

Dylan cleared his throat. "We, uh, made a bet. If she can increase the customer base in two months, she wins. If not, then I win."

"What do you win?"

"I'm not really clear on that," Dylan admitted. Technically, if he won, then the boutique was history, but that wasn't much of a prize, therefore his prize was being right and the store continuing to slide downhill sales-wise.

Mike's perplexed frown was back, drawing his thick gray eyebrows together. "What does she win?"

"A date."

"With…?"

"Me."

Mike's eyebrows came together again. "Let me get this straight. If you win, then you don't know what you win and if she wins, you get to go out with an attractive woman."

"That's not quite the way it is." At least it wasn't the way he'd intended it to be. But since Jolie was involved, things had gotten twisted around.

"I can't understand how you lose in this deal… unless of course you win. Then I think you lose."

"It looks that way, but it isn't," Dylan said, tilting his head back. "She's giving me payback."

"For what?"

"Jolie and I…we have a history."

Mike's hand stopped moving over Speck's rough coat.

"High school," Dylan continued, feeling a bit foolish. "We were lab partners. It didn't go well."

"Lab partners in high school." Mike spoke on a note of gruff disbelief and Dylan had to admit it sounded lame.

"The year from hell. I was trying to get scholarships. She was working against me—or at least it seemed like it…" His voice trailed off before he added, "You had to be there."

"Do you guys get along any better now?" Mike asked with enough irony to make Dylan feel like a twelve-year-old. "Other than her threatening you with payback dating?"

"She thinks I'm controlling, which isn't helping things."

When Mike didn't answer Dylan shot him a look then smiled at the expression on his grandfather's face. "I prefer to think of it as being a take-charge kind of guy."

"That's fair." Mike started stroking Speck again. "Not much for you to take charge of at the store. I mean compared to your other job."

"It's not a bad change."

"Really?" There was no missing the doubt in Mike's voice.

"Yeah." Dylan rubbed a hand over the back of his neck, trying to sound sincere as he said, "I needed a break. If Finn had to be deployed, this wasn't a bad time."

"The accident?"

"It drove me crazy being assigned to a desk and until I get a medical release, that's where I'll be." Now he did sound sincere. Maybe a bit too much so.

"Are you going back to Lanesburg," Mike asked, "if you don't get a release?"

He was 99 percent sure that the release was a given. He'd been working the leg twice daily and while it still ached at times, he had no issues using it. He just wished his grandfather didn't sound as if he hoped Dylan didn't get clearance.

"I'm sitting for the detective's exam there."

Mike picked up the remote and changed the channel as a particularly obnoxious commercial came on. "There's always law enforcement here... I think they also have detectives."

Dylan had a feeling this matter was going to come up sooner or later and he couldn't blame Mike for trying to get his grandkids close to him again. "I'm halfway to my full service credit in Washington. I don't want to screw up my retirement there."

"So I suppose going back to school—finishing your degree—isn't an option, either."

Dylan stared at his grandfather. That ship had sailed so long ago that he was surprised Mike had even brought it up. "I like my career. I just…need a breather."

"Yeah, you've been through a lot of stuff in a short amount of time." Mike shifted his attention to the television. "I'm glad you're here."

Dylan was glad to be there, too. For the time being. As he'd said, he'd needed a breather; a moment to catch his breath before going back for another round.

He felt as though he was doing just that, too, until early the next morning when he got the call. It was from Sadie Warren, a dispatcher who lived a few blocks from him in Lanesburg. He knew the minute he heard her voice that she had bad news; his gut automatically twisting as he waited for her to tell him that one of their fellow officers had been shot. The news, as it turned out, was not that dire, but it wasn't anywhere near good.

"It's none of my business, Dylan, but I thought you should know… I think Pat has moved in with Lindsey."

Pat? As in his former partner? It took Dylan a few stunned seconds to say, "Are you sure?"

Sadie cleared her throat. "I don't know for certain."

"Why do you suspect?"

"He's been parking on the side street between my place and yours. He doesn't always park in the same place, but I've seen his car too often for it to be coincidence."

Dylan pulled in a shaky breath as he batted down rising anger. Lindsey had been seeing someone before they'd divorced. Someone she'd never named. If it had been his own partner…the knot in his gut intensified.

"Dylan?"

"Yeah. Sorry. I, uh, thanks for telling me."

"I trust you not to do something stupid."

"No." He had no intention of doing something stupid. On the other hand…he was going to do something.

"I mean it. I wouldn't have called—"

"I know." He thanked Sadie again for the information, swore another oath not to do anything rash, then hung up and called Phil Murray, an ex-cop he knew who did private investigations.

A quick conversation, a PayPal transaction and a handful of aspirin later, he headed off to work. The terms of the settlement were clear—Dylan only had to make house payments as long as Lindsey lived there alone. If she was not…well, things were going to change.

CHAPTER SIX

DYLAN ARRIVED EARLIER than usual on Tuesday morning, but Jolie still managed to beat him to the store. She'd had a hard time sleeping and had finally given up around 4:00 a.m. just as the sky had started to lighten.

She'd moved her cattle wearing her pajamas, fed Dani's horses for her, then showered, dressed and headed to the store hoping to get a start on the display area. She hadn't expected Dylan to arrive so early, and felt a little cheated of quiet time when he yanked open the door.

"Morning." The word came out as more of an announcement than a greeting as he strode by the counter, dented lunch pail in hand. Jolie didn't bother responding since the office door closed behind him a few seconds later. Apparently she wasn't the only one with issues weighing on her mind. Not that she needed to worry about her sister as much as she was. Gabe was a good guy and Dani was a smart woman when the hormones weren't beating on her; everything would work out.

But Dani was her sister. It was her job to worry

about her. Besides, turnabout was fair play. Dani, she knew, had spent more time worrying about her than vice versa because Dani had always made careful life choices whereas Jolie had a tendency to race into situations half-cocked.

Not a bad way to live when one had no real responsibilities, but life had caught up with her. She was approaching thirty with a college degree in a field in which she'd be hard pressed to land a job and that meant no more screwing around. Failure—on the ranch and in the jobs that paid the bills—was not an option. If things continued as they were, she'd soon be the only person living on the Lightning Creek. The person in charge. The person who wasn't going to mess up.

There was a bang inside the office but Jolie ignored it. It hadn't sounded like a body hitting the floor and Dylan could handle his own emergencies. If he needed help, she was there for the asking—although she was fairly certain he wouldn't ask. At least he hadn't yet.

Their days at the store consisted of Dylan holing up in his office or out in the warehouse and her handling the computer work, accounts and stocking shelves. It also consisted of her cleaning those shelves more regularly than the cleaning crew. Therefore it was something of a surprise when Dylan came out of his office and crossed to the counter.

Jolie looked up with an inquiring expression.

"When do you plan to open this boutique or gift shop or whatever it is?" he asked in a clipped voice.

Damn. What happened to you?

Jolie fought back the question. One, he wouldn't answer it and, two, she wasn't certain she wanted to know the answer.

"I, uh, hoped to open it as soon as the display is built and the commissioned items arrive."

"Which will be?"

She pulled a paper toward her and glanced down at it. "I have items coming in all week. Marti won't bring hers in until she okays the display area."

When Dylan lifted his eyebrows, she explained, "Marti doesn't want her work hanging just any-where. That means that everything should be here by Saturday and I'll have a mini grand opening a week later."

"Which entails?"

"Food," she said with a wry twist of her lips. "A few plates of cookies. Some coffee. I've made some flyers and will post them later today."

"And it's on the Facebook page?"

"This morning."

Dylan glanced down at his boots. When he met her eyes again, some of the hard edge was gone. "Mike liked the idea of the commissioned items."

"I hope that doesn't mean that the bet is off?"

Jolie asked. "Because I'm a competitor at heart, and that would take a lot of the fun of it."

It looked as if Dylan wanted to smile but couldn't quite get all the parts moving. The frown settled back into place. He gestured at the cedar fencing boards Jolie had salvaged. "I assume you now have a set plan?"

"I have a sketch. A few shelving units need to be moved, but I thought I could do that today."

"If I promise not to take over, can I see the plan?" Dylan asked.

Jolie opened the notebook and slid it across the counter. Dylan frowned even more deeply as he studied it. For a second there Jolie was fairly certain he was going to tell her it wouldn't work. Instead he put the notebook back down and said, "We should get started."

"We?"

He leaned on the counter, his blue gaze intent as he said, "I'd like to help, okay? You call the shots, I'll do the lifting."

Jolie hesitated before saying, "Sure."

"But you'd rather do it alone."

"No offense, Dylan, but I'd kind of hoped to enjoy myself building this thing."

He quirked an eyebrow. "And you can't do that if I help?"

"Your mood at the moment is very reminiscent

of chem class." She raised her hands in a wait-I-have-more gesture. "I'm not judging. I just—"

"Want to enjoy yourself." He walked over to the stack of boards, studied them and looked back at her. Tension snapped between them for a moment before he said gruffly, "It'd go a lot faster if I help."

He was asking permission. Well, that was a flipping first.

Jolie came around the counter, relinquishing her barrier. Why she needed one, she wasn't certain, but lately it had seemed safer to put the counter between them. Dylan had been doing the same with his office door, but now he'd abandoned his office and was challenging her to do the same.

"All right," she said. This wasn't a battle she wanted to fight. It would go faster and maybe he needed to do something to distract himself from whatever had put that dark look on his face.

He stood studying her and she finally realized he was waiting for her to tell him what to do. Another first.

"Let's unload the shelving units so we can shift them. I assume you want to handle the one with the horseshoe nails."

"Funny," Dylan muttered but, despite the cloud that seemed to be hanging over him, he didn't sound all that annoyed.

It took more than an hour to remove all the

items off the three units that needed to be moved, push them to their new locations and reload them; during which they exchanged all of ten or fifteen words. But, oddly, it wasn't a totally uncomfortable silence. It was more like a necessary silence and they were both aware of the fact.

They'd just finished when a customer drove in. Dylan loaded him up then returned as Jolie was propping boards against the wall.

"I'll be back," he said, disappearing outside again. He returned with two long 1x2 boards. "I think we should attach these to the wall then attach the cedar boards to them."

"Like a fence," Jolie said.

"Like a fence," he agreed.

Jolie shrugged. "Good idea. Fewer holes in the walls. Do you have another drill? One for pilot holes, one for screws."

"Yeah." Dylan went out into the warehouse and came back with another drill and a case of bits. "I take it this isn't your first time building a fence."

"It's what I do after work a couple nights a week. Fix plank fencing along the north boundary."

She took hold of one end of the board as Dylan held the other and placed the level on top. "This look okay?" he asked.

"Yeah." She gave a soft snort.

"What?"

"This may be the first time in our joint history that you checked something with me before proceeding."

"Possibly because this is the first time you have a stake in the outcome?"

"I had a stake before...it just wasn't as serious as yours." It wasn't an apology, but rather an acknowledgment.

Jolie held her end of the board then exchanged drills, giving him the one with the screw attachment. When he'd finished attaching his end of the board to the wall, she checked the level and drilled a pilot hole. Another drill exchange and she screwed her end of the board to the wall.

They put up the second board a few feet below the first without a word, simultaneously stepping back to assess.

"It'll do," Dylan said.

"Yes."

He picked up a cedar plank. "Rough side out or in?"

"What do you think?"

"Out."

"Agreed."

"So what's with you?" he asked gruffly after attaching the plank to the supports they'd just put up.

"Me?" She shot him a look.

"You seem distracted."

She gave a short, brittle laugh. "You come in

here looking like your dog died and you're telling me that I look distracted?"

For a minute she thought he was going to argue with her, but instead he picked up another board and went to work attaching it to the wall. Jolie decided not to mention that he was squeezing her out.

"Why all the fence building?" he asked.

"Because the ranch is in rough shape."

"Hard times?" It wasn't an insulting question. Most ranches went through hard times now and again.

"Lazy ex-brother-in-law."

Dylan handed her the drill without comment and stepped back.

She put up two boards then returned the drill.

"Not bad."

For a moment they stood side by side.

Since he hadn't pressed matters, Jolie said, "My sister's ex-husband was a dreamer rather than a doer. The ranch fell down around his ears while Allie was out trying to earn a living. Dani moved back home and is using it as a base for her horse training business."

"But you're fixing the fences."

"She has a lot on her plate and—" she moved to pick up another board "—I like doing it. She likes training animals."

"You're the homebody?"

"Don't sound so surprised. But, yes, I am. Although it's more of being a ranch-body. I'd like to get the fields back into shape. Lease them out. Increase the cattle herd. I've already doubled it. All five of our cows had heifer calves. We have nothing to sell but ten head of breeding stock."

"You'll take a loss feeding those heifers until they're breeding age."

"The meadow hay looks good this year and if I can get the baler running, we're going to mow and bale. That'll help. Then I'll just have to pray for a few bull calves to take the financial pressure off next year."

She turned toward him, taking in his speculative look. "I could ask why you're staring, but won't."

"Because?"

"I know the answer."

"Which is?"

"You're surprised that I have a plan." She put the board in place and drilled the pilot hole.

Dylan waited until she was done to ask, "Why would that surprise me?"

"Because in your head, I fit into the slot marked 'incompetent'?"

"I never called you incompetent." He handed her a screw and then traded drills.

"You just treated me that way."

"I thought we were going to bury this."

"I guess it left a bigger mark than I thought it had. I still have a few issues I need to lay to rest."

She put more weight than was necessary behind the drill as she put in the screw.

"I always thought you were capable."

"I don't believe you."

"Why?"

She put a hand on her hip. "I don't know. Maybe the way you mocked me when I was trying to brainstorm ideas to improve business?"

"Feed store luau?"

"I was shooting from the hip," she said through her teeth. "I told you I hadn't put anything together."

"For the record I thought you were intelligent but easily distracted. I thought that you misused your intellect."

"Like some superhero gone wrong?"

"Exactly."

"Huh." She pressed her lips together and narrowed her eyes, trying to read him. He seemed sincere. "So what brought your black mood on today?"

He seemed surprised at the quick change of topic. "Just…issues at home."

"Which home? Mike's or your other…home?"

"The other."

Jolie shifted her weight, the drill still hanging from one hand. "I'm approaching none-of-your-business status again, aren't I?"

"Edging in on it," he agreed. His eyes slid down

to her lips and something shifted inside her, causing warmth to start pooling low in her abdomen. Her breath caught and she had to force herself to let it out low and slow, so he wouldn't realize the effect he was having on her.

"Sometimes it helps to talk," she said, hoping he didn't hear the husky edge to her voice. "Believe it or not, I can keep things to myself." The door opened, startling both of them, and Morley Ames entered.

"Do you have more of that hand cream?" he asked almost before the door had closed behind him.

"I do," Jolie said, moving toward him, escaping.

"The wife loves it."

"And it looks like your hands are in better shape, too."

"A little. But I let her use most of the samples."

"How many tubes?" Jolie asked with a smile as she walked around the counter where she kept her private stash.

"Better make it four."

Jolie blinked at Dylan then grabbed four containers of hand cream out of the box on the lower shelf. "Anything else?"

"Nope. I'll be back for my regular feed order next week."

"By that time we should have the gift store up

and running," Jolie said as she rang up the cream and put it in a bag.

"Gift store?" Morley asked, sounding a touch shocked. "Here?"

"Western gifts and home items, made by local artisans. High-quality unique items." She picked up one of the brochures she'd made and popped it into the bag. "Mother's Day is coming up. And you have a grandson graduating soon, don't you?"

"I'll tell Lillian."

"I'd appreciate it. Bring her in. I also have some samples for other items from the hand cream line."

Morley cleared his throat. "Maybe I could take them now."

"You bet." Jolie reached into the box and pulled out a few samples of gentle dish soap, laundry soap and face cream. "See you next week."

Jolie waited until the door closed behind Morley before saying, "The store owes me eighteen dollars."

The phone in Dylan's pocket rang before he could answer. He pulled it out and glanced at the number, his mouth tightening. "I need to take this."

"Sure," Jolie said. The stormy look was back on his face and she hoped whatever it was didn't tip Dylan over the edge.

DYLAN DIDN'T SAY much after returning from the office. Jolie had put up the remaining boards and was standing back, debating how many more she needed and how best to use the dusty window space, when he crossed the room to join her. She didn't as much as look at him, sensing he needed his privacy. His expression was grim, but not that much grimmer than he had when he'd walked into the store that morning.

"I'll find a couple more usable boards," he said, heading for the door without waiting for her to agree.

While he was out there, they had an unusual rush of customers. Apparently the break in the rain had brought out the shoppers. By the time they'd taken care of the last one, it was time to close up shop.

Dylan disappeared into the warehouse while she gathered her purse and locked the main building and she found herself hoping that whatever was eating at him would soon be resolved.

Dani was working a horse in the round pen when Jolie got home. Since she didn't feel much like talking, anyway, Jolie put on her work clothes and headed out to cut the weeds that had shot up after the rains and threatened to short out the electric fence. She came in late, after dusk, and Dani opened the front door just as she started up the walk.

"I thought I was going to have to send out a

search party," she said, pulling her sweatshirt around her more tightly.

Despite her good intentions, Jolie's gaze dropped to her sister's midsection then slid away before it became obvious that she was speculating. "The weeds are shoulder high in some places."

"I can put in an hour or so tomorrow."

"Yeah? When?"

Dani's schedule was booked solid and if she was pregnant, Jolie was fairly certain that exhaustion wasn't helping matters. This was the first time that she could remember when she and Dani hadn't been totally open with one another, but that was the way life went. Things changed and you rolled with them.

"I can come early."

"No. I actually like being the one in control of weed maintenance," Jolie said. "As the youngest, I rarely experienced that thrill."

Dani smiled a little. "Suit yourself. Two jobs and ranch maintenance. That should keep you out of trouble."

"Nothing," Jolie said with a half smile, "has ever done that." It seemed that if she didn't run into trouble, she made her own—and she had a feeling she was inching toward trouble with Dylan Culver, but not in the usual way.

Dani pushed a hand through her hair. "Sorry for all the emotion lately."

"It happens."

"Not to me."

Jolie pushed her jaw sideways. "I beg to differ."

"I'm pregnant." The words came out in a rush. "I didn't know until yesterday."

"I guessed. You didn't drink your wine that night we had the toast."

"I wasn't feeling well. I—" she gave a small shrug "—had no idea. We're careful. We had a plan. This—" She stopped abruptly and pulled in a breath that made her shoulders rise a good inch. Then she shook her head.

"How's Gabe doing with this information?" Jolie asked gently.

Dani's gaze flashed up to hers. "I haven't told him because I want him to decide on this job—"

"What? Without all the facts?"

Her sister's face went a little pale. "No. He made a huge sacrifice for me. Us, really."

"It was all you," Jolie corrected. "If Allie and I had lived on this ranch and he'd never met you, trust me, there'd be a resort and water park next door."

"All right. He did it for me. I want him to take this job. *He* wants it."

"Then tell him you'll go with him. And then go. You could have done the long-distance thing if you hadn't been pregnant, but since you are—go."

"I don't want him to think I'm going just because I'm pregnant."

"You are."

"Exactly! And he won't want that and then…"

"So it's not perfect. Stop overthinking. Go tell Gabe he's going to be a father."

Dani pulled the sweatshirt around her again. "We had this plan…"

"I'm sure." Gabe was a rampant planner, the result of a chaotic childhood.

"Children happen in four years."

"Guess again."

"Yeah." Dani dug her hands into her pockets. "I just hate screwing up the plan."

"I think that took both of you." And Jolie couldn't believe she was valiantly pushing her sister out the door when she really didn't want to run the ranch alone. But, as she'd said, things changed.

CHAPTER SEVEN

DYLAN WAS MANNING the counter when Marti Kendall came in with a stack of artwork wrapped in brown paper late Friday afternoon. Jolie had been waiting for said artwork for days and he was glad it was finally here.

"Hey," she said with a wide smile. "It's been a while."

She spoke as if they'd been old friends, but as near as Dylan could remember they'd been passing acquaintances. Whatever. She was an attractive woman, petite with long brown hair and wide hazel eyes. From what he'd heard she was a very talented horse trainer and there was a bit of professional rivalry between her and Jolie's sister, Dani.

"Is Jolie here?"

"At the bank. She'll be back shortly."

He'd been enjoying a brief respite. Jolie had been eyeing him thoughtfully for the past several days and even though she hadn't said anything, it was coming. Despite his Herculean attempt not to let that shit going on with Lindsey and his ex-partner affect his mood, he knew he wasn't fully succeeding and she was keying in on it.

"I'm on kind of a tight schedule," Marti said with a smile. "Maybe you could help me hang these?"

"You could leave them for Jolie."

Marti shook her head as if that wasn't even close to an option. "I'd rather hang them myself. Make certain it's done right."

"Okay." Dylan came out from the behind the counter, remembering now why he and Marti had never been more than acquaintances. "I'll get the ladder."

She smiled at him. "Thank you."

Dylan brushed the ladder off before hauling it into the store. By the time he got there, Marti had her paintings unwrapped and set out on the counter. "Those are nice."

They were actually beyond "nice." He didn't know much about art, but the swirling colors that flowed out of the manes and tails of running horses were masterfully done. "You have a distinctive style."

Marti beamed as she held up the first painting. "Thank you. If I didn't train horses for a living, I do think I could have a career in art." She gave him a winsome look. "I don't have time to do both well at the moment, so I paint when I have some downtime in the winter."

She held a painting out at arm's length, raising and lowering it a few inches as she regarded the wall behind it. "This one first. I think the nail needs to go just about where that tiny crack is."

Dylan didn't ask which crack since there were several in the old building, which had been settling for the better part of a century. There were freshly painted cracks, however. Jolie had belatedly decided to paint the wall behind the cedar, and had managed to do so without removing the boards.

"Perfect," Marti said as he drove the nail and then took the painting from her and carefully settled it in place. That was when he got a good look at the price sticker and decided he'd be really surprised if any of Marti's artwork went out the door if they were all similarly priced. He moved the ladder and Marti handed him another painting after he'd driven in the nail.

When he'd hung the last work, he lowered the ladder to lay on its edge along the aisle and they stood back to admire. Yeah. The art definitely added a touch of class to the place.

Dylan settled his hands on his hips. "Looks good," he said.

Marti smiled up at him. "Thank you."

She glanced around the store but they both turned toward the door when it swung open and Jolie strolled in. She stopped abruptly when she caught sight of the paintings.

"Those are fantastic, Marti."

"Thank you. I have them all marked with prices. I assume you'll let me know if something sells? I don't have to check in or wait until the contract is over?"

"Of course," Jolie said, sounding surprised that Marti would even ask such a question. She headed for the counter and Dylan was about to follow when Marti circled around him, essentially blocking his path.

"I was iffy about this idea," she said, "but I really think you've done a great job here."

"It was mostly Jolie."

"Great job, Jolie," Marti called brightly. She glanced down at her watch, a silver-and-rhinestone concoction that perfectly suited her. "I've got to run. New client consultation." She smiled up at Dylan. "I might have to start buying more of my feed here." Then, with another smile and a pat on his upper arm, she sauntered past him to the door. She stopped before she opened it. "Maybe we could discuss sometime?"

He raised a hand. "Sure. Sounds great."

MARTI KENDALL WAS a piece of work. Jolie could handle her being beautiful and talented and an excellent horse trainer. What drove her crazy was Marti's assumption that everyone was in awe of her. That and her occasional lapse into mean-spiritedness when she felt as if she wasn't being properly admired.

Jolie came out from behind the counter to take a look at the art. She'd love to own a piece, if she could separate the painting from the creator in her head, but she didn't know that she could do that. And it was amusing how shifty Dylan appeared, as if he expected her to make fun of him for being the object of Marti's flirtation.

Jolie saw no reason to let him down. "We should put your picture up next to the Culver Ranch and Feed sign on the side of the building."

He gave her a perplexed look.

"'I might start buying all my feed here,'" she said, doing a pretty good imitation of Marti's throaty drawl. His mouth tightened and Jolie continued. "Maybe we could jump-start sales that way." She bit her lip as she ran an appraising gaze over him. "Maybe you could wear a Speedo."

"We wouldn't know if new customers are coming in because of my picture or your gift shop. That would affect our analysis of who wins the bet."

She felt her mouth drift into a smile. "Maybe we should put your picture up and forego the bet."

"Is that fear talking?"

"Never."

"Then…"

"Just giving you an out."

He leaned on the counter, bringing his face

closer to hers, so close she could see the flecks of navy in his blue eyes. So close that his scent filled her nostrils, making her hormones stand up and take notice. "Why would I need an out?"

"You're going to lose. Look at that awesome display."

"Doesn't do you much good if it doesn't get people in to see it. I don't think this is a case of build it and they'll come."

"That's why I'm having the raffle."

He straightened but left his palms on the counter. He had nice hands. Strong and callused…

"And what, pray tell, are we raffling off?"

"A silver necklace and a couple bags of feed."

Dylan frowned. "This isn't supposed to be costing me money."

"It's not. I'm buying that stuff."

"That's not fair."

"How so?"

"You're bribing people to come in. We could have done that without the boutique."

"Why didn't you?"

"Never thought of it."

"People like giveaways."

"No doubt. And if we could afford it, we'd do a lot of them. But giving things away is the opposite of selling them."

"You know what I mean."

"Yeah."

"Do you want people to come in?"

"I want customers."

"Give me free rein for a while and I think we can get some people in. We can drop the bet."

"That's the second time you've said that."

"Is it?" She stared him down, forcing herself to look as though she didn't want to lean closer and simply inhale. His frown intensified, as she'd hoped. "You're in a better mood today."

"Guess this is your lucky day."

"I'm used to your moods. Heaven knows I saw a lot of them back in the day. No. Make that one mood. Cranky."

"My dad was dying. I needed straight A's to get scholarships. I wanted him to watch me walk across that stage when we graduated and take home as many scholarships as I could. He was worried about my future."

Jolie felt as though someone had just smacked her. She'd been aware that his father had been sick but hadn't known that he'd been dying while she and Dylan had been lab partners.

"Why didn't you tell me?" she finally asked.

He gave her a "Really?" look. "It was a painful topic."

"No doubt." Jolie tore her eyes away from his and stared off across the room. "Sorry to have been so…unaware."

"It's all right."

"It's not." He was shutting down fast and she didn't want him to shut down. The atmosphere at the store was so much better when they were communicating. And, even though he'd been preoccupied over the past few days, every now and then they'd had a decent snippet of conversation. Like now. "Just let me apologize once. I didn't know. I'm sorry."

"You had no way of knowing. Apology accepted." He spoke gruffly in the tone of a guy who wasn't used to talking about the things he held inside. Jolie had a sneaking suspicion that this wasn't the only thing he was holding inside. Something else had made him distracted and angry of late and she couldn't help but wonder what it was.

"Maybe we should make a new bet," Dylan said.

"What kind of bet?" Jolie couldn't keep the note of suspicion out of her voice.

"If I win, we keep the boutique, but you take all of Mike's excess animals."

"That will cost *me* money," she pointed out, glad that he was making an effort to lighten the mood. It didn't make her feel any better about being so blissfully unaware of the circumstances of his life back then, but at least he was communicating.

"Well, you do work at a feed store and there is that employee discount."

She smiled and slowly he smiled back.

"Mike got a decent offer on his place. He'll probably take it, but he's starting to stress a little."

And perhaps this was an explanation for his recent preoccupation...perhaps. "I'll put out the word, see what I can do," Jolie said. With a wry twist of her lips, she said, "I see a lot of animal lovers in the course of my day."

Dylan patted the counter. "Mike will appreciate it."

And that, of course, was why she was doing it. For Mike. Not for the guy on the other side of the counter/barrier giving her one of his rare smiles and making her heart melt a little as he did so.

DANI PACED TO the living-room window, stared out at the horses in the pasture, then turned back to Jolie who sat on the sofa, waiting for her sister to talk herself down. "I know it's not fair to leave after asking you to come back and work with me—"

"I want you to leave," Jolie said patiently. "You belong with Gabe."

"You're sure."

"Would it matter if I wasn't?"

"Yes."

"Then good thing I'm sure. When do you go?"

"Gabe takes off in a week."

"Short notice."

"Speaking of which..." Dani bunched the gray

fleece she'd finally found into a wad. "Can you get Wednesday off?"

"I...don't know."

"Gabe and I need a witness. We're going to the courthouse."

"To get married?"

"No. To get fishing licenses."

"Hey, now." Jolie raised her hands. "Just checking." She reached out to loop an arm around her sister. "Congratulations. Mom is going to kill you if she's not there."

"I've explained everything to her."

"And she's not stepping onto a plane at this very moment?"

"I'm flying to Florida to stay with her for a week or so while Gabe gets us set up...and, more importantly, we're having the ceremony next summer here at home."

Jolie smiled widely. "Remember how we used to plan our weddings? Your ceremony was going to be down by the river and mine was under that big oak that Daddy planted when he and Mom got married."

"Uh, yeah. That's why we're getting married here."

"Careful, sis. I may not get the day off to help you procure those fishing licenses."

"Please?" Dani asked before smacking Jolie with a small pillow.

"Fine. Yes. I think Dylan will let me off for something like that."

"And if he won't?"

Jolie wrinkled her nose. "Drag the JP down to the feed store. You can do it there."

"Good idea," Dani said, getting to her feet. "You want to come over for dinner? Gabe grills a mean hamburger."

"You go," Jolie said. "I want to run Jenabelle a little. Then I'm going to move the cows and have an early night."

"Okay." Dani frowned, then closed the space between them and hugged her sister hard. "Thank you for holding down the fort. We need someone here at the Lightning Creek."

And that was when it struck Jolie how very alone she was going to be for the next several months.

For once Dylan beat Jolie to work. He was sure she wouldn't be late. It was Tuesday and she didn't work at the bar until Thursday, so her sleep-deprived days hadn't started yet. He paced to the window then back to his office. Finally he heard her truck pull in and went to meet her at the door.

"Hi," she said, apparently surprised by his being there.

"Yeah. Hi."

"One more time with feeling," she said as she breezed by him toward her workstation.

"I didn't mean to sound…" He muttered a low curse. "Look. Mike accepted the offer for his house last night."

"I hope he got a good price."

"He did. Contingent on closing the deal ASAP."

"Meaning?"

"I need a temporary home for all those damned animals."

"I don't know that wild cats do temporary," Jolie pointed out.

"I have every intention of finding permanent homes in the near future. I've been contacting 4-H leaders and, as you know, I put up the posters. There are ads in all the papers I can think of, on craigslist—"

"Yes."

Dylan blinked at her and then realized what she was saying and smiled. "Thank you." He let out a breath. "Thank you."

"How long?"

"Just until I find homes."

"And how long might that be?"

"A week?"

She nodded slowly. "Can I have next Wednesday off? My sister is getting married."

"Kind of sudden, isn't it?"

"They've been engaged for a while, but Gabe got a temporary job back east and…well…" She made a gesture.

"They decided to get married before they left."

"It was either that or fishing licenses."

"I'm not even going to ask."

She smiled. "You had to be there. I assume that's a yes?"

"I couldn't really say no, could I?"

"I don't think you would anyway."

"Know me that well, do you?"

"I honestly don't think I know you at all. Had you asked me a month ago, I would have assured you that I knew you all too well."

"What changed your mind?"

"I've found out you have a mood other than pissed off at me."

He leaned on the counter, as he seemed to be doing more and more. "I wasn't always pissed off at you."

"But you were at the ready." She cocked an eyebrow at him. "Admit it…you had a hair trigger where I was involved."

"And who honed that trigger?"

Jolie placed a palm upon her chest. "Yours truly?"

He couldn't help smiling at the wicked glint in her eyes that belied the innocent look on her face. "I admit that I thought I had you all figured out, too. I didn't. I still don't."

That seemed to catch her interest. "What would you like to know?"

Probably more than an employer should want to know about an employee, but, truthfully, he didn't think of her as an employee and he was certain she didn't think of him as a boss.

Her lips tilted wryly as the silence stretched. "No questions?"

"Whatever I want to know, I'll find out in my own good time."

CHAPTER EIGHT

"SHE'S GOING TO take them all?" Mike asked for a second time after Dylan had come home with the happy news that he'd found a home for Mike's girls.

"I think the cats are staying here. The real-estate agent is going to check with the new buyer and see if they mind having cats in the barn." He'd have taken them to the warehouse to live and hunt, but that wouldn't be fair to Marcel, who'd never been very social with other cats.

"That's fine with me. I didn't bring the cats here in the first place. They just kind of started moving in." Mike grinned as he pulled up the footrest on his lounger and then stretched out to full comfort position. "What a load off my mind."

"Yeah." There was no way Dylan was breaking the news that the home he'd found was temporary.

"I'm going to celebrate by not packing."

"There's not much left to pack," Dylan said. All the rooms in the house were stacked with boxes. With the exception of the kitchen and bedding, his grandfather was ready to move. Only the area immediately surrounding his beloved lounger and television remained untouched.

Speck jumped onto Mike's lap and the two settled into news shows while Dylan sat in the other lounger and attempted to study for the detective exam that was coming up in another couple of weeks.

Attempted being the key word, since his thoughts persistently crept back to Lindsey and Pat. There was no reason to assume that Pat and Lindsey had been involved a year ago. That Pat had been the unnamed other guy...but the possibility ate at him. He couldn't stop thinking back, analyzing if Pat's behavior had changed at all prior to the accident that had ended their partnership. He came up with no answers. Finally he closed the lid of his laptop and looked over at his grandfather.

"Hey, you want a beer?"

"In the worst way." Mike gave his usual answer, then frowned, his silver eyebrows almost touching. "Something wrong tonight?"

Dylan shrugged and set the laptop aside. "It's been a while since I've studied."

"You'd think it's kind of like riding a bike."

"You'd think," Dylan agreed as he got out of his chair. And it might have been had he not had other things on his mind. He went to the nearly empty fridge and broke into the new six-pack he'd picked up on the way home. "Chips?" he called into the living room.

"Let's go wild," Mike said.

Dylan smiled as he dumped a bag of chips into a big plastic bowl. Finding a home for the goats and cow had definitely lifted his granddad's mood.

Dylan settled back into his chair, set the bowl of chips on the table between them and popped the top of his beer. Then he leaned over to touch his can to Mike's. "To the future."

Mike tilted his can at his grandson. "To the guy who kept my girls together and found them a good home."

Dylan's smile became a little strained, but he touched aluminum to aluminum again and then took a long drink. Things would work out—not that they always did, but in this case he had to keep the faith.

JOLIE TOOK WEDNESDAY morning off to attend her sister's wedding, leaving Dylan to man the store solo. He dealt with a few regular clients, all of whom asked about Jolie and commented on what nice things she was doing to the store. They were right. She had made the place more inviting, but he still thought it was illogical to expect frou-frou items to affect sales at a feed store. People came to buy grain, not to shop for gifts. He had to admit, though, that the customers were taking long, hard looks at the artisan items, especially the iron work, before drifting to the counter to order grain or hay or minerals. And they smiled and chatted more.

Go figure.

He also noticed on the Facebook page that morning that Jolie had advertised the raffle, which he still thought gave her an unfair advantage, but as Mike had mentioned, it was hard for him to lose in this deal, unless one considered the fact that a night out on the town with Jolie had the potential for danger.

When he was around her, he felt off balance and it was in a different way than in the past. His body was encouraging him to move closer, touch her, stake a claim. His mind was telling him that was a very bad idea—they worked together, even if it was temporary and…well, Jolie was Jolie. He wasn't in the market for a relationship and he couldn't see having a brief, hot fling with Jolie. No sense making things awkward, especially when they were often the only two people in the building.

Unfortunately the forklift was purring like a kitten and he'd finally gotten the office sorted out, so he didn't have a lot to fill his time at the store except for studying. He wasn't in the mood to study.

He leaned back in Jolie's chair and stared out the window, hands clasped behind his head. Finn loved running the feed store, puttering around, doing who knew what, which was nuts because his cousin had been so wild growing up.

Jolie also puttered around, making the store homier. She was on the verge of painting the rest of the store. Several times he'd seen her studying color chip cards and he didn't think she was painting at home. It was kind of fun to watch her busy herself around the store when they had no customers and when he wasn't putting distance between them by hanging out in the warehouse.

He was not a putterer, nor was he meant to sit at a desk. He stretched out his leg, flexed it. Almost 100 percent. Surely good enough to be released back to active duty. Best-case scenario, he'd get his medical release, pass the detective exam, Detective Murdock would retire and Dylan would slip into his position.

Worst-case scenario, he would stay at the desk and support his ex-partner who was secretly living with his ex-wife. The prick.

The dark thought had him sitting up in the chair and digging his phone out of his pocket. He'd told Phil that he'd wait to hear from him, but he was tired of waiting. Surely the PI had discovered something.

Phil answered the call himself. "I thought you were going to wait to hear from me."

"Were you ever going to call?"

"Not until I got another week's pay out of you,"

Phil said in his laidback way. "Actually, I was about to call. Your suspicions have foundation."

"Lindsey's seeing Pat?"

"When he's on day shift, he spends the nights there with her."

"What about other shifts?"

"I've only had time to observe him for a shift and a half, but when he's on graveyard, no. He sleeps at his brother's place. He drops by to see Lindsey when she gets home from work, then goes on shift."

"Why not sleep at his place?"

"He rented it out."

"No shit. But he only sleeps with Lindsey when he's off at night."

"Harder to hide a vehicle during the day. He never parks until after dark. He's usually gone by daylight."

Pat always had been slick. He could think of three ways around a problem, which had been handy when they'd worked together. Not so handy now.

Dylan knew he was lucky that Sadie had noticed and liked him enough to give him a heads-up. The thought of subsidizing that asshole, a guy he'd trusted, fried him. He pulled in a long breath through his nose as he fought to control his temper. "I'll be there in a couple of weeks. I'll need something to hand over to my lawyer." And hopefully to get the split mortgage agreement adjusted.

"I'll email a report as soon as I get it together."

"Thanks." Dylan hung up and carefully set his phone on Jolie's desk so that he wouldn't throw it across the room. He hated being played as a chump.

He got to his feet and paced out from behind the counter, shoving his hand through his hair. It would feel so damned good to get into his car, drive to Lanesburg and confront his ex-partner...except that he couldn't risk giving Pat time to cover his tracks. Dylan couldn't think of exactly how Pat might do that, but the guy was good. Better to get Phil's report to the judge than get the satisfaction of a face-to-face. Or a fist-to-face.

The bell above the door rang and a couple of teenage cowboys came in, looking for bandannas. Dylan had to deliver the sad news that they didn't carry bandannas and he didn't have an answer when one of the kids asked why. They'd barely left when another customer came in to buy a supplement they did carry. And all he could think as he put on his polite cop face and rang up the sale was that Jolie seemed tuned in to his moods and was not shy about calling him on the dark ones. He needed to act as normal as possible when she returned so she wouldn't ask questions he really didn't want to think about much less answer.

THE WEDDING WASN'T FANCY. The bride wore a knee-length, green-silk shift, the groom a sports jacket. But the way they looked at one another, the way Gabe's eyes skimmed over his wife-to-be and stopped ever so briefly at her midsection, made Jolie clear her throat more than once as she fought back emotion.

The justice of the peace was the father of one of Jolie's high school friends and they caught up for a few minutes before the brief ceremony. Jolie encouraged him to stop by the feed store next time he needed dog food and handed him a ten-percent-off coupon.

"Really?" Dani said as she took her place next to Gabe. Jolie just smiled, resisting the urge to hand her sister a coupon. It was her special day, after all.

The ceremony was short. The kiss that followed was not. Dani was so damned happy, even if getting married in the courthouse hadn't been part of their original plan and kids were supposed to happen in four years. She and Gabe held hands tightly as they left the courthouse and the three of them celebrated with lunch at the Jameson hotel.

"Well, Mr. and Mrs. Matthews, as much as I'd love to linger and be the third wheel, I need to get back to the store." Jolie insisted on paying the check then slung her purse over her shoulder.

"Aren't you going to give us some coupons before you leave?" Dani asked.

"Hey, I have a bet to win. I have to drum up business where I can. You guys are already part of our customer base."

Although she very much wanted to win that bet and to hear Dylan tell her that she was right and he was wrong—for once—she was beginning to suspect that she'd chosen the wrong prize.

When she'd first thrown down the gauntlet and named her prize, she'd envisioned having some fun telling Dylan where they would go and what they would do—pretty much bossing him around the way he used to boss her around. And she'd assumed he would play along, as well as he was able to play, anyway. Lately, however, she'd discovered that not only could Dylan play, but that she enjoyed playing with him. The beauty of their situation was that Dylan was one guarded guy; he'd only let things go so far before reining them in. So she was free to push a few boundaries—play with him a little—but she was beginning to see that she needed to be careful about how far she pushed things.

When she got back to the store, one look at Dylan's face told her there would be no playing today. Granted, his dark expression cleared some when he glanced up as she came through the door. He was making an effort. Cool. But she couldn't help but flash on the fact that the last time he'd

looked this way was when his father was dying—
and she hadn't known.

He shifted his weight as she approached, as if
he was uncomfortable being trapped behind the
counter. "How was the wedding?"

"Quick, but the bride and groom seemed pleased.
They're going to have a big ceremony next summer
at the Lightning Creek and right now they're on
their way to Flathead Lake for a three-day honey-
moon before flying to Florida to celebrate with
our mom."

"Sounds cool." But clearly his heart wasn't in
the comment. The divorce maybe? Could it be that
Dylan no longer believed in happily-ever-after?
Her sister, Allie, didn't after her rough five-year
marriage had ended, but her other recently married sister, Mel, was enthusiastic.

"How was business?" she asked, setting her
purse on the counter. It seemed odd to have their
positions reversed with Dylan on the inside and
her on the out. So she leaned on the counter as he
always did.

"We had some customers. One lady was ready
to buy one of Marti's paintings."

"Then she saw the price."

"Hey. She didn't faint."

Jolie smiled as their gazes connected. Held. And
even though he was smiling, too, the expression in

his eyes was both distant and wary. As if he was hiding something. "Everything okay?"

Even as she asked, she knew that Dylan would shut down rather than respond.

He did not disappoint. "Nothing."

Nothing her ass. He looked as if he was about to write her a ticket. All cool and distant. Guarded.

"Mike's okay with the sale?"

Dylan's expression cleared a bit and she knew she was on the wrong track and he was glad of it. "Oh. Yeah. Now that the girls have a home, he's good with it. I think he's looking forward to being closer to his sister."

"And you'll live with him?"

"For now."

She leaned her chin on one hand, really wanting to dig deeper, to see if she could cajole his secrets out of him, but knowing he wouldn't let go of them easily. The distant polite-cop look still masked his expression, but there was definitely something there that he couldn't quite cover. Pain? Anger?

Damn it. She wanted to know.

"Well," he said, "I have an order to finish."

"Facebook page to update," she said as they exchanged places. She set her purse under the counter and watched as Dylan disappeared into his office.

Leave it be.

Good advice. She hoped she could follow it.

As it turned out, she could not.

At home that evening she received Finn's long-overdue reply to her most recent email to him, over a week after she'd sent it. He asked about the bet and how she and Dylan were getting along. He hoped the store wouldn't look like a battleground when he returned.

She wrote back telling him that the store was fine, she would certainly win the bet and that she and Dylan were working together surprisingly well, even if he was seriously defensive about certain issues. Such as his recent past. What on earth had happened to him? What kind of mystery accident had he had? Was Dylan also keeping it a secret from Finn? And what had happened to his marriage?

She clicked Send and wondered if she'd already have the answers to those questions by the time he wrote back, which would no doubt be in another two weeks. She doubted that she would.

Dylan was a vault and, honestly? She was spending too much time wondering about him and his secrets—perhaps because with Dani gone, she didn't have a whole lot else to think about during her nights off, except for ranch repairs, of course.

Jolie turned off her computer and wandered toward the kitchen, stepping over Gus, who'd passed out in the doorway. If anyone had asked her if she was afraid of being alone, she would have answered no with a straight face. But she wouldn't have been being totally honest. She didn't mind *being* alone, but she did not like coming home to an empty house.

For some reason the emptiness took her straight back to the days after she'd lost her father, when the house had seemed to echo whenever she walked inside, despite her sisters and mother being there. She had been her father's favorite, the baby, and she'd loved it. But her sisters had all had a longer time with him, even if it had only been a year in Dani's case, and Jolie felt cheated because of it.

Damn but she still missed him. All these years later, even though she now had to look at a photograph to remember what he looked like, she still remembered what it felt like to be near him. Safe. Warm. Loved.

Then all that comfort and security had been snatched away.

Gus gave a yawn and stretched out to his full length. Rolling over onto his back, he "grinned" up at her as if sensing that she needed someone to break the grim mood descending upon her.

With a soft smile she knelt to rub his belly. His eyes shut in an expression of pure canine bliss. Jolie gave his belly a pat and straightened again.

She was good. She was fine. Living alone again was going to take some getting used to, but she'd adjust. It wasn't as if she didn't have a lot of chores, both at work and at home, to keep her busy and help her fall into bed exhausted at night.

For that she was grateful.

JOLIE KNEW THE instant she walked into the store after her lunch break that something was off. Dylan emerged from his office as she walked in the door and took a stance. Everything about him, from his body language to his closed expression, read anger.

She stopped several yards away from him. "Bad news?"

"There's something we need to get straight," he said as he folded his arms over his chest.

"Apparently so," she replied, ignoring the sudden hammering of her heart as she walked to the counter to set her purse down. She turned back, telling herself there was no reason for her heart to beat harder...but she also couldn't think of one thing they needed to get straight, or a reason for him to look so angry.

"You and I work together. You have no right to be making inquiries into my personal life. Of my cousin or anyone else."

She gaped at him. Finn had ratted her out? "I was concerned." Her voice was huskier than usual and she had to swallow after speaking.

"It's not your place to be concerned." Dylan's jaw went tight for a moment. "How would digging into my life alleviate your concern?"

"I—" Had no answer. She also had no defense. There was no use pretending that she did.

"So," he asked coldly. "What did you find out?"

"You know what I found out. Nothing."

He took a few steps closer, but if he thought she was going to back down or shrink into herself, he had another think coming. "Is it that bad?" she asked, trying for bravado. "Whatever it is?"

"What it is, is private. I'm private. If I want someone to know something about me, I tell them. I didn't tell you for a reason."

Jolie blinked, feeling something that felt ridiculously like tears. It sucked to be so wrong, but it sucked just as much to be attacked because she'd cared enough to try to find out what was making this man so freaking defensive and unhappy. "I understand," she said stiffly. "Enjoy your misery, Mr. Culver. If you need me for some *professional* reason, I'll be here. At my computer. Working."

She marched around the counter, put her purse away and pulled back her chair with quick, deliberate movements. She turned to see if he was still there or if he'd retreated to his lair. He was still there, standing stiffly, regarding her with a somewhat conflicted expression.

And then it dawned on her…he'd probably just recalled that he was supposed to deliver his grandfather's menagerie to the Lightning Creek that evening.

The power had just shifted a bit and she wondered what she was going to do with her very slight advantage.

Let him suffer awhile. She turned back to her computer and shook the mouse to wake it up, taking a seat as she waited for the screen to light. She hoped he didn't ask about the animals because, truthfully, she didn't know what her answer was going to be. What she did know was that she was done with Dylan Culver. Maybe she shouldn't have asked about him, but it hadn't been with malicious intent and she wasn't going to waste her breath trying to explain that particular fact to her jerk of a boss.

The bell rang over the door and Jolie got back to her feet, ready to take an order from the elderly couple that walked into the store. After that, customers showed up in a steady stream, one after another, giving her and Dylan no real time to talk.

Jolie sold a couple of picture frames and a bridle, which should have lifted her mood, but didn't. She was polite and friendly to the customers, but felt as if she was outside her own body, watching herself go through the motions of making people feel their business was appreciated. And she was good at it, too—much better at hiding her true mood than Dylan was. However, she made no effort to hide her feelings about him the few times they'd had to speak. Coldness was not a natural response for her under general circumstances, but cold was what Dylan got. And it felt good to give him a little of his own.

Dylan loaded the last customer, one of his former high school cronies, a few minutes after closing time and Jolie took advantage of his preoccupation to slip out the side door, get into her truck and drive away. And she turned her phone off for good measure. She had no idea how Dylan was going to handle the animal issue, nor how she would respond. The ball was in his court and she was curious to see what his next move was going to be.

CHAPTER NINE

MIKE CRANED HIS neck as Dylan turned into the gate leading to the Lightning Creek Ranch. His grandfather was practically squirming in his seat in his anticipation to see where his girls were going to call home. All Dylan could hope for was that, one, Jolie didn't order him off the property and Mike didn't find out tonight that this was only a temporary home.

He hadn't even thought about Jolie being the foster keeper of his granddad's girls until after she'd mentioned that he was free to talk to her about any professional matters. He'd been so damned hot when he'd received Finn's email a few minutes before she'd arrived that he hadn't been thinking straight at all. What if she did throw them off the property? How was he going to explain that to Mike?

Any concerns he had about Jolie's welcome evaporated when he pulled the truck and trailer to a stop in front of the barn. Jolie came out of the house and went directly to the passenger side of the truck to open the door for Mike. She didn't as much as look at Dylan.

"This way," she said with a smile after Mike closed the truck door. "Let me show you the pens."

She led the way into the barn, leaving Dylan wondering whether he should wait outside or follow them in. Deciding that Mike might notice something was off if he stayed with the truck, he trailed along behind them.

"This is for the goats," Jolie said, showing Mike a stall that led to a square-wire pen outside. "A remnant from my 4-H sheep days."

"Looks fine. It's a lot more grazing than they have right now. They'll be happy."

"And your cow—"

"Karen."

"I'd like to eventually put Karen out with the other ladies." She glanced over at Mike as she spoke, her gaze clashing with Dylan's before she asked, "Are you all right with that?"

"Shouldn't hurt none. It's been a while since she's seen another cow." That was evident from the way she was bellowing in the trailer.

"She's halter broke?"

"Did a couple of years of 4-H with the neighbor kid."

"Great. Maybe your grandson can lead her into the pen opposite the goat pen."

"I'll get her," Mike said, shooting a look from one of them to the other.

Great. Dylan smiled tightly at him. "I'll get the goats."

"I'll help," Jolie said, following the two men to the trailer.

The animals went into the pens more quietly than Dylan had expected, given the strange new surroundings and the cows bellowing back at Karen. Once the gates were latched, Jolie ran her hands down the sides of her pants.

"I'll take good care of them," Jolie said to Mike.

From the way Mike was beaming back at her, Dylan wondered if she might not be in line for a raise in pay.

"I appreciate you taking them. I know it's a big commitment. I just about gave up on finding them a permanent home. Most people wanted to eat them."

"Yes," Jolie said, once again meeting Dylan's gaze. "I'm glad to help. Please, feel free to visit any time."

"I don't know if I need to do that," Mike said, "but if you don't mind, maybe I will. Sometime."

"Maybe after you settle into your new place," Dylan said.

"Yeah."

"Can I offer you anything before you go?" Jolie asked. "I have beer and cola."

"We still have to haul a couple loads to the new place. But, thanks," Mike said, reaching out to take Jolie's hand. For a minute Dylan thought he was going to kiss it or something, but instead he squeezed it and then let her go.

"I'll, uh, see you tomorrow," Dylan said to Jolie.

"No doubt," she said, the words dropping coldly from her lips.

He and Mike got in the truck. Mike shot him a look, but Dylan focused on backing the trailer in a three-point turn. They drove by Jolie, who waved at Mike. Dylan nodded at her because Mike would think it odd if he didn't.

"What in the hell is going on between the two of you?"

"What?"

"Don't give me 'what'?" She's steamed at you and you looked like you wanted to be anywhere but there."

"Nothing's up," Dylan said.

"Bull."

"Nothing important. We just had a disagreement. It's nothing big."

"It is if that's the way you two are in the store. Customers are going to leave if they feel uncomfortable."

"They're usually only there for a few minutes anyway." Although most were now taking the time to browse the gift section and Jolie's hand cream was becoming more and more popular—although the store didn't get jack for that because she sold it at her cost and he'd brilliantly told her that the store didn't want to carry it.

"You two patch things up." It was a direct order. "It'll be fine."

But part of him said that having her angry at him was a good thing. They'd proved today that they could be civil to each other while the customers were there. And could retreat to their neutral corners when they were alone. Surely they could continue this routine until Finn returned.

Yes. Civil would be fine with him.

ONCE DYLAN AND his grandfather drove away, Jolie went into the barn to visit her new animals.

Mike was obviously under the impression that the Lightning Creek Ranch was a permanent home to his pets. While she could understand why Dylan hadn't told Mike the flat-out truth, it put her in a situation she hadn't signed on for and she and Dylan would address that in the morning.

One of the goats nudged her from between the bars of the panels and she reached out to rub its bony head. Jolie sighed as the other goat crowded up for attention, ignoring the feed she'd given them, their little tails wagging a mile a minute.

Of course she was going to keep the animals, but she and Dylan were going to discuss his tactics all the same. And the bet. There would be no more bet. That had been made in the spirit of friendly competition. She saw now that friendship wasn't going to work with them. They could be acquaintances. That would work.

Jolie left the goats to their feed and made her way to the house. Now that Dani was gone and the lights of the Staley house were dark, Jolie felt oddly restless. She'd already put Jenabelle through her paces and now she had nothing to do but retreat inside, kick around the house and wish that she'd given more thought to taking up a hobby.

Gus stuck close by her side, apparently sensing that she really hated going into the house alone. Allie was only a couple hours' drive away. All of her sisters, except for Mel, were as close as a phone call, as was her mother, but she wasn't going to call. Not tonight. Instead she was going to tackle this melancholy feeling on her own. She was at a place she loved, and it wasn't as if she minded being alone...

But still she felt off. Unsettled.

There was nothing to do for it except put her head down and muscle through. So she'd messed up with Dylan and they would have some awkward moments ahead of them. Those types of things had never bothered her before and she wasn't certain why they were bothering her now.

The only thing she was certain of was that she was still pissed at Dylan.

She saddled Jenabelle again, took a quick ride to the river then worked on the plank fencing behind the house until dark, putting a lot more pressure on the drill as she inserted more reinforcing screws than were totally necessary. When she finished, the boards were all reinforced, so the next step was to come up with a couple hundred extra dollars for paint. That meant she had to continue showing up for work at both the store and the bar. And that meant she needed to work out a peace treaty of sorts with Dylan.

She gave the matter a lot of thought that night. She would be polite. A model employee. It was her only course of action.

Dylan beat Jolie to the store again the next morning. Jolie sat in her old truck for moment, gathering strength before yanking the keys out of the ignition and making her way inside.

The store was dark except for the light in the office and Jolie decided that it would be best if she took the offensive immediately. She went to his office and knocked once on the door frame, something she'd never done before, but somehow it seemed appropriate now. When he looked up, she said, "The bet's off."

He started to speak and she held up her hand. For once she was going to lay out the way things were going to be. The way they should have been from the beginning. "I'll put in my hours and I'll do my job. Please don't expect anything else from me."

"What else might I have expected?" he asked gruffly.

"Pleasant conversation? Witty repartee? Help cleaning up after a failed lightbulb change? No more of that." She shook her head and she meant it.

"A straight working relationship."

"As if we were an officer and enlisted man."

"I wouldn't go that far."

She gave a tiny snort through her nose. "I would."

Jolie sold one of Marti's expensive paintings a few hours later, which made her very glad she'd told Dylan that the bet was off. They were definitely getting more customers coming in to browse the boutique and new artisans were now calling her. If this turned out to be a successful venue for Marti's work, she might bring in more paintings and she might throw more of her well-to-do clients' business their way.

Yes. She was definitely glad the bet was off.

Dylan came in after loading a truck, stopping at the counter on his way to his office. "You sold a painting."

Jolie's hands stilled on the keyboard, which was fine, since she wasn't so much typing as looking busy. "Yes."

The single-word response hung between them for a moment and once again Jolie felt her heart do the slow *thump-thump-thump* as she waited for him to respond. Or leave.

Dylan's mouth tightened momentarily. "You made Mike really happy by taking his animals. I'll pay for their keep."

Jolie's eyebrows shot up. "I consider them my animals now and I'll pay to feed them."

"Jolie."

"I plan to breed Karen and get a nice Jersey calf out of her."

"Jolie…"

"What?"

"I didn't tell him it was temporary because he's under a lot of stress as is. I planned to tell him."

"Did I complain about that? Have I said one word? No. Now if there's nothing else, I have work to do."

She waited until he said no before turning back to the computer screen and pretending that the stuff on it made sense.

This, she told herself angrily, *is why you don't get too friendly with the boss*. It made work uncomfortable. If Dylan wasn't her temporary boss, she'd probably look for another job, even though she enjoyed the store, the customers. Thankfully it wouldn't be that long before Dylan would be out of there. All she had to do was put in her hours, wear her own equivalent of the cop face and endure.

DYLAN DID NOT like dealing with closed-off Jolie, even though he knew that this relationship was much better for both of them. He just wished he didn't feel as if he'd lost something. And he didn't like the fact that being at work didn't feel nearly as pleasant as it had only a few days ago.

He brought up his computer program and scrolled through his inventory. *Pleasant.* When was the last time going to work had felt pleasant to him? He couldn't remember a time prior to taking over the feed store.

When he'd been on patrol, work had felt both satisfying and frustrating. Frustrating in that there was no way the police could address all the wrongs in the city, but satisfying in that at least he was doing his small part. But pleasant was a new concept and that had been exactly how he'd felt right up until he'd found out that Jolie had been asking questions of Finn.

Finn hadn't seemed to think it was a big deal, but Finn's partner wasn't sleeping with his ex-wife. Sneaking around so that Dylan kept blithely paying his part of the mortgage. He felt stupid and screwed over and…raw. Yeah. He felt raw. He didn't want anyone to know that two people he'd cared for were now playing him as a sap.

And that's what it came down to: broken trust, feeling like a failure and not wanting anyone to know. Even Finn didn't know. The only people who had a pretty good picture of the situation were himself, Phil the PI and maybe Sadie. She was certainly bright enough to put the pieces together.

The bottom line was that this really all came down to hating to fail.

He'd always hated to fail.

He didn't see Jolie for most of the day. Where he used to go out and hang around her counter a little, to see what she was doing, now he only saw her when he loaded a customer and even then she pretty much ignored him. Not that she didn't treat him with respect. She was actually treating him with way more respect than was normal for an informal working environment. He'd noticed more than one customer shoot him a look when Jolie spoke to him in a cool, almost formal tone that was very unlike the one she used with the customers. Respectful, yes. Friendly…not even close.

He was going to have to learn to live without friendly because he couldn't shake the feeling that this uncomfortable relationship was better for both of them in the long run.

The store lights were out when he finally left his office at 5:45 p.m. He grabbed his lunch pail and headed out the door, stopping to lock it behind him. He rounded the corner of the building and found Jolie in the final stages of changing a flat tire on her truck.

"You should have got me," he said as he approached.

She gave him a look over her shoulder. Wispy tendrils had escaped from her reddish-blond braid, giving her a messy, sexy look. "Why?"

Part of him said to just keep his mouth shut and walk on. He didn't. "So I could help change the tire. You're not dressed for it," he added.

"I did fine," she said as she stored the jack. "I do this a lot."

"Maybe you should buy new tires."

"Maybe," she agreed shortly as he set down his pail and hefted the flat into the back of her truck without asking permission.

"Thank you," she said in a cool voice. "I've got to hurry if I'm going to move the cows and make it to the bar on time."

"Do you need help?"

He wasn't certain why he asked, especially when it meant a drive five miles out of his way and he already knew the answer to the question.

"I can manage," she said in the same polite tone as she got inside the truck. She closed the door without saying goodbye, started the truck and, after checking to see where he was standing, put it in Reverse.

Dylan watched her pull out of the lot before heading toward his own truck.

Last week she would have asked for help and he was having a hard time convincing himself that this honestly was a turn for the better.

JOLIE LOOKED IN her rearview mirror before turning onto the highway and saw Dylan standing right where she'd left him, staring after her.

What right did he have to look so offended that she hadn't come running to him for help when she'd found her tire flat? If she needed that type of help she turned to friends. Dylan had made it very clear that he was her boss, not her friend...that she did not have the privileges of a friend, such as the right to feel concerned and voice those concerns. She hadn't asked questions of Finn to hurt him in any way. Maybe it had been wrong to try to get some answers, but her intent had been good. She was worried. She wouldn't waste her time worrying about Dylan again.

She just wished it was easier to shove him out of her thoughts.

When she got home, it was to find her escape artist, the little black heifer, on the wrong side of the fence, her mother pacing, calling to her. If she didn't want to have to fix the fence, she needed to get the baby back on the other side before mama crashed through it.

This is number two, she thought as she got out of the truck and started herding the calf back toward the fence. What would be the third annoying incident of the day?

The calf galloped ahead of her in little spurts, her tail kinked sideways. Finally her mama gave a warning bellow and the calf popped under the wire. Okay. Easy fix.

Jolie opened the electric wire gate and let the ladies through to their new section of pasture, then headed back to the house to grab a quick bite and change. It was payday at several of the local establishments, so it was probably going to be a raucous night, which meant it would pass quickly. It also meant that she was so very glad that she had a short day ahead of her tomorrow—because she'd be tired and because she'd only have to deal with Dylan for four hours.

Now that his animals had a home, Mike threw himself into moving with a more positive attitude. He made several trips to his new house while Dylan was at work, hauling smaller items, arranging his kitchen, staking out the area he wanted to make a garden. When Dylan got home, Mike grilled a couple of steaks and they sat on the porch instead of watching the news.

"Did you patch things up?" Mike finally asked.

Dylan had been expecting the question and had a ready answer. "We did."

Hell of a lot easier than trying to explain the nuances of his relationship with Jolie. And it wasn't really a lie—they now had a working relationship. It may not be the most comfortable relationship, but they knew their roles.

So why did he keep feeling this nagging urge to fix things. Or at the very least to apologize?

Because she hadn't asked for his help fixing the flat? It made no sense, but it still niggled at him and he knew that she probably hadn't had time to get it fixed. She'd be driving around late at night with no spare and bald tires and he didn't like that idea at all.

He waited until Mike got out of his chair and announced it was time for bed before mentioning that he was going out for a while. Mike looked at first surprised then mildly approving.

"You didn't need to stay home on my account."

"I know. I just thought there was no sense going out too soon."

"Meeting someone?"

"Checking in with a friend. I won't be out long."

"I'm not your keeper," Mike said with a wave.

Good thing. Dylan waited until Mike's bedroom door closed, debated for another half second, then grabbed his keys off the hook and headed out to his truck.

IT WAS TWO hours till closing and the place was busy, but not so busy that she didn't notice Dylan come in through the side door. He paused briefly then headed for one of the small tables in the back that a couple had recently abandoned to play pool. He eased back in the chair, propping a shoulder against the wall and eyed the crowd.

She tried to ignore the fact that he was there, told herself that if he wanted something he could come to the bar, but that wasn't the way Jim ran his establishment. So when she did her sweep of the room, picking up empties and checking to see who needed refills, she stopped at his table.

"Here alone?"

"Appears so."

It was on the tip of her tongue to ask if he was meeting friends, but it was really none of her business. "What can I get you?"

"Draft."

She wound her way back to the bar, stopping at two more tables and willing herself not to glance in his direction. Wondering why she even felt the need. If he wanted to stop in, have a beer, then good for him. It had nothing to do with her.

Or so she thought until she brought his draft to the table and set it down. Their eyes connected and she felt a jolt as she looked into the blue depths. She slowly raised her chin, pissed at herself, and asked if he needed anything else. When he shook his head, she abruptly turned and walked on to the next table.

"Are you all right?" Jim asked as she came back around the bar.

"Fine. Why?"

"You wandered unusually close to Maddox and his cronies."

She glanced over her shoulder at the group of guys sitting a few tables away from the bar. Maddox touched the bill of his cap at her, but his expression was carefully distant. She turned back to Jim. "Maddox and I had a discussion last weekend. I don't think he'll get friendly again."

"Especially not with your feed store boss there giving him the dead eye."

She couldn't help it. She turned to see what he was talking about, but Dylan wasn't looking at Maddox. He was looking straight at her. And he didn't look away.

"Excuse me." She took a few steps toward Dylan, then stopped and looked over her shoulder at Jim. "Can I take my break now?"

"Sure."

"Thanks." She went back to set her tray under the bar, then headed across the room and pulled out a chair at Dylan's table.

"What are you doing here?" she asked.

He nodded at the beer.

"So you're not stalking me."

She'd hoped for a bit of outrage, but instead the corners of his mouth tilted up. "Hardly. But I was worried about you driving that truck here with no spare."

"How do you know I have no spare?"

"Do you?"

Her jaw clenched before she said, "No. I'll have one tomorrow."

"Which won't help you tonight."

"Listen, I don't need you taking care of me." She leaned forward to continue in a low voice. "Here's the deal. I thought we were becoming friends. I was mistaken. So I backed off. I don't want you butting into my life any more than you want me butting into yours."

Dylan exhaled heavily. "I just want my private life left alone."

"You made that abundantly clear. And for the record, I wasn't digging. I asked Finn a simple question." That, for some unknown reason he'd passed along to Dylan, which still annoyed her. She stabbed a finger down on the table. "But you were right. We work together and we need to maintain a business relationship."

"That wasn't what I said."

"Well, that is what I heard and that's the way I want things to be. I see now that's the way things *should* be."

"Is that the way they are with Jim?"

She simply stared at him. She was good friends with Jim, but that was different. She wasn't attracted to Jim. "That is really none of your business."

"No. It's not."

"So why did you ask?"

"Because maybe I didn't handle things well between you and me in our workplace."

Tension wrapped around them as they silently regarded one another for a long moment.

Jolie suddenly felt the need to move, to put distance between them. The small table didn't provide enough of a buffer. "No," she said as she stood. "You handled things perfectly." Because she'd been slipping into the realm of temptation, thinking about him a little too much. "My break's almost over."

"Short break."

"Busy night."

And it was a night that stayed busy, but Dylan continued to hang. A couple guys joined him at his table and Jolie recognized them as deputy sheriffs who'd worked with her ex-brother-in-law, Kyle, before he'd taken a job elsewhere. They settled in, talking shop, no doubt, shared a round and then shot a couple games of pool. Beccie, the other bartender, saw to their needs, which left Jolie responsible for Maddox's table, which was fine.

As she'd told Jim, they'd gone a couple rounds

the previous weekend after he'd made one sexist comment too many and she told him where his nuts were going to be if he didn't stop. And she'd taken care to tell him alone as he returned to his table from the men's room, so that he wouldn't feel the need to defend his honor in front of a group. Maddox was the perfect example of a guy who'd peaked in high school and she had a feeling that he knew it and was self-conscious. Not that he'd ever let on, of course.

Jolie had gone onto shift early that afternoon, despite the tire and the calf, so she was able to hang up her apron an hour before closing, leaving Beccie and Jim to man the bar. The crowd had thinned as people moved on to other bars or private parties, but the place was still fairly packed—enough so that Dylan, who was still playing pool, probably wouldn't notice her absence. She just wanted to get away. To stop glancing over at him. To stop being so freaking aware of the guy.

She stepped out of the kitchen entrance and walked quickly to her truck parked a few yards away under one of the pole lights that lit the parking lot. She'd unlocked the door before she noticed that the rear tire rim was sitting on the ground, the tire itself a sad flat black puddle beneath it.

"Shit!"

She'd known it was stupid to drive the truck

when she had no spare, but what were the odds of two flats in one day?

Given the state of her tires, pretty decent.

Annoyed that the tire was flat, that Dylan had been right, that the third bad thing had happened, she kicked the tire and then jumped a mile when a male voice said, "I'll help you with that."

She whirled to see Maddox's older brother, Wyatt, coming toward her from the main entrance of the bar. Wyatt, who was pushing forty and roughly the size of a battleship.

"No need," Jolie called as she took a few steps toward the side door. Wyatt continued in her direction with a purposeful stride, his big arms swinging at his sides. His ball cap was pulled low so she couldn't read his expression, couldn't tell if it was friendly or whether he had other things in mind. He *might* be there to help, but after her run-ins with his brother, she was taking no chances. "I've got it. Thanks anyway," she said when she'd reached a point midway between the kitchen entrance and her truck.

"I don't think you do," Wyatt said.

"She does."

They both turned to see Dylan standing next to the door she'd been heading for and Jolie hated the fact that she was glad to see him. Putting a guy in his place in the bar was one thing. In a parking lot a lot of other factors came into play.

Wyatt squinted at Dylan for a moment. "Culver?"

"Yeah."

"Mind your own business. I'm going to help this lady with her tire."

Dylan started toward him. Jolie stepped aside as he walked past.

"I'm getting Jim," she said as she started for the door.

"No need," Dylan replied easily. "Wyatt's going back into the bar. One of his brothers is going to drive him home."

"Are you sure about that?" Wyatt asked.

Dylan stood with his weight on one hip, looking totally relaxed. In control. "You know what I do for a living now?"

"Uh-uh."

"I'm a cop."

"Good for you." But Wyatt rubbed his jaw. "All I was doing was offering help."

"That may be, but when a lady says no, that's what she means."

"It's a damn tire, Culver."

"She likes to change them alone."

Wyatt let out a disgusted breath. "Whatever," he muttered, turning and walking back into the bar.

Once he was gone, Dylan turned to Jolie who'd walked a few steps closer, trying to look as though she hadn't been spooked. "I hate that you work here," he said matter-of-factly.

"Well, guess what? You have no say. My life is private. Just like yours."

"Private or not, you're buying new tires. I'll loan you the money if that's what's holding you back. And I want to pay you to feed that damned cow of Mike's."

Jolie drew herself up. "We need to get a few things straight, you and me."

He cocked his head politely.

"One, I took the animals because I wanted to. Two—" she pointed a finger at his chest "—you are not going to finance anything in my life except the paycheck that I earn from your store. Three, I have a truck with brand-new tires, but I didn't feel like unhitching it from the horse trailer. Four—" She pointed the finger again, but never got the rest of four out of her mouth because Dylan took her hand in his and pulled.

Jolie, caught totally off guard, stumbled half a step forward and the next thing she knew she was wrapped in his arms and his mouth was on hers.

There was never a question of whether or not she would kiss him back. She did, and as his arms tightened around her, she had the most stunning feeling of coming home. Of being where she belonged.

It scared the crap out of her.

Roughly she pushed away, needing space. Now. Once she was a couple feet from him, she pressed the back of her hand against her swollen lips. Then, realizing how vulnerable that made her appear, she quickly dropped it to her side.

"No," she said, swallowing hard after the word came out. "No."

CHAPTER TEN

DYLAN STEPPED BACK, giving her space, disturbed
that he'd upset her to the point that all she would
say was no. He'd seen too many instances where
some asshole assumed that *no* meant *maybe* or *yes,*
or took it as a challenge to show a woman she
didn't really mean it.

So he took another full step back, his mouth
tightening as he wondered how he, who thought
everything through, had allowed this to happen.
Had allowed feelings to boil to the surface and then
acted on them without any kind of analysis at all.

But that was what being around Jolie did to him.
It knocked him off-kilter, as she'd so aptly put it.

She'd responded, though. In a big way, as if she'd
been waiting to kiss him for a long, long time. And,
damn, but she could kiss.

That didn't matter. Now she was backing off.

"I didn't mean to upset you," he said.

"What did you mean to do?" she asked as she
rubbed her upper arm with her opposite hand, as
if trying to look casual and unaffected by the very
thing that had rocked his world.

He shrugged. "Kiss you?"

"Why?"

"What kind of answer do you want me to give, Jolie?"

"The truth?"

He took a cautious step forward. She no longer seemed threatened by him, which made him wonder if she found the threat in him or in herself.

"The truth. Well, I'd say the truth is that I'm attracted to you. And I would also risk saying that you might be somewhat attracted to me."

Her eyes widened. "And surely you can see where this could become awkward if pursued."

"I backed off."

"It's still awkward."

"So is being around each other all day long, feeling this…"

She twisted her lips into a speculative expression and waited for him to find the words.

And that wasn't all that easy. He frowned a little as he finally said, "Attraction?"

"Here I'd hoped for a really great synonym," she said without one bit of humor.

"Sorry to disappoint. And it won't happen again." He cleared his throat, held her gaze, half afraid that she was going to start walking home or something to prove how independent she was.

Instead she pulled her purse up higher on her

shoulder before asking stonily, "Are you going to give me a ride home or what?"

"Ride home," he said, feeling a surge of relief. He jerked his head in the direction of his truck and started walking. A moment later Jolie followed.

JOLIE LEANED BACK against her front door, listening to the fading sound of Dylan's truck as he drove away. It'd been a silent trip home. Uncomfortably silent. But what had there been to say?

It was just a kiss. A great kiss, but a kiss all the same.

Jolie pushed off the door, dropping her purse on the chair on her way to the kitchen. She'd overreacted. Long day; stressful, busy night. Wyatt lumbering toward her... Yeah. Overreaction. She poured a glass of tap water and held it against her heated forehead for a moment before drinking.

This was a blessing. Yes, it was. Now that the kiss was over, they no longer needed to wonder. They knew.

She snorted. Yeah. They knew enough not to do it again or it might get away from them. With another guy, Jolie might have gone for it. With Dylan...not an option.

She couldn't put a label on the reason why, so decided to go label-less. To go with her gut, which said, *For your own safety, keep your distance from this guy.* She'd do that. At the store, she'd be friendly but distant. Shouldn't be that hard, what with Dylan holing up in his office or the warehouse. A couple more months and he'd be out of there and the kiss would be a faded perhaps even pleasant memory.

Gus padded into the kitchen, probably wondering if she was ever going to bed.

"Coming," she murmured, setting down the glass and turning off the light on her way out of the kitchen. It occurred to her as she went up the stairs that she'd been so preoccupied by kissing Dylan that she hadn't even thought to check the closets for monsters. She really did hate living alone, but Dani was happy and she needed to toughen up.

Jolie was the first one at the store the next morning and while she should have gone to work facing shelves and dusting, she paced, duster in hand, nerves thrumming. It wasn't as though she and Dylan had had drunken elevator sex and now had to face the reality of the day after.

But still she paced, feeling the need to burn off nervous energy she shouldn't have early Saturday morning after a night at the bar.

Last night she'd fallen asleep almost as soon as she'd crawled into bed and, of course, she'd dreamed of Dylan. But the dream had had nothing to do with kissing him or having her way with him sans consequences. It had been about his injured leg.

He'd been in the path of something big. Awful. Frightening. Something he couldn't escape because he couldn't move fast enough. It rolled over him. Destroyed him...

Even now her gut twisted at the thought.

As she'd driven to work that morning, in the truck that actually had tires, she'd wondered briefly if she was the force that was going to roll over him, destroy him, because he was at a disadvantage.

As lovely a thought as that was, she knew it wasn't the answer. Then what? And why had the dream bothered her so much that she'd awoken to a burst of relief? Only a dream. Not real at all.

That was why it shouldn't still be bothering her.

JOLIE WAS DOING the Saturday-morning cleaning when Dylan arrived at the store. Saturdays were one of their busier days, but it was also the day they did the work the janitorial service had overlooked in their twice-a-week visits. Little things like dusting all of the shelf space.

Between the two of them, they did a good enough job that Dylan had suggested to Mike they drop the service. At least for a while. Mike had given his blessing and as soon as the current janitorial contract expired, they'd be the only cleaning force.

She stopped dabbing the lamb's wool duster over the display of ironwork when he opened the door, then went right back at it, perhaps with a bit more force, after nodding a quick hello.

"Let the awkwardness commence?" he asked in a low voice.

The dabbing stopped and Jolie looked at him over her shoulder. "By all means." She lowered the duster and turned to face him.

Dylan shifted his weight, noting that Jolie was more blinged-out than usual this morning with rhinestones on her shirt, back pockets and belt. Her armor?

"I'm not sorry I kissed you," he said. "It was coming and now it's over."

"Is it?" Her voice was as cool as it'd been over the past week.

"Yes." He was fairly certain they both realized that getting physical, developing a more intimate relationship, was not a good move on either of their parts. He wasn't ready to trust, to share, to let down his guard. He had issues to deal with and he didn't need to haul anyone else into the muck and mire.

"Good." She didn't speak in an insulting way. Or maybe they were so clearly on the same page that he simply knew it wasn't meant as an insult but rather as an expression of relief.

She regarded him uncertainly for a moment and damned if he didn't feel the urge to move closer to her. Touch her. This was going to be a rugged couple months until Finn came home.

"I dropped the spare off at Bobeck's this morning," she said as she took a couple of wipes at a piece of pottery. "It should be ready at noon. They're even going to take it to the bar and switch out the flat on the truck and then repair it, too."

"What's that costing you?" he asked, glad for the change of topic. Glad for anything that helped them ease into a more comfortable working relationship.

"Barrel lessons for his daughter. I also get tires at cost."

"I'm impressed." He smiled a little. "There was a time—"

"When you assumed I was too rattlebrained to manage my life effectively?" Her tone might have been mild but her gaze was sharp.

"That's not what I was going to say, and I think you know that."

It was pretty obvious what she was doing: cruising for a fight, even a minor one, so that they once again had a reason to back off to neutral corners. Quite possibly because she also felt the heat steadily building between them. The kiss hadn't solved anything. He could say that the matter was over and done, that they'd had their experiment and now they were moving on, but it didn't feel that way. And the way Jolie was reacting told him that she was thinking the same thing.

Her mouth tightened and she shook her head. "Sorry. You're right."

He crossed the room to set his lunch in his office, then leaned back out the door. "How are you getting to work tonight?"

"Beccie is picking me up."

He gave her a long look. "Will you give me a call if you need a ride home—for any reason?"

"Yeah," she said after a brief hesitation. "I will."

And that was good enough. A bit of a truce, but enough tension to keep them from getting too close. He closed the office door, but only halfway.

When he got home from work Mike handed him a beer, then told him to take a load off while he finished barbecuing the hamburgers.

Dylan complied, thinking that it had been one long uncomfortable day. He'd barely started drinking when Mike professed that he had a hankering to see his girls. Tomorrow would be good.

Dylan shot him a disbelieving look over his beer.

"You don't need to come," Mike said. "I'm totally capable of driving to the Lightning Creek. Besides, you have that exam to study for."

Dylan grabbed the excuse not to go. Again, he didn't think Jolie needed to see him at her ranch, in her domain. Mike, on the other hand… She seemed to have a soft spot for his grandfather. Her expression warmed a little whenever Dylan mentioned him, just as it warmed when Morley Ames or his wife came into the store. As far as he knew Jolie had no living grandparents so, yeah, why horn in on Mike's visit?

"I got the truck rented for the move," he said. "And Gordy Sawyer said he'd help us with the big stuff."

"The big stuff?" Mike coughed and Dylan couldn't hold his smile. Gordy was Mike's friend Cal's grandson, sixteen-years-old, tall and rail thin.

"He's tougher than he looks." At least that was what he'd told Dylan when he called and asked if they needed help in the warehouse earlier that day. Dylan had regretfully told him no, but that he'd keep him in mind if anything opened up. And then he'd gotten the brilliant idea of hiring the kid to help move Mike's furniture. Gordy had been more than happy to help.

Mike shrugged. "I guess what he lacks in bulk, he makes up for in enthusiasm."

Dylan lifted his beer. "Here's to enthusiasm." And finally getting this move over and done with.

LATER THAT EVENING, after Mike had gone to bed, Dylan drove to McElroy's Tavern. He didn't go inside, even though he recognized Jess Moody's Jeep in the parking lot. They'd had a decent time catching up and playing pool the night before, and Dylan could have used a beer, but he didn't think Jolie would be all that happy to see him. Not after the long day they'd shared pretending the other wasn't in the building.

He drove past Jess's Jeep to the back of the building where he was pleased to see Jolie's truck parked next to the rear entrance under the light, all four tires fully inflated. Jolie wasn't stupid. She wouldn't risk her safety and the fact that she'd parked as close to the building as possible made Dylan feel a little better as he drove away.

Even though he hated driving away.

It's the way things were. His test was coming up. He'd received his confirmation and had set up a meeting with the captain to discuss his future. He also had an appointment with his lawyer to address the matter of Lindsey entertaining a steady houseguest and thus breaking the terms of their mortgage agreement. In other words, he had a shitty trip ahead of him, but one that was necessary to put his career and his finances back on track. He had no doubt that he could rebuild his life in Lanesburg, maybe even to the point that he could see about establishing a new relationship. Who knew how things might eventually play out with him and Jolie?

But now was not the time to see.

WYATT SHOWED UP at McElroy's the day after he'd pretty much set the stage for Dylan to kiss Jolie in the parking lot, lumbering in as if he owned the place. Jolie had no intention of meeting him in the parking lot again, ever, so she told Jim what had transpired the night before, leaving out the kiss. Jim then had a word with Wyatt and returned to tell Jolie that he didn't foresee any further trouble with either Wyatt or his brother.

One worry down.

Dylan's friend Jess was there again with a group of off-duty deputies, which made her fully expect Dylan to walk in at any moment, but he didn't. At eleven o'clock, when the deputies left the establishment, Jolie finally relaxed. No Dylan encounters tonight. No kisses in the parking lot. No rather vivid dreams to follow, leaving her feeling frustrated and unsatisfied.

As she cleared the deputies' table she thought about how she had no trouble thinking of Jess Moody as a cop, even though he'd been kind of a nerdy kid in high school. But Dylan? Not so much. That side of his life, the side he was going back to, seemed unreal to her. Totally unreal. She knew nothing about his life and the one time she'd tried to glean information had backfired.

Yet she was still curious.

Her lips curled a little. One would have thought she'd learned her lesson about curiosity.

The next morning she slept in, waking only when Gus shoved his nose into her face and demanded to be let outside. No dreams, yet she still felt anxious for reasons she couldn't pinpoint. Dragging herself out of bed, Jolie let Gus outside and made herself a pot of coffee, letting it brew while she showered. She'd just finished her first cup when Gus let out a couple of "stranger danger" barks and she went to the window. Mike Culver was fending off the big dog and Jolie instantly went to the door to save him.

Mike raised a hand as she shouted at Gus to get off the poor man. "He's fine."

"He's not fine," Jolie said as she came down the path. "He's rude. I assume you're here to see the girls?"

"Separation anxiety."

Jolie laughed and Mike smiled back. She gestured toward the barn. "I'm a little late feeding, so I'm sure everyone will be happy to see us."

The goats raced to Mike when he approached their pen, bleating a welcome. Mike grinned at Jolie.

"They missed you," she said as he reached over the fencing to rub their heads.

"They've lost weight."

"They'll be healthier because of it."

"I did try to kill them with kindness," Mike agreed.

After several minutes with the goats they went out to the field to see Karen. As soon as he called, the cow's head came up and she ambled over.

"You're like the ruminant whisperer," Jolie said.

Mike laughed. "Always a dream of mine," he said, patting Karen's neck. "So…how's my grandson treating you?"

Jolie blinked at the sudden change of subject. "No complaints," she said, wishing her voice didn't sound so brittle.

"He can be intense at times."

"No arguments there."

"He has this big exam coming up. It's important to him."

Jolie was fairly certain that Dylan's intensity came from his DNA.

"It's the detective's exam," Mike explained. "He wants to get off patrol. Well, actually, he's not on patrol because of his leg. And between you and me?" Mike raised his thick gray eyebrows. "I hope he never goes back on patrol. I want him to go back to school, but he seems to like law enforcement, so I'm hoping he makes detective."

"I never saw Dylan becoming a cop," Jolie confessed.

"Kind of happened by accident," Mike said. "I heard you were lab partners at one time."

"He told you about that?" Jolie was surprised—unless, of course, Mike simply remembered Dylan complaining about her years ago.

"In a roundabout kind of way." He looked as though he was going to say something else, but instead he gave Karen's neck one final pat and started back to the truck.

"Would you like some coffee?" Jolie asked. "I made a full pot and can usually only drink half."

"I'd be glad to help you out with that."

Mike stayed for two cups of coffee, asking about the store and the boutique she'd put in. He mentioned that his wife had once thought of doing something similar. He talked about the final move to his new house coming up soon, and how cutting ties with the old place was difficult.

"But it's a good thing," he concluded. "That old place was too big. It was getting away from me."

When he left, Jolie once again felt the emptiness start to close in around her, so she saddled Jenabelle and let the mare race full-bore through all of their practice runs. They both needed to blow off steam and a hard practice was the easiest way to do that.

After she released the horse into the pasture, Jolie still felt unsettled. Anxious.

The ranch was too damned empty without Dani there. Her sisters were scattered and she was alone. It shouldn't bother her, but it did. And after asking Dani in their phone conversation a few days before if living alone on the ranch had ever gotten to her, Dani had been mystified. Then she'd suspiciously asked if Jolie was all right.

Jolie told her that she was simply having rough

days at work, which wasn't a total untruth. "I guess I just like having someone to vent to when I get home and my ventee is on the other side of the country."

"Well, call anytime," Dani said. "No. Don't call after six o'clock your time. But other than that, call anytime."

Jolie hung up wondering just what was wrong with her. Did any of her sisters have this issue? Obviously, Dani did not. Mel, her second oldest sister, was the picture of independence. Her husband, KC, had had his work cut out for him getting her to give up her solitary ways. Allie loved being alone as she healed from her broken marriage. She was alone by choice, as Mel had been… and maybe that was it. Jolie hadn't chosen to be alone. It had been thrust upon her by circumstances beyond her control.

Jolie hung Jenabelle's bridle on a peg, then sat on the step and soaked up the late-afternoon sun. She was going to have to get a grip. It wasn't as if Dani wasn't coming back and it wasn't as if she couldn't talk to any of her sisters at a moment's notice. She was being ridiculous. Everyone's life came with circumstances beyond their control. She simply needed to deal with it.

CHAPTER ELEVEN

JOLIE WAS WORKING on the plank fence when she heard the distant sound of the phone ringing inside the house. It stopped before she reached it, but she recognized the number and hit Redial.

"Dr. Hartman," she said as she perched on the edge of the chair. "How's vacation?" Her former college roommate and rodeo partner, Faith Hartman, was now conducting classes in equine science at U of M Western in Dillon.

"I'm not totally done, but I finally have time to practice." Faith gave a small laugh. "Hard to believe I sweat blood to get this job that's making me sweat blood. I just called to see if you were planning to go to the rodeo in Ennis over the Fourth and if so, could we share a trailer?"

Jolie felt an instant lift in her mood. "And not travel by myself? Share gas? Hmm. Tough choice."

"Yeah. I know. I prefer to break down alone, too," Faith said with a laugh. It seemed that they'd broken down at least once a season on their rodeo team trips during college.

"I'm going and I'd love to have you along. I'll drive."

"Great. I can drive the next trip."

"Are you going to Glennan or Big Timber?" Jolie's first two rodeos; she'd love to have someone with her.

"Can't," Faith said regretfully. "I have some faculty stuff to deal with, but after that I'm free for the rest of the season. You still plan on a fairly full season, right?"

The last time they'd spoken, shortly after Jolie had moved home, she hadn't been certain how many rodeos she'd be able to do working two jobs, but had managed to arrange things with Jim so that she could get the Fridays and Saturdays she needed to compete. She was going to take a hit in her paycheck, but the plan was for her to eventually start giving barrel clinics and the exposure would definitely pay off.

"I plan to go to as many rodeos as possible. I'll make a list."

"I'm so glad. I just…need to spend some time away from Dillon this summer, but I don't like traveling to rodeos alone."

"Is everything all right?"

"Everything's fine." Faith spoke a little too

brightly, giving Jolie the impression that things were not fine, but she knew better than to push matters. Unlike most of her sisters, who held things in, if Faith needed to talk, she would.

Jolie hung up a few minutes later, glad to have a travel partner, glad to have places to go this summer. Her life had become a tight world of work at the store and the bar, ranch repair and animal care. Getting out, hitting the road for a day or two, sounded heavenly. Not being alone and sharing some conversation sounded even more so.

That night she dreamed of Dylan again. And not a sensual dream, which would have at least have been pleasant while it was occurring, even if she did wake up frustrated afterward. No. Once again she'd dreamed of him being overcome by a dark force, this time a twisting funnel cloud that engulfed him, tore him away from her as she desperately grabbed on to him, trying to keep him from being pulled away. She woke as he'd cried out for her, her heart hammering.

Jolie could accept that she was a literal dreamer, but why Dylan? Why would she be afraid for him? Because he was going back to being a cop? Because Mike had mentioned a fear of having him go back on patrol? Whatever the reason, it left her with an ominous feeling she wasn't able to shake and when Dylan came into work twenty minutes after she arrived, Jolie actually felt a surge of relief to see him in one piece. She nodded a hello then focused on her keyboard.

This was nuts.

JOLIE LOOKED AS if she hadn't slept much, even though she hadn't worked at the bar. She kept yawning and Dylan wanted to ask her if something had happened on the ranch. He didn't.

They'd developed a wary truce, behaving civilly, edging around each other, but not getting too close. Close was dangerous. Especially when he wanted to reach out and just…touch her. Brush his fingers along the edge of her jaw…run a casual hand down her arm…lean closer—

"Are you all right?"

Dylan snapped back to reality, felt his color rise a little as he took the ticket Jolie had just written up for an elderly customer waiting in her car.

"Fine," he said abruptly before heading to the door to deliver the cat food and the receipt.

When he came back, Jolie was on the opposite side of the counter—his side—waiting for him, arms crossed over her chest, a no nonsense look in her eye.

"Is something wrong?" she asked. It was the most personal thing she'd said to him in more than a week.

"No. And I was about to ask you the same thing."

"Mike said you have an important test coming up."

"I do." Funny how they'd never talked about his other life when they'd been on friendlier terms. Or rather, he'd never talked about it. Probably because he preferred not to dwell on matters that couldn't be settled until he returned to Washington. "Detective's exam. I'm tired of desk duty."

"Don't detectives do a lot of desk duty?"

"Higher caliber," he said shortly.

She opened her mouth then closed it and he wondered if she was thinking about how he'd taken her to task for asking Finn about him. He'd been a jerk, plain and simple. An embarrassed jerk who'd just discovered his partner was sleeping with his ex-wife and had taken it out on her. And he needed to address that.

"I, uh, want to apologize to you for taking your head off when you tried to find out what had happened to me. My leg." *And his marriage.* She'd asked Finn about that, too, but he doubted she'd do that again. He idly ran a hand over the side of his thigh.

"None of my business."

"It's no big secret and I'm sorry I was so touchy. It's just…the accident was kind of a painful turning point in my life." One of many that had occurred in too short a period of time. "Long story short, I stopped a car. Once I was out of my cruiser, they took off. I caught up with them, no problem, then the passenger leaned out the window and shot out my windshield."

Jolie went so instantly pale that Dylan wished he'd kept his mouth shut. "You got shot at?"

"The car got shot at."

"You just happened to be driving it."

"It was an unusual occurrence."

"All the same…" She glanced away, frowning deeply, then seemed to bring herself back together, shooting him a very dark look. "And you're trying to go back on patrol?"

"If I don't make detective. I truly prefer it to being in Logistics."

"I think you're insane."

He reached out to take her upper arm without thinking and Jolie didn't step away. She looked stunned and the muscles in her arm beneath his palm were taut.

"We're trained to deal with these situations. Someone has to do it."

"Why does it have to be you?" she challenged, turning and walking around the counter.

Dylan's hand dropped to his side and he was struck by the fact that Jolie seemed overly concerned— about him—even though she was now hyperfocused on her computer screen, typing madly.

That was something he needed to think about.

DYLAN HAD BEEN shot at. Jolie couldn't keep the thought out of her head as she rearranged her display in an attempt to keep herself busy. Couldn't stop thinking about the what-ifs, seeing the image of Dylan lying bloody in his cruiser and feeling a little sick, until finally she told herself *enough*. He hadn't been hit by the bullet. It had been a fluke incident. It was over.

Besides, he was fairly brilliant in the academic sense, so he would pass the detective exam and after that he'd be wearing a suit to work instead of driving around chasing bad guys.

But she didn't feel all that much better.

Finally she called her sister Allie, who'd been a law enforcement officer's wife before she divorced her husband. Allie had listened then told Jolie matter-of-factly that being shot at was an unusual occurrence and that it was unlikely to happen again. When her ex, Kyle, had been a deputy, he'd gotten himself into trouble a few times due to his attitude, but never came close to being shot at.

Jolie thanked her sister, exchanged news of Mel and Dani and then hung up feeling as if she'd been overreacting—for days. The past was the past and Dylan was going to pass his exam.

End of story.

And, thankfully, she didn't dream of Dylan that night. That gave her hope that she was getting a handle on the situation.

The next day she was surprised to see Mike's truck at the store when she got there. It was the first time she'd seen him there since Finn had hired her. She'd gone to dinner at Mike's house a couple times, but he'd never ventured to the store itself after her interview.

He came out of the office as she walked in the front door and nodded a hello.

"Hey," she called back.

"Just thought I'd stop by to brush up on operations before Dylan takes off for his exam."

Logically, given all that had happened between them, Jolie should have felt relieved at the thought of Dylan returning to his old life, but she didn't. Because of the shooting, she told herself, even though she suspected it was more than that. Suspected, but wasn't going to investigate, since she didn't want to know the answer.

"Will you be taking over?" she asked Mike.

He smiled warmly. "Nope. You'll be in command. I'll be around in case of emergencies. You know, in case someone orders rolled oats and gets whole."

"That won't happen on my watch," Jolie said.

Mike laughed as Dylan entered through the side door. He bounced a look between them.

"Inside joke?"

"You might say that," Mike replied as Jolie went behind the counter and stowed her belongings.

"Just talking rolled oats," she said, trying to look as if she wasn't feeling conflicted. It was stupid that she was feeling conflicted and she wished now that she hadn't found out about his accident. Ignorance truly was bliss in some cases.

Mike stayed for about an hour, chitchatting with Jolie and any customers that came into the store. He was definitely more hands-on than Dylan and Jolie enjoyed watching him catch up the few old friends who'd stopped by for feed. He went home a little after 10:00 a.m., leaving Jolie alone in the store and Dylan in the warehouse.

And that was when Jolie felt her good mood evaporating. Finally she left her desk and went out to the warehouse where Dylan was going over an invoice on a clipboard. He looked up as she approached.

"It was good seeing Mike," she said.

"You two get along well," Dylan commented.

"Yeah. Well, you know, we share custody now."

Dylan smiled and she wished she could smile back. But she was having a hard time when she was totally drawn to a guy who was so totally wrong for her.

People shot at him, for Pete's sake.

THE BIG MOVE went better than Dylan had anticipated, mainly because Gordy was stronger than he looked. When he easily picked up his end of

Mike's zillion-pound sofa sleeper, Dylan vowed he would keep the kid in mind if business got so good that he needed to hire additional warehouse help. If things continued as they were, it was a definite possibility, and he'd mention that to Gordy before the night was over.

After they'd packed up the final bits and pieces from the old house, they drove the truck to the new house, where Mike's friend Karl Evans lent a hand with the furniture arranging. Cal Sawyer and his sister, Lois, showed up shortly thereafter with a dinner of fried chicken and potato salad, and the six of them ate sitting on Mike's new deck. A nice-size creek flowed just behind the chain-link fence, separating the housing development from the fields behind it, and Karl joked about Mike being able to fish without leaving home.

"You do have a fine back yard," Cal said, gesturing at the mountains behind the field. "As long as no one buys the field and plants houses on it."

"Federal land," Mike replied. "No worries there."

Lois got to her feet and started gathering paper plates. "Gordy and I will help you do the final cleaning before you turn your keys over to the real estate agent," she said as she took Mike's plate. "Just tell us what time to be there."

Mike accepted the offer and then the four old friends drifted into a conversation about how Eagle

Valley had changed over the past forty years. A sudden thought struck Dylan and he caught Gordy's eye. A few seconds later the kid followed him into the kitchen.

"I have to make a trip soon, and it occurred to me that I need someone to cover the warehouse while I'm gone. It'll only be for a couple of days. Are you interested?"

Gordy's thin face broke into a smile. "Yeah. Totally."

"Can you stop by early tomorrow before you and your aunt go to Mike's place so that I can show you what's what?"

"Yeah."

"And…nothing certain here…but if I do need to hire someone, you're first on the list. We can even work around school." He'd certainly worked around school back in the day. Before school. After school. It'd kept him busy.

"Great! I mean…great!"

Gordy was beaming when he went back out onto the deck, leaving Dylan with one fewer problem to solve before his exam. And if he could somehow force himself to stop wondering why the dynamic had changed between himself and Jolie after he'd told her about his accident, he'd be ahead of the game, focus-wise.

Maybe things were better this way, with Jolie

taking a step back. No more distractions. Yes. That made sense.

Dylan walked down the short hallway to the bathroom, glancing into the guest bedroom where he'd be staying until he moved back to Washington. His two duffel bags sat on the bed, reminding him of how temporary his time was here in Montana.

Soon he'd be six hundred miles away.

Soon it wouldn't matter why Jolie was distancing herself from him. He'd be gone.

JOLIE'S FIRST RODEO was coming up and Mike was disappointed that he wouldn't have a chance to see her run the barrels. It was in Glennan and he didn't feel up to driving that far with his new hip still not fully healed. Dylan commiserated, thinking that his grandfather and Jolie must have had quite the bonding conversation when he'd gone to visit his girls.

Frankly, he wouldn't mind seeing Jolie run the barrels himself, which was an indication of how unsuccessful he'd been at chasing thoughts of her out of his brain. But he had to focus on this test, which was coming up soon. Too soon, maybe. Tests were his thing; he always thrived under that kind of pressure, but this test was different. He felt nervous, inadequately prepared.

Probably because of his lack of concentration lately. And then there was the matter of Lindsey and Pat. His lawyer would handle the matter with Lindsey. He wouldn't even have to see her, but when he did go back to work, he'd have to deal with Pat on the days when their shifts overlapped.

Awesome prospect, that, but he could deal. It might put a cloud over his professional life initially, but the cloud would dissipate in a matter of time and no one would ever be able to say that he'd left his job because he couldn't handle being around the jerk who'd had a hand in ending his marriage. He wasn't a guy who ran away from stuff like that. Even if there were times that he was tempted to tell Mike that he wouldn't mind managing the feed store full-time.

That smacked of backing down and he wouldn't go there. Besides, Finn would expect to take over the reins when he got home.

He came in from the warehouse to find Jolie staring at her nearly empty boutique display case, holding the hair back from her forehead with one hand, frowning deeply.

"You okay?"

"I'm trying to rearrange to best effect, but it's hard when I'm almost out of stock. I have more coming, but not soon enough." She let go of her hair and it settled back around her face, the sunlight coming in through the front window making it glint with red and gold lights. "I don't want to lose momentum."

"I guess we can say that the boutique is a success."

"Yes." She smiled a little, but it was guarded, as all of her smiles now were. He missed the spark of their former relationship, before he'd kissed her, but accepted that this was how things were going to remain—with too much sexual tension and no relief in sight.

"Cal's grandson is going to load while I'm gone next week."

"Gordy? Teenage awkwardness incarnate Gordy?"

"That's the kid."

"I like him and all, but I hope he doesn't get crushed under a bag of grain," Jolie said dryly.

"I'm sure you can rescue him. Besides, he's stronger than he looks. Trust me. I know."

"You know, I handled the store just fine during the week before you took over. Drove the forklift and everything."

"I know. But I don't want you to do that for five days."

The words hung for a moment then Jolie said, "Nervous for your test?"

"A little."

The bell rang over the door and they turned simultaneously. Jess Moody walked in wearing his deputy tans.

"Thought I might find you here," he said as he approached Jolie's display area.

"Am I in trouble?" Dylan asked.

"Depends on your definition of trouble."

His preoccupation with Jolie?

Jess turned to Jolie. "Nice display. Dylan mentioned your project when we were out conferring on other matters."

She smiled at him with more warmth than Dylan had seen in a month. "Would those matters involve green felt, sticks and sixteen balls?"

Jess raised his eyebrows in feigned surprise. "They would."

She laughed and then said to Dylan, "I'll let you guys talk. I need to check Marcel's dish."

Jess waited until the door closed behind Jolie before saying, "We got that grant I was telling you about."

Yeah. The grant. Dylan had to admit that he'd only been listening with half an ear when Jess had been filling him in on the employment issues at the local sheriff's office at the bar the first time they'd hooked up. He'd been too busy watching Maddox and his fat brother, Wyatt, watching Jolie.

"That's good news."

"I think so." Jess shifted his weight. "How bad is that leg of yours?"

"Uh… I see the doctor when I go to Lanesburg. He'll let me know if he'll sign off, but in my opinion, I'm close to one hundred percent."

"Any chance I could talk you into applying for this position?"

Dylan didn't answer immediately, so Jess went on. "We have a bunch of local douche bags knocking on the door. Guys we don't want but may have to take if we can't get someone we do want. The guy who had the position before we lost funding was Jolie's brother-in-law. Well, ex-brother-in-law. He was a piece of work."

"There's got to be some decent candidates out there."

"There are…but I know you. I think I could work with you."

"I'm sitting for the detective's exam next week."

"Yeah. You said."

"I can't give you an answer right now," Dylan said honestly. He needed to see how things worked out in Lanesburg.

"I figured. We won't post the job for a couple of weeks, but I wanted to give you a heads-up. Something to think about, in case you wanted to stay closer to Mike. And—" Jess's gaze drifted toward the door Jolie had gone out of a few minutes before "—whoever else might be here."

Dylan wasn't exactly surprised that Jess had noticed him watching the jerks at the bar who'd been watching Jolie. Or that he'd come to a logical conclusion. It wasn't a fully accurate conclusion, but Dylan wasn't going to correct him.

"I can't make any promises. I'm halfway to full-service credit in Washington."

"You could start over here and still make full-service credit before you hit minimum retirement age, plus have whatever you get from Washington."

"Aren't you the helpful little bunny," Dylan said and Jess laughed.

"Hey, just keep it in mind. I'll let you know when it's posted and you do what you gotta do."

"Thanks," Dylan said as Jess started for the door. "I really do appreciate the heads-up."

"And I appreciate that you have a lot to consider before making a jump."

CHAPTER TWELVE

As DYLAN APPROACHED LANESBURG, the city he'd protected and served for the past decade, he had no sense of homecoming. No sense that he was back where he belonged.

All he felt was stress. Jaw-clenching, stomach-knotting stress. The doctor, the exam, the Lindsey/Pat/mortgage business. And yet he was also thinking of Jolie. Wondering how she was doing with Gordy and Mike, who'd assured Dylan that he'd stop by the store, now that he was more ambulatory, and make certain that Jolie was handling matters all right on her own.

Dylan had mentioned that she was quite capable, but when Mike persisted, Dylan figured he was doing it more to get out of the house than for any other reason. He had been a captive for a long time while that hip of his healed.

What he didn't think about was Jess Moody's offer. Maybe because it was too easy of an out and Dylan avoided easy outs.

Or maybe he didn't trust easy outs. There was always a price to pay, and in his experience, the easier something appeared, the steeper the price eventually became.

He pulled into the motel, checked in, stashed his bag in his room then headed straight to his doctor's appointment. Where he waited. And waited some more. Flexing his leg, assuring himself he'd hit the point where he could run and carry a load. Do the stuff he needed to be able to do physically to reclaim his old job.

Finally he got called into Dr. Burke's office and within ten minutes had exactly what he'd hoped for—a release and an "attaboy" for sticking with the therapy program.

Too easy, which made him feel edgy.

He spent the next hour at the station, talking to the captain and nailing down exactly what his future would be with or without the detective's badge. Passing the exam meant that opportunities for transfer would open up and if he didn't want to stay in Lanesburg he would have options.

"If you don't mind me asking," he said to the captain, "are you hinting that I should pursue other options?"

The captain's gaze shifted down for a brief second then back up again.

"I know about Pat and Lindsey," Dylan said before the captain could answer. "It won't affect me."

"How can it not?" the captain asked. "Realistically it will. Under the circumstances."

Dylan shook his head. "This can't be the first time something like this has happened."

"No," the captain agreed. "But I've never seen anything good come of it."

"Nothing will happen."

The captain fell silent again and Dylan's mouth tightened. How was he supposed to convince this guy of his ability to remain professional when he'd already made up his mind? Then it struck him. *Under the circumstances.* Personnel being reassigned. "Pat's getting promoted?"

"He'd be your immediate supervisor if you remain in your old position."

"Which means if I don't pass the exam you'd keep me in Logistics." A nod. "And even then you'd like for me to transfer."

"You could transfer even if you do pass the exam. I'll do what I can to help."

"I haven't done anything wrong."

"No. No one is saying you have."

Dylan jammed a finger down on the table. "Why should I pay the price because my ex-partner—" he stopped himself from saying *screwed* "—took up with my ex-wife?"

"Because you suspect they were together before your marriage broke up and you hate the son of a bitch?"

In a nutshell.

"And because rumor has it they're living together now in your house and you're going to do something about it."

The guy had no mercy.

"However," the captain continued, shifting his gaze briefly down to the pen he held, before once again fixing Dylan with a stern look. "You don't need to do that because I addressed the issue." His expression clearly said "Do not ask questions."

Dylan wished he was not in front of his captain, being told not to worry about his dirty laundry, the stuff he wanted no one else to know, because it had been taken care of for him. "How?"

"Let it lie." The captain spoke in a way that brooked no opposition, but Dylan ignored the warning tone.

"They're not living together in my place anymore?" He somehow managed to keep his voice carefully modulated, his temper under control.

"No."

Now it was Dylan's turn to study the ground. This wasn't humiliating or anything, having the captain intercede in his personal affairs. But no way was he going to show how much it bothered him, so he tried for a matter of fact tone when he looked back up and said, "That takes care of one issue, although I had kind of hoped to get out from under the mortgage."

The captain didn't answer and Dylan pulled in

a long breath. "I'm not interested in a transfer at this time."

"And I'd like my department to run smoothly."

Dylan opened his mouth to tell him that it would but closed it again. He wasn't going to win this battle right now. The best thing to do would be to sit for his exam and take things from there.

"You have another four weeks of family leave." Dylan had tacked together family emergency medical leave, his vacation and his own sick days to come up with enough time to cover for Finn. The captain had been very accommodating when Dylan had requested to take all of his leave at once, which meant even then he'd known something was up between his partner and his wife while Dylan'd been happily oblivious.

"Yeah."

"Regardless of what happens with the exam, I suggest you use that time to think about what's best for you and the department."

"Right." Dylan got to his feet, fully aware that the clipped answer hadn't sounded all that respectful. What was best for him was to get his job back and continue as he'd been. He definitely wasn't going to back down where Pat was concerned. The department wouldn't suffer…but he wouldn't mind if Pat did.

"And, Dylan?" He glanced back over his shoul-

der at his captain's grim face. "While you do that…
try parking your ego at the door."

THE STORE FELT empty without Dylan in a way it
hadn't felt empty after Finn left. And that bothered
Jolie. She told herself that it was because she'd been
so on edge while he'd been there that she didn't
know what a relaxed work environment felt like.
Of course she was lying. She missed him and she
was worried about him. Like it or not, she was attracted to him and that meant she had to decide
what to do about it. Ride it out until he left? Or
indulge herself?

After weeks of delays, the crew finally showed
up to build Dani's arena the day after Dylan left
for Washington, which gave Jolie something else
to focus on. It would also give her a place to practice when her outdoor arena was too muddy. A few
days later the walls were up, the canvas stretched
over the frame and a half foot of sand covered the
floor. Jolie sent photos to Dani, showing her the
fruits of their labor and promising not to have too
much fun in it until her sister got back. Funny how
one made plans, then fate intervened. Dani had
worked so long and hard for her arena and now
she wouldn't be able to use it for a year and a half.
But Jolie would put it to good use. Her first rodeo
was coming up soon and she had eight more over

the course of the summer. When the rains came she could still practice.

Friday was unusually slow at the bar, nothing like the previous Friday, which Jolie preferred not to think about, although nothing stopped her from dreaming about it. Was it because her life was in a state of flux that her dreams, both the good and the bad, were so vivid? She never had trouble sleeping, but in the mornings she often felt as if she hadn't, because the dreams were so exhausting. And in some cases frightening. But her new tactic was to push the feelings aside, which was way better than living the terror or, on occasion, the sensual longing, over and over again.

She worked until eleven when it became obvious that there would be no swell in the crowd prior to last call and Jim told her to go home. The tips were nil and her hourly wage wasn't but a drop in the bucket, so Jolie thanked him and went for her coat. It felt light without her phone inside, which she'd left in her desk at work in her hurry to get home in time to change for the bar.

Mike had come in and spent a good half hour after closing talking about Karen and the goats and his new house. Jolie hadn't had the heart to shut him down, especially after he'd asked for help picking out some pottery for his new kitchen, but once she'd gotten him into his truck and on his way, she'd had to race to get home herself. As it was, she'd barely had time to feed and ended up going to the bar in the clothes she'd worn to the store that day. And she'd realized too late that her phone wasn't in her pocket.

It was only a short detour to the store on her way home and Jolie left her truck running as she went to the door. She'd hoped the cleaning crew might be there on one of their last missions before the contract officially expired, but the building was dark. The yard light next to the warehouse was on, coloring everything a washed-out bluish color.

Jolie used the light on her key ring to find the right key and get it into the lock. She snapped on the overhead as she went inside, pausing to cast a cautious eye over the interior of the store. Her father had always teased her that she was the most cautious about things that weren't likely to be a danger and the least cautious about those things that were.

So be it. She didn't like dark, lonely places, even if the chances of something being there were slim to none. It was amazing how creepy a feed store could be at night. Dylan's office door was cracked open. Had she left it that way? Probably, even though it was her custom to leave the door wide open so she could see inside the office.

Finally, Jolie lifted her chin and headed toward her desk where her phone was in the top drawer. Her footsteps sounded unusually loud in the store—louder even than she remembered them in the morning when she was there alone. She slid open the drawer, pulled out the phone, then jumped a mile as the bell above the door jangled. Her heart slammed against her ribs, then the next thing she knew she was in flight, heading toward the rear exit.

"Jolie!"

Her hand was on the dead bolt when Dylan said her name a second time and she realized that the intruder was someone she knew...someone who was supposed to be in Washington. Or home with Mike. Definitely not here.

She turned back to see him standing in the middle of the store, an expression of concern on his handsome face. She pressed a hand to her hammering heart and for a moment she thought she might, for the first time in her life, pass out.

"You scared the bejeezus out of me!"

Dylan took a couple steps closer. "Did you ever think to lock the door behind you?"

"No," she muttered, feeling stupid. "I didn't think anyone would be lurking." She cocked her head. "Why are you lurking?"

"I was driving by on my way home and saw lights where there shouldn't be any and drove in to investigate."

"Alone? What if I'd been some crazed burglar?"

"Driving your truck?"

"Point taken."

"Besides," he said dryly, "investigating is kind of what I do."

"Do you have a gun with you?"

"Yes."

That gave her pause. Dylan carried a gun. Had he always? Like, here at the store?

She didn't want to know. Guys who carried guns were guys who courted danger and she didn't want to think about Dylan being in danger.

"I should be going. I left my truck running."

"I noticed."

She didn't move. "How was the test?"

He slowly shook his head in a way that didn't exactly smack of confidence. "I don't know."

"But you're Mr. Test. How could you not know?"

"I was...preoccupied."

"By?"

"Way too much stuff." He reached up to rub his hand over the back of his neck, his eyes closing briefly as his fingers worked the muscles there.

Do. Not. Do. This. "Anything you can talk about?" The words came out of her mouth anyway. They had to. There was no way they were staying put. Not when Dylan looked like this, as if he was one tautly stretched nerve-snap away from imploding.

His chin hit his chest and Jolie thought she had

her answer and was about to back off when he said, "Got an hour or two?"

"Maybe."

And maybe there was no good reason that her heart was still beating a little harder, but she sensed she was approaching some kind of threshold and she couldn't stop herself from easing over it.

When he lifted his gaze, his expression was resigned. To his fate? Or to finally spilling his guts to her? As she looked into those blue, blue depths, she decided she didn't care which. And even though part of her insisted that she march past him, out the door, get into her truck and drive to safety, she knew she wasn't going to.

"I need to shut off my truck."

She half expected him to use that as an excuse to drop the pretense that he was actually going to talk to her, but he didn't. "I'll get it," he said. "Mine is running, too."

"I didn't see your headlights when you drove in."

"Probably because I turned them off."

"Snuck up on me."

"Old cop trick." He let himself out and Jolie told herself that she didn't need to be thinking that he looked as good in slacks as he did in jeans.

"What other old cop tricks do you have?" she asked when he came back in and handed her the keys.

"Too many to mention." He leaned against the shelf that held the horseshoe nails. Seeing that they were making themselves comfortable, Jolie boosted herself up onto the cabinet, crossing her booted ankles. Pretended that he was just Jim telling her the woes of his day at the bar.

"How did you come to be a cop, Dylan?" It seemed a safe way to dive in, even though she didn't really expect him to answer.

To her amazement, he did.

"Grieving process," he said shortly. "I couldn't handle school after dad died. I'd been doing a work-study job with campus security and because of that I got a chance to enter police officer training school." He scuffed his shoe along a crack in the floor in front of him. "Granddad wasn't thrilled. He wanted me to continue in forensic biology, but I wasn't ready." He gave a small shrug. "I love being a cop."

Something in her stilled, the same as it had when he'd told her about his windshield being shot out. "What about the potential for danger?"

"With the proper precautions…" He shrugged again, seeming to think danger wasn't an issue. "I'm a field training officer. I ride with the rookies, which means that I know what I'm doing."

"Huh." Jolie studied her bare knees for a moment.

"Something wrong?"

She looked up, forcing her expression to clear. "No." Nothing she felt like talking about. Like the way her stomach was turning inside out at his seeming disregard for danger. This was his time to talk. "What happened in Washington?" Because something had clearly happened.

"I got the all-clear to go back on duty."

Again she felt a small twinge of anxiety. "Congratulations."

"Took my test. Dealt with some other matters." He glanced down at the cracked tile again. "Found out that my supervisor wants me to transfer."

"What? Why?"

"A guy that I have potential issues with would be my immediate superior. I told the captain it didn't matter, but he has hesitations."

"What's the solution?"

"He thinks it's a transfer. He said he'd make it easy."

"How do you feel about that?"

"Honestly? Like shit. I didn't do anything to justify..." He shook his head. "Long story."

He moved then, coming to stand closer to her. Because she was sitting on the counter their eyes... their mouths...were at the same level. He leaned in another fraction of an inch and for one wild moment she wondered if he was going to kiss her, because if he did, she wasn't going to stop him. Not tonight. But instead he leaned on his forearm, close to her thigh, and looked out across the room. He was close, too close, yet somehow not close enough.

"It felt kind of strange going back."

"I think that's pretty normal. Plus, you've been through a lot of…I don't know…trauma?"

"More like drama. Don't get divorced."

"No intentions of ever doing that," she said and he glanced up at her.

"Neither did I." His softly spoken words made something shift inside her. "But, Lindsey and I… I don't know what happened. I did my best but it quit working."

"Maybe it worried her. You know…" Her voice softened. "Being married to a guy who spends a lot of time in harm's way."

Dylan considered her theory for all of a heartbeat. "I don't think that was a major concern."

"Why?"

"She hooked up with another cop. Before we split up. My, uh, partner. The guy who will be my supervisor if I go back to my old job."

Jolie's stomach had twisted as he spoke and now a heavy silence hung between them and there wasn't much to do about it. She couldn't think of anything to say—nothing that would help, anyway. No wonder he'd seemed lost in dark thoughts. She glanced down at her rose-embroidered boots then looked up and said, "I see why you wanted your private life left alone."

"It was pretty damned humiliating. I mean, my own partner and my wife? The killer part was that I thought I'd been doing all right." One corner of his mouth tightened. "I steered away from the booze, the groupies. Tried to make our time together count." He exhaled. "We talked, tried to explain our needs...but it was like we weren't speaking the same language."

Jolie's lips parted. She understood what he was saying. Most of her short-lived relationships—flings, really—hadn't ended well because of it. She'd tried to explain what she was and wasn't looking for, but she may as well have been speaking gibberish. Guys didn't understand her need for space. And a lot of it. So when they closed in too tightly, she did the only thing she could do and walked away.

"So what happens now?"

"I wait to hear the results of the detective exam. Make a few decisions about where to work."

"Everything is in limbo."

"At the moment."

"Makes me glad I've finally made a commitment to the ranch. To staying." She swung her foot back and forth. "I like having roots. Like working for something."

"Can you see yourself leaving?"

There was something more to the question than what he was asking on the surface.

Therefore Jolie considered her answer before saying, "I'm not going to say I'll never leave the Lightning Creek, but for right now being there works for me. I like being there. Where I grew up." She took in a breath. "Where my dad died."

"There on the ranch."

"I was nine years old. He had a heart attack at a ridiculously young age. Just…died."

"I'm sorry."

She reached out and put her hand over his without thinking, covering his warm work-roughened fingers with her own before once again settling her hand back on her thigh. "I could say the same. Although…you were probably grieving before you lost your dad."

"For a couple years." He shrugged. "We had a good relationship and I'm grateful for that."

"I never asked about your mother," she said with a sudden frown.

"No need to. She and my dad never married. She basically left me with him when she found a guy she liked better. I have very little contact. My dad and grandfather raised me."

"They did a decent job," Jolie said, a little shocked that she'd never known this about him. He seemed so together, so centered. Yes. His dad and grandfather had done an excellent job.

It was getting late. Too late, yet she had no desire to go home to her lonely house to check for monsters in the closet. Maybe she and Dylan could talk in the feed store until it opened for business. Then she could go home at noon and fall into bed. Forget about practice and sleep until it was time to work at the bar.

"What?" She raised her eyebrows at Dylan's question. "You're smiling."

"Thinking about not sleeping until tomorrow afternoon."

"We're probably both going to be useless tomorrow morning, which happens in, oh—" he glanced at his watch "—not that long from now."

Jolie eased off the counter. "Yes. I need to get home. Gus will be worried about me."

"Gus?" There was just enough suspicion in his voice to make Jolie smile.

"My big fluffy black-and-white dog."

"Oh, yeah. I remember him."

"Should I ask why you sound relieved?"

"Probably not," he said, smiling down at her.

"What do we do here, Dylan?"

He didn't pretend not to know what she was asking. "I don't know...be friends?"

"I like that idea."

"I wouldn't mind having someone I trust to talk to every now and again. If the mood strikes."

"I wouldn't mind listening." He smiled at her. A heart-stopping, take-his-face-in-your-hands-and-kiss-him-hard smile. She didn't take his face in her hands, but his mouth was suddenly way too close to hers. Or maybe it just seemed that way. "Don't kiss me," she said, her voice husky and low.

"Why?"

"I really want to try this friendship thing and if you kiss me, you'll ruin it."

Jolie held her breath, utterly conflicted. Either way it went, she could handle it, but one way would be better for her peace of mind. Fortunately that was the way Dylan chose. Slowly he eased back, putting himself out of range.

"Friends. Not the kissing kind. Agreed." But his breathing was uneven. "Come on. I'll walk you to your truck."

MIKE INSISTED ON making Dylan breakfast the next morning, even though all he wanted was a lot of black coffee to make it through his four-hour work-day. Mike chatted about how well Gordy had done in the warehouse and about meeting his new neighbors, Joe and Marion Bradford. Apparently he and Joe had been acquainted years ago when Joe had operated a service station not far from the feed store.

And the entire time his grandfather was talking, Dylan had the feeling he was leading up to something. So he drank his coffee and waited.

"Things go okay over there in Lanesburg?"

Mike asked as he set a plate of scrambled eggs, toast and bacon in front of him.

"I don't know how I did on the exam, but the doc gave me the all-clear for active duty."

"Well, good." Except Mike didn't sound all that pleased.

Dylan was not going to ask why. Honestly, he was half afraid to ask why. Besides that, Mike would broach the matter when he was ready.

"Did you straighten out all that mortgage stuff?"

All Mike knew was that Dylan had been having some difficulty with the house. He'd been purposely vague about the matter and his grandfather hadn't pushed. Dylan hoped he didn't start now.

"Better than I'd hoped, but my advice is to never get divorced."

"Does this mean you're never getting married again?"

Dylan shot him a what-the-hell look and Mike said, "Just asking. No need to get your back up."

"My back isn't up."

"Spent some time at the store," his grandfather continued conversationally.

"Yeah?" Dylan purposely kept his response casual, since this was obviously going somewhere.

"Jolie's made it nicer."

"She has."

"The customers like her."

"They do."

"Don't scare her off."

Dylan's fork stopped a few inches from his mouth. "What?"

"You heard me. I like her. Don't scare her off."

"What makes you think I can scare her off even if I wanted to? Because, trust me, I did my best in high school and it didn't work."

"Just a feeling I had. She got kind of funny when I mentioned you. And, well, you guys did have that dust-up a while back."

"I don't want to chase her off. The store needs her." He recalled how she'd made that very statement the first time they'd met in the store and he'd scoffed at her. He wasn't scoffing anymore. He also wasn't saying any more.

Mike was giving him a look that made him a tad uneasy.

"Do you mind if I come to work with you today?"

"No," Dylan said, surprised. "It's your store."

"Was my store. Now it's yours and Finn's."

Dylan finished his eggs and got up to put his plate in the sink. "You'd better grab your coat. We're going to be late if we don't get a move on."

Somewhere along the line Mike had developed a real soft spot for Jolie. Maybe it was because she'd given his animals homes and provided him daily updates. Or maybe she reminded him a little of his wife, Helen, who'd also been a warm, outgoing woman with a wicked sense of humor. Whatever it was, over the next several days Mike came to work with Dylan more often than not, and whatever Jolie was doing, he was right there, chatting her up and helping her out.

Dylan was definitely the odd man out—which, he told himself, was a good thing. Mike was enjoying his days at work and he provided a buffer between Dylan and Jolie. Not that he was so certain they needed a buffer anymore. Something had changed since the late-night confessions in the store. Since they'd decided to be friends.

Some of the edge was gone, the sense of not knowing what the other person was thinking. He felt different when he was around her. Happy, really. But he was also well aware that she had a clear boundary that he wasn't allowed to cross. Not yet, anyway. Friends. Not the kissing kind.

And he told himself he was good with that. The last thing he needed was another complication in his life. Nope. He was going complication free just as soon as he figured out how to handle his job situation. His lips curled as he hefted a bag of grain onto a stack. Or, at least, what parts he would be allowed to handle and what parts would be decided for him.

He hefted another bag with more force than necessary. Oh, yeah. He could deal with having Pat as his superior. Dylan gave a soft grunt as he picked up another hundred-pound bag of grain.

All right. It wouldn't exactly be a pleasure going to work, but he *could* handle it. Eventually the gut twisting would diminish. And, besides, he wanted Pat to have to deal with him on a daily basis. Look into the face of the guy he'd lied to at the beginning of every shift. Yeah.

He tossed the last bag up and it skidded off the top of the pile, hit the ground on the other side and broke, scattering molasses-coated oats across the dusty floor. He muttered a curse as he went for the broom and an empty burlap bag. He hated the idea of Pat being promoted over him, but he wasn't going to back off because that was what Pat wanted him to do.

Unless the captain forced the transfer, he was going to push to return to his old job as a field training officer. Screw Pat. He was a professional. He could do this…and the captain was going to have to come up with a decent reason to keep him away from a job in which he'd received several commendations.

That fantasy lasted a day and a half. Sadie the dispatcher called him again and he was beginning to get the idea that she was interested in him, which was ironic, because at one time Pat had pursued Sadie and had been super pissed when she'd shot him down. So he'd apparently moved on to

Lindsey and now Sadie might be interested in him…yeah. No complications there.

"There's been no announcement yet, but rumor has it they're cutting back on the field training officer program."

That meant there might not be a patrol position for him to go back to, which meant continuing in Logistics. He thanked Sadie, agreed to look her up when he was back in town, then jammed his phone into his back pocket. He'd barely let go when it rang again.

He let out a breath as he recognized the number. Lanesburg Police Department. He hit Accept and brought the phone to his ear. The bastards worked fast.

"WHAT'S WRONG?" JOLIE asked when Dylan came into the store looking dazed.

He raised those blue eyes, shook his head and said, "Kind of your good news, bad news scenario."

"How so?"

"They're cutting back on the number of field training officers."

"Meaning you won't be on patrol?" She did her best to keep her voice even, but the truth was that she silently cheered at the idea of Dylan not being on patrol, even in a training capacity. She kept having those dreams every couple nights. The one where Dylan was overwhelmed by whatever awesomely evil force her mind managed to cook up. The evil entities changed, but the result was always the same…she lost Dylan.

And that made no sense because she didn't have Dylan.

"Doesn't look like it. Not without a fight, anyway."

"What's the good news?" Jolie asked, hoping no customers arrived before they finished their talk.

"That *was* the good news," Dylan said with a straight face.

"Sometimes you need a smack," Jolie replied darkly, but inwardly she was smiling. She loved it when he played. Such a change from the times not that long ago when he was closed off and defensive.

"I just got the call about the test. I passed the written exam and now I have an oral board exam."

Jolie felt her face light up. "One step closer."

"I'll be in the pool for the next job opening if I pass."

"How do you feel about that? Your chances of passing, I mean."

"Pretty confident. Now."

Jolie reached out and patted his upper arm. The flannel of his shirt was soft and worn. The muscles beneath rock-solid. It was kind of hard to drag her hand away and she had a feeling that he was well aware.

"When's the board exam?"

"Two weeks."

"I have a rodeo next week. We can be nervous together."

"I wouldn't have thought you were the nervous type."

"Why not?" she asked with a smile, leaning on the counter, feeling almost as good about him passing the written exam as he probably did.

"Because you're the competitive type."

"How would you know?"

"I can read the signs."

"I am an awesome competitor," she said with a cheeky smile. "But I get nerves. Right up until they open the gate and Jenabelle and I do our thing. Then it's all autopilot."

"You don't steer?"

She laughed. "Yeah. I steer. Kind of. More than that, I shift my weight, keep my toes away from the barrels when Jenabelle hugs in, then I urge her on home."

"And this takes…"

"Seventeen seconds. On a good day."

"Ah. Well worth how many hours of driving?"

"This trip is only four hours—round trip. Not bad, really." She drew a pattern on the top of the counter. "It's worth the time and gas to me." Her expression sobered slightly as she met his eyes and said simply, "I'm good and competing kind of completes me."

"I'd like to see you race," he said, holding her gaze.

"Then you should come with me."

"I guess I'll do that."

And Mike had better get his ass out of the office before she did what she swore she wasn't going to do—take Dylan's face in her hands and have her way with that sexy mouth of his.

"Okay." She cleared her throat, tore her gaze away and called for backup because things were feeling too intense for the middle of the day in a feed store. "Mike?" Her voice was thinner, higher than usual, and held a note of urgency. The old man poked his head out of the office. "Dylan has good news for you."

"Yeah?"

"I passed the written and now I take the oral."

"Hey," Mike said, smiling. "That is good news." But somehow he didn't look that thrilled.

Well, it was good news, Jolie told herself after the two men drifted into the office to talk. If Dylan made detective and got the job, then it wouldn't be as likely he'd get back in a patrol car. This was very good news.

And as for Dylan traveling with her…given the circumstances, that wasn't bad, either. Yes, the sparks were once again flaring, but now that she was looking at him leaving in a matter of weeks, she found that maybe she wasn't so anxious to keep her distance. She wasn't going to sleep with him, but she liked being with him, feeling that sexual edge. He would honor her wishes, she knew that instinctively, even if he hadn't demonstrated it behind the bar the night Wyatt had tried to change her tire. They could have a nice trip and who knew…maybe at some point in the future…

No. She didn't think that would happen.

Too complicated. But no reason she couldn't enjoy the here and now.

EVEN THOUGH HE grew up in a rodeo town, and the high school had a rodeo team, Dylan could count the number of rodeos he'd attended on one hand. It just hadn't been his thing. He'd gone to motocross instead with his dad and when his dad had gotten too sick to travel easily, he'd gone with Mike or Finn and his uncle. Toward the end of high school, he'd given up motocross and spent all the time he could with his dad in the garage, working on cars that his dad would never get a chance to drive.

They pulled into Glennan and drove through town to the rodeo grounds on the east side of the river. There Jolie parked in a grassy field already crowded with gooseneck trailers and big trucks. There were horses tied to the sides of almost every trailer and a group of kids raced past them as Jolie turned off the engine, the kid at the rear swinging a lariat, trying to rope one of the boys running in front of her.

Dylan stood back as Jolie unloaded her buckskin mare who raised her head as soon as all four feet hit solid ground and gave a loud whinny. Several horses whinnied back and the mare seemed satisfied to know that there was more of her kind in the area. Jolie tied her up, then told Dylan she needed to check in and she'd meet him back there in ten or fifteen minutes. She pointed to the coffee stand. Dylan took the hint, grabbed the empty thermos from the front seat and headed off on his own mission.

"We're going to get home late," she said as she came back from the office, a bunch of papers clutched in one hand. "I'm the second-to-last competitor in the last section. Just before the bulls."

"Then I guess you'll know the time you have to beat."

"That's an advantage," she agreed, "unless you let it mess with your head."

"Do you do that?"

She blinked at him with those wide green eyes. Eyes he could kind of get lost in.

"No."

He laughed. The Jolie he'd thought of as so scattered was actually not scattered at all. At least not about things that mattered to her, such as her ranch, the store, barrel racing. Most of the drive to the rodeo had been quiet and Jolie had apologized, telling him that she'd make up for it by talking his ear off on the way home. Before a competition, she liked to go over the run in her head and pretty much let her mind drift. Not too difficult with so many miles to drive. And this was only the beginning, she'd told him. She had a rodeo almost every weekend between now and Labor Day. Mike had agreed to handle the store on the days she needed off.

Dylan wasn't surprised. Mike was a little in love with Jolie, in a grandfatherly way, and he also seemed to enjoy being at the store now that customers came in to hang out and visit. He'd even put in a coffeepot near Jolie's desk, which was proving quite popular with the older guys.

"I don't mind getting home late," he said. "I'd kind of hoped to watch the bulls anyway."

"Sounds good," Jolie said. "Maybe we can grab a burger. I usually don't stay much past my event. A lot of times I'm pushing on to another rodeo the next day."

"How do you afford that?"

"If I start giving barrel clinics next summer as planned, once Dani comes back, I may be able to write it off as a business expense. But right now, I just hope to win enough money to break even or not lose too much on travel." She gave a small shrug. "Hey. All hobbies cost money, you know."

He thought of the rusted-out Mustang that he and his dad had restored. That had cost a lot of money and in the end they'd sold it at a small profit—nothing close to covering their time. He reached out to run a hand over her shoulder, felt the tension in her muscles.

"Do you relax more as the season goes on?"

She lifted her eyebrows in an amused way. "More like I develop a what-the-hell attitude."

He let his hand fall away, told himself that he needed to stop touching her, but she also needed to stop looking at him like that.

The past week at the store had been…interesting… to say the least. Mike had showed up every day, acting as an unwitting chaperone. His presence reminding Dylan to keep his distance from Jolie while they were on the clock—as much as he could anyway. If the chance to get close presented itself…well, more often than not, he took it.

She wasn't stepping back emotionally as much as she had prior to confession time, but neither was he.

When his lawyer had called and told him that she'd sent a letter to Lindsey requesting one month's mortgage reimbursement for the month that they could prove she'd had a roommate, he'd shared the news with Jolie. And a few days later when the real-estate agent had called to say that there had finally been an offer on the house—a low offer, but an offer all the same—he'd shared that, too. It was as if he was approaching *The Oprah Winfrey Show* status in the sharing department.

Jolie, on the other hand, hadn't been so open. She teased when the opportunity arose; she didn't back away when he got close. And more than that, she hadn't withdrawn her offer of letting him travel to the rodeo with her even though there had been three days between her offer and the actual event. She seemed to like their new status as friends— not the kissing kind—but from the way her gaze kept slipping to his mouth, he wondered how long that was going to last. How long he was going to let it last.

She was driving him crazy and, if he were honest, he was loving it.

As his dad had told him, what was worth having was worth waiting for.

CHAPTER THIRTEEN

JOLIE WASN'T CERTAIN whether having Dylan at the rodeo with her was a blessing or a curse. She liked being close to him, would have been lying if she said she didn't enjoy the tension snapping between them. It seemed that once she'd made her decision to enjoy it, it made it possible for her to do just that. He was a friend. A hot, hot friend. Nothing wrong with letting a hot friend add a little zest to one's fantasy life.

In a few weeks he'd be back in Lanesburg, she'd be at the store and maybe they'd see each other on the holidays. Maybe she'd hear about him via Mike. He'd get his detective's badge, work in a position where he wouldn't be in that cruiser tempting fate, and she'd be happily building her ranch. Running barrels. Waiting to become a doting aunt.

She glanced over to where he was standing near the front of the truck, watching the contestants as they made ready for the day. The roping kids raced toward him and he had to take a quick step sideways to avoid being roped before they charged on. He laughed and looked back at her and she felt a slow tumbling in her midsection. Damn but he was gorgeous.

He ambled toward her, hands in his jacket pockets. "Cute kids."

Who would grow into hunky cowboys, no doubt. "Yeah," she agreed.

"What do you do until you compete?"

"Warm up. Sometimes I shop at the vendor booths if I'm feeling flush. Catch up with old friends."

"And today?"

"Warm up. And I'll probably watch the first half of the rodeo with you."

"Want to grab something to eat? Or are you a nervous-stomach performer?"

"Just the opposite. I feed my stress."

He laughed, his teeth flashing white against his tanned face. He held out a hand. "I'll buy you some lunch."

Jolie hesitated ever so briefly before putting her hand in his. He squeezed her fingers and she returned the pressure. Friends.

WHILE JOLIE WARMED UP, Dylan watched the competition. It was a smallish venue, but the stands were packed—because it was Memorial Day and one of the first rodeos of the season, Jolie explained. He had to admit to thinking that maybe he'd missed something by not attending more rodeos. Or maybe he just appreciated the fact that a guy could get the snot beat out of him by a bronc then stand up, dust himself off and wave his hat to the crowd as he walked off, doing his best to look as though he felt no pain. Kind of what he did in the line of duty.

Yeah. He admired these guys.

As her event approached, Jolie took on the same look as the steer wrestlers and the ropers—one of grit and determination. And when Dylan watched her charge out into the arena, one small woman atop a thousand pounds of churning horseflesh, he felt his mouth drop open then snap shut as he silently rode with her, helping her around those barrels, then bringing her on home. It was all he could do not to jump to his feet as she crossed the barrier then pulled her mare to a sliding stop. The crowd cheered. She wasn't the top time, but missed it by only fractions of a second. In the money, which was what she'd hoped. Dylan got to his feet and made his way to her gooseneck, all thoughts of watching the bulls gone.

"Way to go," he said as he approached.

Jolie was not smiling. She looked exhausted. "Yeah. I'm happy." She didn't sound like it, but he realized she was coming down after her performance and probably felt about the same as he did after successfully chasing down a runner.

She unsaddled Jenabelle as if on autopilot, her look distant, and he had the feeling she was still going over her run in her head, analyzing. Tweaking. He took the saddle from her and she looked surprised but didn't fight him for the honor of storing it away in the tack compartment. A cheer came up from the arena and she glanced at him as he stepped out of the compartment.

"If you want to watch the bulls, you better get back to the stands."

Dylan simply shook his head.

"Then…you want to grab something to eat?"

He wanted to grab something, all right. And she was standing right there in front of him. Slowly he hooked his thumbs in his belt loops, curling his fingers loosely against his jeans.

"Yeah." That palpable…something…was once again there. Hanging between them. Neither of them moved.

Finally, Jolie let out a long, low breath. "Dooley's is good."

"Dooley's it is."

Dooley's was good. And so was the company. Dylan was to drive home, so he didn't drink, but Jolie had a tall beer and as the glass emptied, she began to talk more. About the circuit. About the ranch. About her plans for the future.

Dylan listened, suspecting that she was talking about one subject but thinking about another. And he was doing the same.

She fell asleep on the drive home, startled herself awake at one point, shot him a fearful glance, which made him want to ask whether she'd had a nightmare, then she let out a shaky breath and settled back against the door and closed her eyes again.

They stayed closed until he drove into her yard where his truck was waiting next to the barn.

Jolie got out of the truck without a word and went back to unload her mare. She released the horse into the pasture, where it loped off to meet her equine buddies.

From the fenced yard, booming barks reverberated, making Jolie smile ruefully as she returned to where Dylan was waiting for her, coiling and recoiling the lead rope as she walked. She laid it on the hood of her truck and continued on to where Dylan stood near the gate post.

"Good thing I don't have close neighbors," she said.

"Yeah." He looked down at her, once again hooking his thumbs in his belt loops.

Jolie took a step forward and covered his hands with her own, holding them as she rose up on her toes and kissed him.

"Thanks for coming with me."

"What happened to being non-kissing friends?" he asked. Having his hands held down was making him hard.

"I guess I'm not totally against kissing."

"What changed your mind?"

"I guess we have this time right now and I'm afraid that when you go back to Washington, I'm going to regret not taking advantage of it."

"Are you sure about that?"

"Are you going to keep talking?"

"Just making sure it won't get awkward again."

She nipped his lower lip and there was no more getting hard. He *was* hard. Rock-hard, ready to go.

He unhooked his thumbs from his belt loops and pushed his hands into her hair, holding her as he answered the nip with a crushing kiss that had them clinging to one another. There were no more questions. No need for answers.

When he lifted his head, Jolie eased herself out of his embrace and reached for his hand. Linking their fingers together, she led the way across the driveway. And, Dylan imagined, paradise.

Gus ambushed them at the gate then followed them into the house, making it impossible to do what Dylan wanted to do, which was to back Jolie against the front door and start a long, slow exploration of her mouth and then start peeling her out of those rodeo clothes.

Jolie greeted the dog that bounded around her, rubbed his fuzzy head, then opened the door and allowed him to gallop out into the yard. He turned, seemingly perplexed that she hadn't followed him, and she closed the door then leaned against it.

Her hair was ruffled, lips swollen and the look in her eyes as she regarded him made Dylan wonder what had taken them so long to get to this point. They'd both known they were heading here and it suddenly seemed as if they'd wasted a whole lot of time jockeying for position.

"Now," Jolie said from where she stood with her hands behind her, leaning against the door. "Where were we?"

Dylan took a slow step forward, carefully placed a palm against the door on either side of her face and leaned close. "I think I was about to do this," he said, brushing his lips over hers in a light kiss. Her eyes drifted shut and he kissed her again, their tongues meeting this time, touching lightly, teasing, before the serious kissing began.

Jolie finally gave a small moan before pulling her mouth away and gesturing toward the staircase with a quick motion of her head.

Dylan did not need a second invitation. He took her by the hand and led the way upstairs. As she passed the thermostat, Jolie cranked it on, saying something about not freezing. Dylan saw no way that freezing was anywhere near possible.

She opened a door and led him into a darkened room, stopping close to the bed. She glanced around her as if looking for something. When she met his perplexed gaze she said, "I'm looking for my boot jack. I'm pretty much stuck in these pants until I get my boots off."

"We can't have that," he said.

"This is the way life is," she said. "Never a boot-jack when you need one." She sat on the bed and held up her foot. "Please?"

"If it'll help get those pants off." Dylan took the foot she offered him and rather expertly pulled off the boot then gestured for the other. Jolie complied and after removing the second boot, he peeled off her socks, running his hands over her bare feet in soft caresses only to have her pull them away.

"I'm ticklish," she said in a voice that was barely above a whisper.

"Good information to have," Dylan said. "What else don't I know about you?"

She leaned back on her elbows, looking up at him. "That I want you naked?"

"I'd almost guessed that one," he said as he started unbuttoning his shirt.

She got to her feet and covered his hands with her own. "Let me."

He dropped his hands to his sides and watched as she unfastened the buttons one after another. Then, smart girl that she was, she lifted each wrist and released the cuffs. Slowly she pushed the shirt off his shoulders, allowing it to fall into a heap on the floor behind him, before skimming her hands over his chest, down his sides. A faint smile curved her lips as she touched him, giving him the feeling that she'd thought about this before, about touching him, making love to him.

She curled her fingers inside the waistband of his jeans, her eyes meeting his in a serious way and he could see that she was feeling as impatient as he was. They'd talk and play and laugh later. Right now he needed her. Needed to feel her underneath him, needed to feel her respond, and convince him that she wanted him as much as he wanted her. He took hold of the edges of her shirt and pulled, unsnapping the pearl fasteners in a series of quick pops.

"Your pants," she muttered as she fumbled with his belt. He helped her out and the next thing he knew his pants were being pushed down over his hips and he was in her hand. He closed his eyes as her palm grazed the length of him then her fingers circled him and squeezed. He stepped back, needing her to be as naked as he was.

Jolie understood and unsnapped her bra, tossing it aside. Her jeans followed and Dylan stepped in to slowly peel down her panties, caressing her as he did so.

Jolie gasped through her teeth, her eyes shutting as his fingers stroked her damp core. "More," she murmured, once again taking hold of him, caressing him, and he returned the favor.

He was sure they were both going to come in a

matter of minutes. There was nothing wrong with that, but he wanted to be inside her. Did. Not. Want. To. Wait.

When he pulled his hand away from her hot center, Jolie's eyes came open, a frown pulling her eyebrows together. "Condom," he murmured against her mouth before turning to find his jeans and dig his wallet out.

Jolie took the package from him, tore it open and slowly, slowly rolled it over his erection. And then she lay back on the bed, pulling Dylan down with her, kissing him long and deep as he pressed against her, gasping against his mouth as he eased inside.

And after that all he was aware of was how perfect and wet and tight she was. How he wasn't going to be satisfied doing this just once. Or twice. How her clever hands kept sending him closer to the brink. And when she suddenly arched against him and he felt her throb around him, seeming to pull him even more deeply inside her, it was too much. He lost control, even though he'd wanted to last so much longer.

Collapsing against her, he let out a long, long breath, closing his eyes as she brought a hand up to stroke his damp skin. He rolled off her, tucked her against him and fell sound asleep.

DAYLIGHT WAS FILTERING in through the sheer curtains when Dylan opened his eyes. His arm was draped over Jolie, so he pulled her closer, drawing the length of her soft body close to his before loosely closing a hand over her breast. She made a small sound and moved against him, making him swell against her backside. She turned in his arms, a soft smile curving her lips as she nestled against him.

"Raccoon eyes?" she asked, blinking at him.

He fought a smile as he rubbed a thumb under the faint shadow under her eyes. "Nothing to speak of."

She rolled onto her back and stared up at the ceiling.

"Regrets?"

"None." But she didn't look at him, which made him wonder. He brushed his hand across her flat belly and she rolled her head to meet his eyes. "Honest. It's just that…well… I didn't expect last night to rock my world as hard as it did."

He felt his eyes crinkle at the corners. "Same here."

He felt warm. Good. And…satisfied to be there with her. As if she'd been the piece missing from his life. He'd never felt that way about Lindsey. He'd loved her and they'd been good together in the beginning, but he'd never had this feeling of oneness before.

Jolie turned toward him to form herself against him. "Is Mike going to wonder where you are?"

"Probably not." His grandfather was no fool.

"Should we think about getting to work?" she asked, a lazy note in her voice.

Dylan brought his forehead down to touch hers. "We could. Or we could be a little late."

"I'm shocked to hear my boss talking that way."

"Yeah?" He murmured close to her ear and then told her exactly why they were going to be late. Her eyes widened and a wicked smile curved her lips as she reached down to circle him with her fingers.

"You're on."

THE NEXT TWO days in the store were interesting to say the least—especially when Dylan suggested that they make use of her box of leftover lingerie party stock.

Oh, yeah…interesting. Jolie couldn't think of another time in her life when she'd spent so much time anticipating. They had a couple weeks left together and she was going to enjoy every minute of it, even if part of her was shouting out a warning that she and Dylan needed to talk. Needed to make certain they were on the same page. The this-is-fun-for-now page.

After her startling realization the first time they'd made love, she refused to allow herself to think along those lines. Yes, she felt for him deeply, but this was no different from any other of her relationships. They'd continue as they were until he left and then that would be that. She wasn't going to Washington and he'd made it very clear to her during their late-night talk that he had some issues to settle there. He had to return. They would part sharing special memories.

And she was beginning to think that the day of parting needed to come soon, because for the first time ever, she had a feeling it was not going to be easy. That it might even be a touch painful.

But better to suffer a little pain now than a lot of pain later.

She refused to think of sleeping with Dylan, of sharing herself with him, as a mistake. Sex with Dylan was one of the most powerful experiences of her life. She was going to ignore the little voice murmuring to her that it was too powerful...to the point of being dangerous.

AFTER MAKING HIS motel reservations for his next trip to Lanesburg, Dylan hung up the phone and was struck by a hard question. Why? Why was he pursuing this plan so doggedly?

Yes, he'd like to make detective. But did he want to live in Lanesburg? Was showing Pat that he wasn't about to back down or disappear with his tail between his legs worth screwing up the rest of his life?

Because what did he have there and what did he have here?

When placed side by side, there wasn't much of a question as to what he had where. On the Lanesburg side he had retirement credit and a job at a desk. The potential of making detective and one hell of a lot of stress until he did. On the Montana side, he had his grandfather and Jolie. No job. No place to live, but that was easily solved…once he got a job.

Once planted, the thought refused to die. Why go back to a life he wasn't certain he even wanted when he could build a new one here—in the place where he was born? His dad had wanted him to leave. To not be one of the guys who never saw any part of the world except for their small corner of Montana. But he had seen the world. Experienced life in a big way. Now he was ready to come back home.

Half an hour later he picked up the phone and called Jess Moody from the warehouse.

"If that position is still open, I'd like to apply."

"It closes day after tomorrow," Jess said. "Only a one-week posting."

"Look… I'm still kind of debating, but I want to keep my options open."

"I understand. You know I'm going to put in a word for you, though."

Dylan smiled a little. "I appreciate that."

Feeling ridiculously optimistic, Dylan went into the store to find Jolie selling a piece of silver to an elderly lady. She smiled at Dylan with such warmth and promise that his heart stuttered a little.

Yeah. He was definitely applying for that job.

CHAPTER FOURTEEN

EARLY FRIDAY MORNING while waiting for a delivery driver to finish paperwork, Dylan got a call from the Eagle Valley Sheriff's Office offering him an interview on the following Monday—three days before his board oral exam.

He accepted the interview, then dropped his phone into his pocket and stood regarding the truck just outside the bay door. He hadn't told Mike about the possibility of staying in Montana because he knew how much his granddad wanted him to stay. No sense getting the guy's hopes up. He hadn't told Jolie, either, for the same reason. He liked to have everything in place before proceeding forward. The last thing he wanted to do was to raise hopes only to disappoint those close to him.

The driver approached and held out his clipboard. Dylan signed and the guy headed back to his truck. Once he pulled away, Marcel trotted out from under a pallet and went straight to his empty food bowl, giving Dylan a hey-stupid-my-bowl-is-empty look.

"You're supposed to catch your supper," Dylan

muttered. The cat skittered away as he approached, but didn't disappear as he used to. Jolie was right—a hungry cat was a friendly cat, and once Marcel figured out that Dylan also knew how to fill a food bowl, he'd started hanging around out in the open more often. The previous afternoon he'd found Marcel sleeping on the seat of the forklift and discovered that there was something satisfying about the standoffish cat coming to trust him in his own distant way. Trust was not something Dylan took lightly.

Mike hadn't come to the store that morning, which left Dylan and Jolie to deal with more customers than usual. He was beginning to think Jolie's theory was correct; that people rushed in to buy feed just before account billings went out. But business had picked up in other ways, so he wasn't complaining. And because Mike wasn't there to BS, his cronies didn't hang around drinking coffee for as long, but there were still plenty of people to fill the store.

By the end of the day Jolie pronounced it the best day they'd had since she's come on board and Dylan suggested a night out to celebrate. "Let's pretend you didn't call off the bet."

"I have a night out tonight," she reminded him dryly. "McElroy's?"

"I was thinking next Sunday, when you don't have a rodeo interfering with my plans. Dinner out.

Someplace with cloth napkins." The only places they'd been to had been the café and McElroy's. Their time together had been a study in informality, but Dylan had a hankering to see Jolie dressed up, smiling at him over a glass of wine.

She considered his offer for a moment, leaning on the counter, chin in her palm, green eyes dancing. "Cloth napkins, you say. Hard to pass that up."

He grinned at her. "I hear they're real nice."

She smiled back. "I'd love to."

He put his hand over hers and leaned in to kiss her just as the bell jangled.

"Hey now. None of that," Morley called across the store.

Dylan stepped back. "Caught me," he said, wondering how long until Mike was notified of what Morley had witnessed.

Jolie came around the counter. "Do you have a list for me?"

Morley pulled a paper out of his pocket and Dylan felt warmth spread through him as he watched her squint to decipher Lillian Ames's faint handwriting.

Soon after Morley left they closed the store and he went home with Jolie to help her feed, then drove her to the bar. There was only one car in the lot—Jim's.

Dylan swung the truck close to the side door. "Looks to be a slow start to the evening."

"You should come in for a while," Jolie said as she gathered her purse and jacket.

"Tempting."

She leaned across the truck toward him, lifted her eyebrows suggestively. "That's me. Ever the temptress."

He closed the distance between them, gave her a quick kiss. "Let's go, temptress."

She laughed and got out of the truck, leading the way through the side door. Jim appeared mildly surprised to see Dylan tagging along behind his server. "Expecting trouble from Maddox and Company tonight?" he asked Jolie.

"I'm buying my boss a drink," she replied lightly.

"Why, thank you," Jim said with exaggerated politeness.

"My bosses," she corrected.

Jim's questioning gaze connected with Dylan's. "Do you ever really feel like her boss?"

Dylan shook his head. "Never have. Probably never will."

Jim gave a commiserating nod and lifted a bottle of Knob Creek. Dylan nodded and Jim poured two fingers and passed it to him. Then he shot seltzer into two glasses, passed one to Jolie and lifted the other himself. "To quiet Fridays—may they be few and far between."

Jolie touched her glass to Dylan's, a smile lighting her eyes, making him wonder for the umpteenth time why he hadn't fallen for her long ago. He needed to make up for lost time and, if things worked out the way he hoped, he'd have an opportunity to do that.

Patrons trickled in and Jolie went to work, while Dylan hung at the bar, talking to Jim between customers. Bartenders and cops had a lot in common, as in they both dealt with a clientele that wasn't always on its best behavior. Jolie seemed to enjoy their swapping of war stories and added a few of her own when she wasn't busy.

"I heard you might be staying," Jim said conversationally after Jolie left the bar to clear a recently vacated table.

Dylan automatically glanced toward where she was loading empties onto her tray.

"She doesn't know?" Jim asked.

"I was waiting until it was official before I told anyone. Even my granddad."

"Ah." Jim's mouth quirked at the corner. "Well, you know what they say about bartenders and secrets."

No, but he assumed that Jim was indicating that he'd keep quiet. The problem was that someone else wasn't keeping quiet—probably Jess—but Dylan hadn't said anything about keeping the application a secret. His fault.

The door banged open, which was a feat considering the size of the big oak door, and Maddox

and Wyatt came in. Jim raised his chin in acknowledgment and the men both gave slight nods back
before heading to a table in the corner. "Good customers," Jim said. "They just need proper care and
management."

Dylan gave a short laugh, then the door opened
again and a large group of guys in their twenties,
dressed in jeans, cowboy hats and western shirts
came in.

"This might not be such a bad night after all,"
Jim mused. Jolie was already at the first table
taking orders when another group came inside.
"Maybe I'd better get Beccie down here…"

The crowd continued to swell and at one point,
Dylan was unloading clean glassware behind the
bar while Jolie and Beccie took care of the orders.
A little after midnight, the bar emptied almost as
quickly as it had filled and a half hour later Jim
told Beccie and Jolie they could go home.

Jolie slid across the truck seat to sit close to him
on the drive home and Dylan rested his hand on
her knee. One thing he'd learned tonight—not to
assume that his personal business was his business in this small community. He needed to talk to
Jolie, fess up about the interview before she heard
it from someone else, but it could wait until tomorrow. Right now, he just wanted to get her home.

She took it for granted that he was coming in,
or so he guessed when she got out of the truck and

turned with a slight frown as if wondering what was taking him so long. He shut off the engine and followed her into the house.

Gus barked. She shushed him then motioned with her head toward the stairs. "It might have been a short shift, but I'm beat," she confessed.

"Sleep's fine with me," he said, following her to the staircase.

"Who said anything about sleeping?" she said with a wicked smile. "I was just calling the bottom."

And he was instantly hard.

The next morning, he woke to find Jolie snuggled against him, lazily caressing his chest. His arm tightened around her and he smiled at her. "Keep that up and we'll be late for work. You know how Mike feels about opening late." As it was, they were going to have to skip showering and wear morning-after clothes—at least until noon, when he was going to suggest a long, hot bath together.

She pulled his mouth down to hers, making Dylan seriously consider not opening on time and having that long, hot bath now, even though they had another delivery due that morning.

Jolie gave him one last, lingering kiss then pushed herself upright and slowly swung her legs around to sit on the edge of the bed. She pulled open her dresser drawer from where she sat and, took out a pair of bikini panties. "I'm going to miss being tempted to play hooky," she said on a sigh as she pulled the panties on, lifting her butt briefly from the bed as she slid them into place.

"Actually, I might be staying in the area," Dylan said as she leaned down for her jeans lying on the floor where he'd peeled her out of them.

Jolie stilled for a fraction of a second then shot him a look.

"How's that?"

"I applied for a position as deputy sheriff."

"Oh." The word came out softly. And she didn't look happy. She looked startled. Deer-in-the-head-lights startled. "A deputy position? Here? What about the detective exam?"

"I'm still scheduled." And if he wasn't mistaken, the color was fading from her cheeks. This was not the reaction he'd expected. Not even close. "What's going on, Jolie?"

Instead of answering, she pulled her jeans on over her long, smooth legs. He put a hand on her thigh, stopping the motion.

She turned to look at him again, her long hair sliding over her shoulder, her green gaze troubled, though it seemed she was trying to hide it. "You're just keeping your options open by applying for the deputy job?"

"I guess you could say that." He pressed his lips together, not liking or understanding this barrier edging up between them, triggering the knot that was forming, hard and tight, in his gut. "Don't look so down. I may not get the job."

"It's not that I don't want you to get the job."

But she was troubled by the possibility that he might stay. That was suddenly and painfully apparent. "All right…"

A brittle silence hung between them. He waited for her to break it; to explain what was going on in her head. Instead Jolie smiled a little and ran her hand over his thigh. "We'd better get to the store. We can talk later."

"I want to know what's wrong."

"Nothing's wrong. You just kind of sprung this on me. I'm…processing. We'll talk later today. After work." She patted his thigh again and reached for her lacy bra.

Dylan wanted to talk now, but instead leaned in and gave her a quick kiss. Her response was at best cool. He wasn't sure why she had to process, why she needed time to adjust to the possibility of him being around more permanently, but if she did, so be it.

She got off the bed and pulled her shirt on. Dylan watched as she continued to dress, her movements quick and methodical. She wanted out of there. Now. He made no move to stop her.

After she was dressed, she took a few steps toward the bed where he still sat, an expression on her face he couldn't read. For a minute he thought

she was going to say something about her reaction
to him staying, to explain, but instead she said,
"You want to swing through the Coffee Spot for
breakfast? We're running late."

"Sure."

"Great. I'll go throw some hay and we can just
make it to the store on time."

She disappeared out of the room and Dylan got
to his feet and grabbed his pants from the floor.
He heard the bathroom door shut, the water turn
on, then shook his head and stepped into his jeans.

What in the hell had just happened?

JOLIE TRIED TO focus on her computer screen, but
a movement outside her window caught her eye.
Dylan wheeling a barrow of old grain off for dis-
posal. She sucked in a breath and brought her eyes
back to the screen.

How had her happy, hot fling transformed into
this unsettling situation? One in which she was
going to have to explain again what she'd thought
she'd already made clear…she was in this for the
here and now. She didn't do long term. She didn't
know if there was something wrong with her, or
if she was simply wired this way, but as much as
she enjoyed friendship and closeness, she believed
in being true to herself. To her instincts. And her
instincts told her she was better off being single.
She'd gotten the strong feeling from Dylan that

morning that he assumed that staying meant that he and she would build a more solid relationship.

That most definitely had *not* been on the agenda. He was supposed to go back to his old life and she was supposed to continue with hers, here, six hundred miles away from him.

Jolie pushed the hair back from her forehead, trying to stave off the headache that hadn't fully responded to pain reliever. So far the day had proved to be a study in mutual avoidance. Dylan hadn't left the warehouse since they'd arrived at the store to find a delivery driver impatiently waiting for them, and there was no way she was going out there as she usually did when things got slow. His office phone rang a few times, but she ignored it. The line was private and it wasn't her job to answer it, as she would have done yesterday.

A deputy.

Why would he want to become a deputy and stay here rather than go back to Lanesburg and have a relatively safe career as a detective? It wasn't that she didn't want him to live close to his grandfather, but—she pressed her hand harder against her aching head—why did he have to become a deputy? A guy people shot at? He'd gotten off lightly once, but to her, this was pushing things. Not that his life choices were her concern, but even though she wasn't going to ride off into the sunset with him, she cared about him. His safety.

Being a deputy wasn't safe. Even Kyle, who'd been with the local office for only a year, had had a few close calls. Of his own making, according to Allie, but close calls all the same. The bells on the door rang and Jolie looked up, feeling a wash of relief when she realized that a customer had come into the store, not Dylan, although she had no doubt that the moment of reckoning between them was coming and it was coming soon.

DYLAN PURPOSELY GAVE Jolie her space that morning, allowing her time to think. Allowing them both time to think. There weren't nearly the customers that they'd had the previous day, but enough to keep them both busy. Between loads, Dylan tried to review for his oral exam, but he had trouble keeping his focus where it belonged—on his laptop instead of on Jolie.

Finally, at eleven-thirty, he closed his laptop and stowed it in his truck. It was a half hour away from the time when he could turn around the Open sign, but the parking lot was empty and chances were that he and Jolie would spend that time alone—unless someone needed last-minute chicken scratch.

Dylan decided to take that chance. He was normally a patient guy, but this situation with Jolie was eating at him. He wanted some answers and he wanted them today. If he waited until closing, there was always the chance that Jolie would take off, despite saying they would talk after work.

He trusted her, yet he didn't. Mainly because he had no idea what was going on. No. That wasn't totally true. He had a few theories, but needed more data.

He rolled down the warehouse door and crossed the graveled yard to the store. Jolie was rearranging the items in the gift display, as she always did after making a few sales. She looked over her shoulder at him as he came in.

"Hey," she said, setting down the candle she'd been holding.

"I think we should talk now. If you have time."

That, she clearly did, since it was still twenty five minutes to closing time.

"I have time." She started to fold her arms over her chest, then stopped and instead loosely clasped her hands in front of her.

He came a few feet closer, trying to look relaxed when he was anything but. "I didn't say anything about applying for the local sheriff's office posting because I didn't know if I'd make the cut for an interview. I did. It's on Monday at eight."

"You should have told me."

"Yeah, I should have," he agreed. He'd never been one for sharing before a deal was done, but maybe he'd have to get over that.

Jolie glanced sideways out the window as if willing someone to drive in and it struck him then that maybe his staying in the area wasn't what bothered her. Maybe it was the fact that he'd done something as major as applying for a local job without telling her. He felt a brief surge of optimism. Maybe she was simply angry at him. That he could fix. "Nothing was, or is, certain," he said.

Jolie looked back at him. "All the same…it would have given me a different perspective if I'd known you'd planned to stay. Affected some of my decisions."

"How?" He regarded her carefully.

Her eyes flashed as she said, "I like knowing all the facts when I become involved with someone."

"The facts changed. It happens." His eyes narrowed slightly. "And I'd like to know how my being here permanently would have changed your decisions." He wanted to hear her spell it out.

"It's hard to explain." Her expression was growing more distant by the second, as if she was hiding a deep, deep secret and he was edging uncomfortably close. "I shouldn't have to explain."

"No, Jolie. You shouldn't." He was surprised at the coldness in his tone. It didn't grow any warmer as he said, "But a few hints would help me get a handle on things."

"I thought I'd been clear on that."

Really? Clear as mud…but the mud was starting to settle a bit as an idea took hold. "This…thing…

between you and me. Was it just a string of one-night stands to you?"

She swallowed before lifting her chin, but didn't give him the denial he was hoping for. "I never promised anything else."

"And I never asked for a promise. But I thought there was a possibility of exploration."

"I have nothing against exploration," Jolie said.

"As long as it's only physical?" And there he'd hit the nail on the head. He could see it in her face.

"I'm not looking for a relationship," she said.

"Ever?"

"Let's just say I'm not in the market."

"Have you ever been in the market?"

When she didn't answer, he asked in a gentler voice, "Did something happen? Did someone hurt you?"

Her expression blanked out even more than before. But, despite her stony expression, he had the oddest feeling that she was close to tears. She shook her head as if his hypothesis was so far off base it didn't even need to be addressed.

"Then what?"

She started to speak then stopped. "I have nothing against you staying."

He started to ask why; thought better of it. "But you don't do committed relationships."

"I do friendships," she said. "The kissing kind."

He lifted one corner of his mouth in a grim half

smile, even though her statement wasn't funny. Not even close. He really wanted to ask her what the deal was, for real, but one look at her face told him he'd get nowhere if he continued to push. Apparently his plan to stay had ruined her plan for an easy out after a few weeks of good sex.

"ARE YOU ALL RIGHT?" Jim nudged Jolie as they stood side-by-side behind the bar during a brief lull. Since he was tall, his elbow hit her upper arm.

"Yeah. Fine." She gave him a quick why-would-you-ask look, even though she knew exactly why he would ask. She'd been spacey all night long; lost in thought as she tried to convince herself that she hadn't done anything wrong in regard to her relationship with Dylan. She'd been up-front. Never once had she indicated that she was looking for anything long term. Even if she'd planned to use his departure as an easy end to a most excellent fling, she couldn't see where she'd led him on in any way, shape or form. Pretty much because she hadn't. That wasn't the way she did things.

So why did she feel like hell?

She glanced at Jim, considered asking for a male perspective, but decided against it as a couple of women approached the bar, holding each other up.

"I'll call a cab," she told Jim since they'd been watching the pair and knew they had no one there to drive them home. She escaped to the office and made the call, then came back to find the women sitting on stools at the far end of the bar. "Ten minutes," she told Jim.

"Hope they make it that long," he said. He was good at monitoring his patrons, but when people were buying drinks for one another, he had no way of knowing who was drinking what and how much.

Jolie slumped down onto a stool to wait for the cab. It'd been a long night and early the next morning she'd load Jenabelle and head out for Big Timber.

Jolie didn't know whether a day on the road with nothing but her thoughts and old country classics was going to make her feel better or worse, but she figured a couple of days without seeing Dylan should help her get her head on a bit straighter. She'd never before had any problem just walking away, but never before had she slept with anyone to whom she had ties—business or otherwise. This was a wakeup call. No matter how hot a guy was, if they worked together in any capacity, he was officially off limits. Starting now.

Jim and Jolie helped the women into the cab, wished the driver luck then stood back as he drove away.

Now. Ask him now if Dylan is being unreasonable.

But she couldn't. Too personal. Even if she

put the question to him hypothetically, as she'd planned, Jim was no fool and she didn't want to let go of too much information. It was probable, too, that Jim didn't want too much information, which left her grappling with her problem alone.

She got home at 1:30 a.m., checked her truck and trailer to make sure everything was ready. Her rodeo clothes were hanging in the back window, her lunch was packed in a cooler on the seat. Sunglasses, hat, water bottle, phone charger. She was set.

Gus didn't bother to bark as she approached and entered the house.

Jolie undressed at the hamper, tossing her bar clothes in and shutting the lid. She didn't bother with pajamas, but instead climbed into bed and was almost asleep when the text came in.

Did you get home ok?

Dylan.
That's it. Stab me in the heart.
She debated then decided to take the high road.

I did.

She almost added, "Good luck with the interview," but that seemed insincere, so she sent the message on its way and powered off her phone.

"I LOVE THIS PAINTING," Lillian Ames said for the fourth time after Dylan climbed down off the ladder and delivered it into her hands.

"It's beautiful," he agreed. "Anything else?" he asked Jolie coolly. It'd been like that between them since he'd returned from his interview on Monday—distant and cool—which was exactly what Jolie wanted, so it made no sense that his stand-offish demeanor ate at her. Except that she really had hoped to remain friends after they'd stopped sleeping together.

"No." She wouldn't have needed him for this if she'd had a ladder handy. They really needed to invest in a five-foot stepladder.

"Great." Dylan didn't bother to look her way as he replied. He dragged the ladder back out the door. Lillian stared lovingly at the artwork in her hands and Jolie tore her gaze from Dylan's retreating back.

And this is why you don't sleep with your boss— at least not while he still is your boss. Awkward, stilted work environment.

Lillian paid for the painting, then took her prize out to show Morley who was waiting in the truck with the load of chicken scratch.

Jolie sat at her computer and for a brief moment propped her face in her hands. Dylan had interviewed with the county two days ago and she had no idea how it had gone. She wanted to know yet she didn't. He certainly wasn't volunteering any information; however, she did know that he was still taking the oral exam for detective in two days. A sign maybe?

He'd be so much better off as a detective, although she understood that he wanted to stay close to Mike, who was getting up there in years. What she didn't understand was how she had so fully lost control of what was happening between them. How they'd moved from a pretty decent friendship into whatever this limbo was that they were currently in. She hated this walking-on-eggshells feeling.

Well, she'd had enough.

After Lillian and Morley drove away she walked out to the warehouse, where she found Dylan sitting on a bag of feed looking at his phone while Marcel lay on the seat of the forklift, sunning himself.

"This is how you spend your days?"

Her attempt at lightness fell flat. He looked up with those very distant, very blue eyes of his and said, "I'm studying for my exam."

Jolie shifted uncomfortably. "Can we talk?"

"Sure." He lowered his phone and stared impassively at her.

When was the last time she'd felt this nervous? "I'd like to remain friends."

"Not a problem." A heavy silence fell, giving lie to his easy acceptance. He made no move to break it and she found she wasn't able to pull her gaze away from his. "Anything else?" he finally asked.

"You have no intention of remaining friends, do you?"

"I'll try."

Jolie's fists clenched at her sides. "Why does it have to be all or nothing with you? Why can't we…?"

"Scratch each other's itches in a casual no-strings manner?"

"Don't tell me you've never been in a relationship like that."

He didn't answer. He didn't have to. She could see the answer in his face. Of course he had.

"Here's the thing. What we were developing, it was more than scratching an itch and you know it."

Jolie's insides went cold but she managed to keep her voice even as she said, "We see things differently."

"I know." He spoke with such certainty that it took her back. Made her feel damaged.

"I'm not into relationships. It's just the way I am," she said with a touch of heat. "The way I've always been."

"I'm not fighting you, Jolie."

He wasn't. But she felt as if he should be, which was crazy because it was exactly what she didn't want. "It sounds as if you're humoring me."

"I'm trying to understand you. Your motivation."

"My motivation? I guess it's to be honest and to enjoy other people while maintaining my autonomy."

"Nothing wrong with that."

"But?"

He shook his head. "No buts. I'll do my best to be a friend." He got to his feet, his movements slow and deliberate as he hooked his thumbs on his pockets, still holding his phone loosely in one palm. "But we're not getting physical."

"I didn't ask to get physical." She could feel heat working its way up her neck. Guilt? Embarrassment at being called out?

"Just thought I'd make it clear. It seems that's how it needs to be with us. Spelled out. Clear."

"I was clear before."

"In your mind."

She opened her mouth to defend herself then realized that she wasn't certain she could do that. Had she been clear? She'd thought so, but he didn't, so she'd have to leave it at that.

"You drive to Lanesburg tomorrow?"

"Tonight. After work."

"If you want to leave work early, I'm sure I can manage."

"I'm sure you can, but I'll stay here."

She shrugged nonchalantly. "Have it your way. Good luck on your exam…just in case I don't see you before you leave."

"Thank you, Jolie. I appreciate it."

It was like talking to a stranger. She didn't like it, but given their situation, there wasn't much she could do about it.

CHAPTER FIFTEEN

DYLAN DROVE OVER Lookout Pass into Montana on his way home from Washington just as the sun was setting behind him. He glanced at the sinking orb in the rearview mirror, thinking that it was kind of fitting.

He'd passed his oral exam easily and was currently the top candidate to replace Detective Murdock upon his retirement next month. The captain was his biggest supporter now that he understood Dylan wasn't going to make things harder on Pat. Replacing Murdock got him out of Pat's sphere and they wouldn't have a lot to do with each other— even less now that the house had finally gone into escrow.

The last tie with Lindsey, and by default, Pat, was about to be severed and Dylan would be a free man. All the planets seemed to be aligning after a year of being seriously out of whack. Despite that, he was certain he wasn't going to apply for Murdock's position.

He didn't want to go back to Lanesburg.

He gripped the wheel a little tighter as he negotiated the curves on the Montana side of Lookout. Hell, who was he kidding? He wasn't going back.

If Eagle Valley offered him the position as deputy, he'd take it. If not, he'd figure something out. Decision made. There were still some hurtles ahead, but this was the right decision. He felt it in his gut. Maybe it was because he'd missed Montana and his grandfather more than he'd realized. Maybe it was because Mike was getting older. Maybe it was because even though they'd hit an impasse, he was hoping that Jolie would eventually see things differently than she was now. Granted, that didn't seem likely. Not with her being so adamant about ending things—except the friendship, of course.

As if he could settle for that. He couldn't go back to being friends when he wanted so much more— which begged the question, why was she so certain she couldn't *give* more? She'd given freely right up until it looked as if she might have to put a name on what they were doing. Until he'd applied for the county job and her escape route evaporated.

So when was the last time Jolie had been in a relationship? Had she *ever* been in one? If so, had it ended badly? Had she been abused? Cheated on?

Dylan had no way of finding out, short of questioning those who knew her well or asking her himself. He wasn't going to do either.

Not immediately, anyway.

Mike was waiting up for him when he got home at ten. Dylan dumped his small suitcase in his room and returned to the living room, taking a seat in his lounger as Mike hit the mute button on the remote.

"You got a call while you were gone. A lady."

His grandfather's announcement surprised Dylan almost as much as the fact that he was still up.

"Jolie?" he asked, feeling a surge of something that felt a lot like hope.

"Nah. Codie James. She left her number." Mike was watching him closely, waiting for a reaction, no doubt. Dylan wondered what reaction would make him happiest. "I think she and Finn went out a time or two."

"So I heard," Dylan said.

"Number's by the phone."

"It's a little late to call. I'll get her in the morning." A look of disappointment crossed his grandfather's face and Dylan said, "I'll let you know what she wanted."

"You d-don't have to do that," Mike sputtered. "So what happens now?"

"With…the job?" He'd already called and told Mike that he'd passed and his grandfather had made the appropriate noises, even though Dylan didn't think he was thrilled.

"Yeah."

"I think when all is said and done they're going to offer me the job I'd hoped for."

"And will you take it?"

"Don't know."

Mike tilted his head, his hand stilling on Speck's back. "You don't know?"

Dylan pulled in a breath. He didn't want to get the old man's hopes up, but he didn't see any reason to hedge, either. "I don't want to go back to Lanesburg. The house is in escrow and… I like it here."

A smile cautiously spread across Mike's face. "Well, the way business is improving at the store, maybe both you and Finn—"

Dylan raised his hand, stopping Mike. "I'm going to try to get on here with the Sheriff's Office."

"Law enforcement here? Just like I asked to begin with?"

Dylan smiled a little at his grandfather's accusatory tone. "I had a plan in my head, granddad. You know how I get with plans."

"Yeah, I do. Just like your dad. You follow them come hell or high water. Even if they're wrong."

"How many wrong plans have I followed?"

"I wasn't exactly in favor of the become-a-cop plan, if you recall."

"No, you were not, but it was a good plan for me."

"It is now," Mike said. "Especially if you're going to live close by."

"I may not get the job," Dylan felt compelled to remind him. "But if I don't we'll talk about how many people the feed store can support."

Mike smiled. "You'll get the job. I know who else has applied." He dropped the footrest and hefted himself to his feet. "I didn't mean to stay up this late, but got suckered in by a movie."

"Glad you waited up for me. Glad we talked."

His grandfather gave a small nod and headed down the paneled hall to his bedroom, Speck trotting close to his heels.

Dylan waited until the door closed before walking over to the phone and glancing at the number written in his grandfather's angular hand. *Call* was written after it with a line drawn under it.

He'd call at a decent hour tomorrow. Codie was, after all, a customer and he didn't want to alienate her. Especially if he and Finn might both have to temporarily survive on the income from the store.

As it turned out, he didn't need to make that return call. He'd barely arrived at the feed store, hadn't even had time to face off with Jolie, who was already at her computer, when Codie's red Dodge pulled up outside the front door,

"We're not open yet," Jolie said, shooting Dylan a look that told him that she was kind of looking forward to crossing swords with him. Had she realized a thing or two while he was gone...such as they did really well together?

"Maybe it's an alfalfa pellet emergency," he said. "Are you going to turn away a customer?"

"You know I'm not." Jolie took the keys out of her pocket and walked to the front door before he could move. "Hi, Codie," she said as if greeting an old friend. "Come on in."

"I know you're closed," she said, smiling warmly at Jolie before shooting him an equally warm smile. "But I'm on my way to Missoula and was hoping to catch the boss in."

"You caught him," Jolie said. "There he is." She nodded in Dylan's direction before walking around the counter.

"Hi," Dylan said. "I was going to call you back first thing this morning. Is there something I can help you with?"

"As a matter of fact," Codie said as she crossed the dusty floor, "there is. Perhaps we could talk privately?"

"Sure." He opened his office door and stood back so that she could precede him into the room. As soon as he stepped inside, she tore her gaze away from tractor girl and fixed a smile on her face. "I wanted to talk in private, so that you could say no if you wanted to without an audience."

"What would I be saying no to?" he asked with a half smile.

"Well," she said, drawing the word out, "I need a favor." She shrugged her shoulders. "My date canceled on me yesterday and I hate going to functions alone. Would you consider escorting me to a dinner tonight? The Mule Deer Foundation. The tickets are paid for and it's a shame to waste one."

"I, uh…sure," he said.

Her face lit up. "Thank you. Like I said, I hate going alone and since you're new to the area, I thought it might work out well for both of us."

"Sounds good," he said, not pointing out that he had grown up in the area.

"It's a jeans-and-nice-shirt type of affair, but a sports jacket wouldn't go amiss."

"I'll see what I can dig up," he said with a smile, "but I won't guarantee no mothballs. My grandfather kind of has this thing…"

She laughed and patted his chest, the smile fading a little as her eyes drifted to his lips then back up to his eyes. "So how about I pick you up…say six-fifteen? Drinks are at six-thirty."

"Can I meet you there? I'll probably be in a bit of a rush since we close at five-thirty."

"Maybe Jolie can close?"

"She has to get to work at her other job, so I'll close."

"I understand. The dinner is in the convention room at the Jameson Supper Club. There'll be a silent auction for all kinds of wonderful stuff, so you might want to bring your checkbook."

"Sounds good," he said as he opened the office door. "Six-thirty at the Jameson."

"SPECIAL ORDER?" JOLIE asked after Codie drove away, even though she'd promised herself she wouldn't say anything.

"Kind of," he said, glancing across the store as if checking something important on the opposite wall. "We're going to the Mule Deer Foundation dinner tonight."

"Ah," she replied. *He* was the special order. Well, good for Codie.

Right. That was why her stomach was twisting. *You can't have it both ways.*

No. She couldn't, but she could look as if she didn't care. After all, she'd been the one to walk, so it'd be very poor form to care. She leaned an elbow next to her keyboard on the desk. "So how were those orals?"

"Don't tell me Mike didn't fill you in." The way he looked at her told her that she wasn't coming anywhere close to fooling him.

"He did, but I thought I'd ask you."

"Because we're friends?" he asked with enough ironic bite to make Jolie shift a little.

"Yes."

"I passed."

"I'm not surprised. You always were good at that stuff." And other stuff, which she really hoped

Codie wasn't going to partake in tonight. Again… poor form.

"What now?" She was talking about the job, however, Dylan chose to misunderstand.

"I have a lot to do in the warehouse." But he didn't move and she didn't like the way he was looking at her, as if he was debating about diving into matters that she felt better skirting right now. Finally he took mercy on her and said, "Don't work too hard."

"As if," she muttered. Because to work hard one had to focus and she had a strong feeling that she wasn't going to be focusing too well today.

And she was right. Half an hour into accounts and she shut down the program and started dusting and facing shelves, silently thanking the janitorial staff for being so inept.

Noon approached, but Jolie didn't slow down, despite her rumbling stomach. Just as she was about to break safety protocol and stand on a lower shelf to access an upper shelf the bell on the door jangled and Dylan strode in, a taut expression on his face.

"What?" Jolie demanded.

"Marcel. I think he's sick."

Jolie's heart jumped. "How do you know?"

"He let me touch him. He's got to be sick."

Yes, he did. Marcel wouldn't even let her touch

him and he was friendlier with her than anyone else at the store. "Where is he?" Jolie asked.

"Hiding between two pallets."

Dylan pushed the door open and Jolie ducked under his arm, heading to the warehouse as fast as she could go.

Dylan beat her there and once again pulled the door open before pointing to where the big orange cat huddled between two pallets of grain.

Jolie approached slowly and Marcel backed up a couple of steps before hunkering down and attempting to glower at her.

"I tried to chase him away so I could move the grain and he just sat there," Dylan said from behind her. "So I reached out and he didn't attempt to shred my hand. Or move."

"We need to get him to the vet," Jolie said.

"Agreed."

"Do you have a carry cage?"

"I have a cardboard box with a lid."

"It'll have to do."

He headed out the door while Jolie crouched and told Marcel that they'd get him some help, but he was going to have to cooperate.

Dylan returned with the box, a towel and a pair of thick leather gloves.

"Done this before?" Jolie asked.

"I had to help Mike with an injured barn cat

when I was a kid. That thing almost took Mike's face off."

Marcel thankfully left Dylan's face alone. He fluffed and growled and spread his feet when Dylan dragged him out from between the pallets, but hardly put up a fight as he went into the towel-lined box and Jolie put on the lid. Dylan tied it shut with a hay string.

"Poor old guy. I hope the clinic can work him in," Dylan said as he pulled off the gloves.

"I'll go," Jolie said, reaching for the box. "You've got that thing tonight and…" She almost said, "You don't want to disappoint Codie," but instead finished with, "Who knows how long this will take?"

"I'm taking him."

"I'd rather be there with him than worry about him."

"I'll call you."

There was no way she was going to win this battle. Jolie could see it in his face. When had he become so attached to the cat? "You call as soon as you know something."

"I'll call." He hesitated then reached out to lightly touch her shoulder, his firm mouth quirking up at one corner. "Soon, I hope."

"Thank you."

As luck would have it, when Jolie truly wanted to be alone in the store with her worries, a flood of customers poured in. The men loaded their own purchases once they discovered that Dylan wasn't there, and the only order Jolie ended up loading by herself, while wearing a short denim skirt, was for a pair of elderly sisters who raised exotic chickens. Her phone rang just as she finished stacking the last bag. She closed the tailgate, raised a hand to wave to the ladies then scooped her phone out of her pocket.

"How is he?" she said instead of hello.

"Massive hairball. They gave him some gunk to help flush it through, but if it doesn't work, then he'll have surgery. He has to stay here tonight."

Surgery. Her heart broke a little at the thought. Marcel was not going to understand any of this.

"But he's going to be okay."

"He's going to be okay," Dylan said with a weary smile in his voice. "See you in a little bit."

"Yeah," Jolie said quietly. "See you." And the sad thing was that she was looking forward to it.

JOLIE JUMPED UP from her computer chair the instant Dylan strode into the store. He crossed to the counter and set his keys down, then gave a small shrug as their eyes met. "Things are as good as they can be. If he passes the mass, no surgery. They promised to call with an update by nine tomorrow."

"So…are you okay with the surgery? It won't be cheap."

Dylan appeared stunned at the question. "Of

course." He gave a snort. "I hope he comes out of this okay. It's got to be rough being in a strange place, feeling like hell."

"Sounds like me at a wedding shower."

He smiled a little as he leaned his forearms on the counter and met her eyes, just as he'd done dozens of times when they'd been working their way to intimacy.

A prickle of electricity danced over her skin, but Jolie did her best to ignore it as he said, "Am I crazy to drop a bundle on an old cat?"

"No."

Dylan looked down at his clasped hands then leveled a surprisingly serious look at her. "Are you good with things being like this between us?"

"What?" Jolie asked, scrambling to catch up with him.

"Because I'm not."

She swallowed and hoped her voice sounded seminormal as she said, "I see."

"Do you think we can…come up with some kind of a compromise?"

He wasn't talking about friendship. She'd bet her ranch on it. Taking in a breath, pushing down the panic, Jolie said, "Compromise?"

"Yeah. Compromise. I won't push you and, in return, you keep an open mind."

"About?" She knew what about, but was trying to buy some time, collect her thoughts. Not screw things up until she was certain she wanted to screw them up.

"Hell, I don't know." He pushed off the counter and stood facing her, his hands hanging loosely by his sides. "Stuff. Us. Just…being…for a while."

Just being. What a great idea. Wasn't that exactly what she'd been trying to do before the trouble between them had started?

Maybe he was coming around to her way of thinking. Or her to his. She didn't know and he had a date with Codie tonight and she had one hell of a lot of thinking to do. "I can try." No promises. But the startling thing to her was that she did want to try.

"I'd like that." He looked over his shoulder almost as soon as he spoke. "Someone just drove in."

"Always a last-minute customer when you need to do something else." But she was not one bit sorry for the interruption.

"Yeah. I'll be in the warehouse if you need me."

If you need me.

Jolie sank into her chair. She did need him. She just didn't know what to do about it.

Maybe…maybe she could try it his way for a while?

Could she possibly be any worse off than she was now?

CHAPTER SIXTEEN

MIKE WAS A big believer in moth balls, to the point that going into the spare room closet usually left Dylan feeling a little dizzy. He pulled his coat out and hung it outside the back door on the deck railing, where it swung gently in the breeze, hopefully dispelling all evidence of camphor.

He checked his watch as he headed through the kitchen and muttered a curse. He hated being late and he would have had plenty of time to get ready if the vet hadn't called him on the way home to tell him that the gunk had worked. Marcel could go home anytime.

Dylan had instantly reversed course and headed to the clinic, knowing that the cat would be a lot happier in his warehouse than he would be hiding in the corner of a kennel wondering what the hell was going to happen to him.

But now he had to bust his ass to get to the dinner on time.

"What are you in such a hurry about?" Mike asked as Dylan headed up the stairs to his bathroom.

"I'm going to the Mule Deer Foundation dinner."

"I thought that was long sold out," Mike called after him.

"Probably is. Codie's date couldn't make it, so I'm going instead."

"Mmm," was all he heard his grandfather say before he closed the bathroom door.

Fifteen minutes later he was in his truck on the way to the Jameson Supper Club. The airing had done the trick on his sports coat, for the most part anyway, and he'd managed to find a pressed white shirt, so all in all, he didn't feel as if he'd embarrass her.

He liked Codie, all right, but ironically he wasn't interested in anything beyond friendship with her. But with Jolie, who only wanted friendship, he wanted a whole lot more. At least she'd said she'd try to compromise...although she'd looked panicked as she'd agreed to try to keep an open mind.

The important thing was that she'd said she'd try and he knew Jolie wouldn't have promised that if she wasn't going to.

THE BAR WAS *s-l-o-w* for a Friday night. It seemed that anyone who was anyone was at the Mule Deer Foundation dinner. Even Jim had attended, which was handy because when he got back, he gave Jolie and Beccie a rundown on who was there with whom. But he didn't mention Dylan, so Jolie did.

"Yeah. He was there with Codie James." He gave her a sideways look as he spoke, which Jolie met blandly.

"What was she wearing?" Beccie asked.

"Some red."

"*Some* red?" Beccie echoed.

"Wasn't much of it," Jim said in a low voice.

"Was he enjoying himself?" Jolie asked as evenly as possible, considering the fact that her blood pressure had just spiked.

"Looked like it."

"Well, I'm happy for him," Jolie said, surprised that she sounded as if she meant it when she really didn't.

Nothing against Codie, but she was all wrong for Dylan. And Jolie was surprised at how important it was to her that Dylan not explore what there was to find under "some red."

She'd put off attaching the name to her feeling, but there was no way around the fact that she was experiencing good old-fashioned jealousy. She was jealous of Codie and pissed at herself for not having a better handle on her emotions. She wanted Dylan; she was afraid of wanting Dylan.

This supposed short-term fling had not turned out the way she'd anticipated and it was turning her inside out.

When she pulled her phone out of her pocket

before heading home, there was a text waiting for her from Dylan.

Marcel is back home. All is well. Good luck at your rodeo.

Jolie gripped the phone tighter before shoving it back into her pocket, glad that he'd taken time out from his evening with Codie to text her, to set her mind at ease.

THE NEXT MORNING Jolie left for Ennis at dawn, stopping briefly at the store to check on Marcel, who sauntered out from behind a stack of grain bags as if nothing had happened. What Jolie wouldn't give to bounce back so easily.

Reassured that Marcel was definitely on the quick road to recovery, she headed south to Dillon to pick up Faith. After loading her mare, they had breakfast, caught up on old times and then hit the road.

Jolie's section ran on Saturday, Faith's on Sunday, so it was an overnighter for them. And, frankly, Jolie was glad to be out of Eagle Valley for a few days. Mike had agreed to cover the store and Jim had gotten his sister to fill in for her at the bar. The hardest part of rodeo was wedging it into a work schedule, but camping out with an old friend, giggling into the wee hours as they had in college, waking up to the crisp, damp air made Jolie feel more like her old self.

Or it would have if she could shove the situation with Dylan out of her mind for any length of time. As luck would have it, Faith had just broken up with her long-term boyfriend, which explained her sudden desire to spend a lot of time on the road that summer, and she needed to vent. A lot. And Jolie listened, trying to equate Faith's situation to her own.

Finally, Jolie asked, "Was it worth it?"

"Worth it how?" Faith asked, rolling over in her sleeping bag to face Jolie.

"Worth the heartache?"

"What do you think?" Faith asked.

Jolie let out a sigh as she stared up at the stars. "I don't know. Honestly, I've been in lust quite a few times, and I have strong friendships, but... I've never had a breakup that bothered me all that much."

Not until recently.

"You've just...walked away?" Faith sounded mystified.

"Yeah. I guess I have."

"Then you've been choosing poorly."

Jolie flopped over. "How so?"

"If you feel no pangs breaking up, then you've either chosen a jerk you can't wait to get away from or someone you never really connected with. Not in a real way."

"Well, hell," Jolie said rolling onto her back again and frowning up at the sky.

"What?"

"That makes a sad sort of sense."

"Then choose better next time," Faith said with a soft laugh. "Find someone to fall in love with."

"I guess." But the thought froze her up. Despite her promise to keep an open mind, she was fairly certain she didn't need what Mel and Dani needed—guys who loved them. She was more like Allie, finding emotional attachments messy, bothersome. Potentially painful—or so it seemed from a distance. Why put yourself through that when one was entirely satisfied with one's own existence?

She couldn't think of one reason, but she didn't say that to Faith because her friend obviously believed in the value of strong emotional ties…and because, like it or not, Jolie did have an emotional tie to Dylan. If she didn't, then the whole situation wouldn't bother her in the least.

She drifted off to sleep and dreamed of Dylan. Dreamed he was there with her, doing those things he did that made her feel so good, and woke up all hot and bothered at sunrise.

Faith was already out of her bag and in the shower room. Jolie pulled her jeans on in her sleeping bag and sat up to tuck in her long sleeping T-shirt. And then for a moment she sat with her forearms resting on her knees, staring at the gooseneck opposite her trailer.

Why couldn't she get this guy out of her head?

She sighed and pushed the sleeping bag aside. At least he hadn't gotten destroyed by a dark force in this dream. But, frankly, the hot dream was almost as troublesome as the dark dream would have been.

JOLIE TURNED DOWN the Lightning Creek road late Sunday night. She and Faith had had a flat on the trailer, even though the tire was practically brand-new, and it had taken a while to change it on the side of the highway. She still had to feed and she was fairly certain Gus was cursing her out for leaving him in the yard and taking Faith to the rodeo instead of him.

She pulled to a stop next to the barn and noticed a truck parked next to her old beater. Her heart jumped.

Dylan was there. Somewhere.

Sure enough, a few seconds later, he walked from the barn toward her truck. She shut off the engine and got out, her heart beating faster.

Find someone to fall in love with. Faith's advice drifted through her head.

Maybe she'd done that…

It scared her to death, but she'd agreed to keep

an open mind and he'd agreed not to push. Could they do that?

Dylan stopped a few feet in front of her, a cautious smile on his face, as if he was very glad to be with her again but afraid of scaring her off if he said so.

"Mike gave me a call on my way home tonight. I guess he called the ranch and when you didn't answer, he thought I should come over and feed Karen. Maybe check on you."

"Karen's on pasture," Jolie said, ignoring the check-on-you part. She was becoming close to Mike, but hated having him worry about her. "But I'm sure you figured that out."

"I fed the goats. And Gus, who tried to eat me through the fence."

"Probably more like lick you to death." Gus loved Dylan. "And thank you." She headed toward the back of her trailer. Dylan followed. She opened the door and he held it as she went inside and untied Jenabelle.

"How'd you do?"

"I won."

"Congratulations."

"I needed a win," she said as she led the mare past him. "I needed to get away, quite frankly."

"How'd that go? The getting away." His tone was mild, but Jolie could read the tension in his body as he waited for an answer.

"Good. No big changes. I'm, um, keeping that open mind."

They approached the gate and Dylan opened it. Jolie released Jenabelle. The mare shook once before ambling off into the darkness. And then it was just the two of them.

"I accepted the position with the Eagle Valley Sheriff's Office. I signed my paperwork today."

His declaration jolted her. It was real now. He was staying. "I didn't realize it would happen so quickly."

"They need someone as soon as possible. There's nothing in Lanesburg for me anymore. Nothing of value, anyway. And Mike needs me here."

"I understand," she said. She did, but that didn't keep her from feeling as if she was being backed into a corner. It wasn't his intent, she knew that, but she couldn't help feeling that way.

"That thing we were talking about at the store... the compromise?"

"Yes?" Her throat went a little dry, but she got the word out.

"I thought we might hold off on that for a bit. I leave in three days for training in Bozeman and then I have another regional training in Boise before I start work. When I get back from those, maybe we can have dinner or something."

"All right."

When she didn't say anything else, he added

on a gentle note, "I guess what I'm saying is that there's no need to move quickly on anything. We can take our time. Address...fears...in a timely manner."

The way he'd spoken told her that he'd been thinking long and hard about this and that he was asking that she do the same. She would. She'd start addressing instead of avoiding. Surely she was strong enough to do that? Especially since he was keeping his word and not pushing.

He stepped closer, put his hands on her shoulders and it was the most natural thing in the world to meet his lips in a kiss that started out tender and then rapidly heated to something more. He pulled her close, deepening the kiss, and even as Jolie lost herself in the sheer sensuality, she felt herself pulling away.

Dylan felt it, too, and slowly released her.

"I wasn't going to do that," he said as his hands fell away.

"Neither was I," Jolie said.

He stepped back, pushed his hands into his pockets. "So we agree...we wait to make any big decisions? Just take things slowly and see what evolves?"

"We agree," Jolie said on a husky note. She walked with him to his truck, realizing that she wasn't going to see him for a while. She wasn't certain she was going to like that, even though she'd been fighting for it.

As he opened the door to the truck she put her hand on his arm. He looked at her and she simply said, "Be careful. Okay?"

He smiled a little and said, "You got it."

DYLAN HAD HELD off telling Mike that he'd accepted the job with the county until after telling Jolie. The last thing he wanted was for her to hear it secondhand—especially now that she'd cautiously agreed to not kick him out of her life.

"It's official?" Mike asked, looking as if he wanted to swing Dylan around in a circle.

"I signed on the dotted line today."

"We need to celebrate," Mike said, pushing up out of his chair and heading for the kitchen where he got the good whiskey out of the cupboard over the refrigerator.

The good whiskey was so old that Dylan was surprised it hadn't evaporated. He pulled shot glasses out, but Mike waved them aside and took out his wife's crystal glasses.

"To the prodigal," Mike said, raising his glass.

Dylan smiled and drank, touched by his grandfather's reaction to him coming home and more certain than ever than he'd made the right decision. He'd counted on Finn to hold down the fort and care for Mike over the past several years, but now he was starting to see that he should have come home more often.

No longer an issue. He finished his whiskey, which was excellent, and was surprised when Mike poured another splash into both their glasses before putting the top on the bottle and setting it back on the shelf. They took their whiskeys and headed to their recliners. For once Mike left the television off.

"I imagine since you're here permanently now, you'll be getting your own place, instead of staying with me."

"Eventually," Dylan agreed. "But it'll be close."

Mike nodded, staring off into the distance. "Not that I don't like having you living here with me, but you need to have a place where you can entertain."

Entertain? Dylan gave his grandfather a slow sidelong look. Mike was still studying something on the other side of the room. He gave a slow nod. "A place where you can settle down with a family at some point."

Ah.

Mike was silent for a moment then asked, "Have you told Jolie?"

"I did."

After a couple of beats of silence, Mike said, "Is she happy?"

Dylan debated but went with the truth. Mike may as well know the lay of the land. "Kind of."

The look on Mike's face made Dylan wish he'd lied to him.

"She has some issues," he said slowly.

"With you?"

"More like with commitment."

Mike frowned deeply. "I thought she was down in the dumps because you were going back to Lanesburg."

The can of worms was now officially opened.

"It's kind of complicated."

His grandfather looked perplexed. "But you like her, right?"

He was pretty damned certain he loved her, which was why the situation between them was so frustrating.

"I like her."

"She likes you okay, too. I can tell."

A bad feeling struck Dylan. Maybe Mike was trying his hand at matchmaking. "Now that I'm home for good, I figure I'll give her time, let her work through some stuff. I see nothing but trouble ahead if I try to push things."

His grandfather thought long and deep on that one. "Yeah. I guess you're right. Not that I'm trying to butt into your life or anything," he added quickly.

"Of course not," Dylan said before downing the last of his whiskey.

Mike picked up the remote and brought the TV

to life, then leaned down to scoop up Speck. "I'm glad you're moving home for good," he said before switching channels.

So was Dylan. Even if he couldn't work things out with Jolie, this was where he belonged. Pat and Lindsey might think they ran him, but screw 'em. He was through fighting battles.

THE NEXT DAY when Jolie got to work, she was surprised to find Mike there, busy in the office. When she poked her head in, she saw that he'd installed a small television.

"You're coming here to watch TV?" she asked in a gently teasing voice, wondering just how lonely he anticipated being now that Dylan would be gone for a few weeks.

"I like the news," he said.

"You can read it on the computer."

"I like to listen," he said.

She was about to tell him that he could listen to it on the computer, then decided against that. If he wanted a television, then so be it. She suspected what he really wanted was company instead of sitting in his lonely house. His little dog trotted up to her and she bent to ruffle the terrier's rough fur. "Good morning, Speck."

The dog smiled at her, curling her lips back over her teeth, and Jolie laughed. When she glanced up at Mike he looked away, but she caught the smile on his face. She was glad he and Speck were there. It kept the store from feeling too empty, although there was no getting around the fact that now that Dylan was gone, the store was never going to feel quite the same again.

She didn't like the heavy feeling of missing someone, didn't like it one bit, but she could deal with it. She told herself she was going to ride this out instead of seizing up at the thought of having a relationship where someone depended on her to be there. She didn't need to know why she felt that way, but instead learn to deal, because there was a very good chance she'd never know why she was afraid to have people depend on her.

Her positive thinking worked to a degree. She chatted with customers and called out orders to Gordy. Mike spent at least an hour in the office watching his television with Speck on his lap, then came out to eat lunch with Jolie during a brief lull.

"I'm kind of wondering about that other job of yours," Mike said just a touch too casually.

"McElroy's?" Jolie asked.

"Yeah. Do you really have to work there?"

"I do if I want to roof the barn. You know how much that's going to cost."

"Oh, yeah."

Jolie carefully folded the paper bag her lunch had come in. "Does it bother you that I have a second job? Because I make certain it doesn't interfere with this one."

"No. But I kind of wish it wasn't that job."

Jolie gave a soft, reassuring laugh, finally understanding where Mike was coming from. "Jim takes good care of us." And then she wondered if Dylan had shared the story of Wyatt trying to "help" her with her tire.

"But he doesn't drive home with you. It's not good going home to that lonely ranch alone that late at night."

"I take precautions," Jolie said, hoping the old man wasn't going to inadvertently spook her. "And I have a gigantic dog."

Mike gave a small nod. "I've met him." He ran a hand over Speck. "He seemed...adequate."

Jolie reached out to touch Mike's arm. "I really need that job if I'm going to start putting the Lightning Creek right again. I've made a start with the cattle and the meadow hay. I need to press on."

"The Lightning Creek used to be a pretty nice ranch, back in the seventies and eighties." He thought for a moment. "Clear into the nineties, really."

"It fell apart when Dad died. And then there were those years when both cattle and hay bottomed out."

"Yeah," Mike said in a considering tone. "Lots

of people wondered why your mother didn't sell and move instead of hanging on by a thread."

"So did my older sisters."

"But not you?"

"I've always loved the place. So does my sister Dani."

"The older ones probably remember…more."

"I think so. And they had more of a burden during the hard times. They did their best to protect us." Jolie smiled a little. "And you'll notice that as soon as my older sister and her husband took over the ranch, my mother married and left the area."

"I don't blame her one bit. She used to come in here, counting her pennies, trying to figure feed down to the last bag."

"And you carried her through some of the tough times. I know that." Jolie idly rubbed her upper arms as she stared across the store. "Maybe that's another reason I want to make the ranch good again. To make her sacrifice mean something."

She glanced at Mike to see him studying her. She smiled cautiously, uncertain of what he was thinking. "Your dad always wanted one or all of his girls to run the ranch. He'd be happy to see you doing that."

Jolie thought about that as she went home and fed in the misting rain. Her dad would be happy to see her bringing the ranch back. She was glad she'd moved home, even if it had introduced a bump in her smooth road. A Dylan-shaped bump.

He'd complete his training, come home and... do his job as a deputy. That didn't mean he was necessarily in harm's way. But it didn't mean he wasn't, either.

She couldn't help it. She hated that he was back in law enforcement and whether Dylan liked it or not, his being in law enforcement was something she had to take time to come to terms with...or not.

If she couldn't, then they wouldn't have a future. But if she could? Lots of women did it. Had husbands in law enforcement. Lived with the risk of loss. Was she as strong as them?

Jolie shoved the thought out of her brain and settled into working on the quarterly taxes. If anything was going to put her to sleep, that was it.

CHAPTER SEVENTEEN

JOLIE HAD A horrible barrel run. Dylan's fist clenched when her mare momentarily lost footing in the mud as she rounded the first barrel, recovered, then knocked over the second. Jolie and the mare charged home after the third and even at a distance he could read the frustration in her expression.

He left the rail where he'd been standing and headed for the trailers. Having arrived only minutes before her run, he hadn't had time to figure out where she was parked, but it didn't take long to find her tying her mare to the side of her trailer.

"Jolie."

Her head whipped around as he said her name, her mouth dropping open before she smiled. Okay. She was happy to see him. This was good, since he'd kind of ambushed her.

"Dylan." She finished tying the mare with a few quick movements then turned back to him, wiping her hands down the sides of her pants. There was mud splattered over her clothing, her hat and across one cheek.

He automatically reached out to wipe the specks off her face and her breath caught as he touched her. Good sign? Bad sign?

"You have mud on your face."

"Occupational hazard. Did you see my run?"

"Pulled up just in time to catch it."

"Too bad you weren't a few minutes later." She started unsaddling the horse. Dylan stood back and watched. Her movements were practiced, but if he wasn't mistaken, her hands were shaking a little. That didn't usually happen when a friend stopped by to say hello.

"I thought you were on your way to Boise." Her voice was all-business now. She dragged the saddle off the back of the mare and Dylan knew better than to try to take it from her. She needed it as a barrier.

"I decided to take a detour. I'm not due there until tomorrow morning." The training had been rigorous, but thoughts of Jolie had kept edging in. He'd needed to see her. It was that simple.

Rain started to mist down again and after Jolie had loaded the horse, she returned to the tack room.

"How was the training?"

"Fine." He was tired, he still had hours to drive and he wasn't feeling like the most patient of men at the moment. But he was careful not to let any of that show.

Careful until she stepped out of the trailer and

came to join him where he was waiting by the rear of her truck.

"I need to get on the road," she said. There was something in her eyes that said she needed something else. Something that made his heart rate bump up and blood start to head south.

He cleared his throat. "Me, too. But I wanted to see you." To reassure himself that she was all right, that she hadn't changed her mind about holding off making big decisions. That she hadn't let her demons take over while he'd been gone.

"I wanted to see you, too. I'm glad you came." She pressed her lips together. "Really glad. I missed you."

And that was an admission. For so long he'd thought of Jolie as being fearless—and she was, as long as her emotions weren't involved, as long as there was no chance of being hurt. Because he was pretty darned certain that fear of loss was what kept her from commitment. It was his job to convince her that he wasn't going to hurt her. That all he wanted was for her to be happy, with him.

He reached out to touch her face again, his thumb brushing over her lower lip.

Jolie sucked in a breath, her eyes holding his as she stepped forward and wrapped her arms around him.

Dylan felt a stab of need as he pulled her close, holding her tightly against him. Damn but he wanted her. Needed her. And she was no doubt aware of that need, which was now pressing against her.

She leaned back and he thought she was going to kiss him, but instead she said in a low voice, "I've been doing a lot of thinking… I think I can do this. I'd like to try, anyway."

"You mean…?" He gestured back and forth between them. "Us?"

"That's what I mean."

Dylan felt himself start to smile, but Jolie wasn't smiling back. Instead she looked down at her muddy boots then up at him and now he could clearly read the need in her eyes. "Faith won't be back for a while. Her section runs last."

He frowned, stupidly wondering what she was getting at, sorting through possibilities, knowing it wasn't what he hoped it was…was it?

A moment later her mouth was on his, taking, giving, and he knew that she'd not only noticed how much he'd wanted her, she'd felt the same. She leaned into him as they kissed, backing him up against the damp side of the truck. He felt the cold on his back through his jacket, but it was no match for the fire that ignited inside him at the touch of her lips on his.

His hands came up into her hair, knocking her hat off. She didn't seem to notice as she pressed herself into him, holding his face, exploring his mouth with a hint of desperation as if the moment could be snatched away from them.

This was a moment in time. Dylan knew it and he wasn't asking for more. Not tonight. Not when she so obviously needed him as much as he needed her. Not when she'd promised to try a relationship.

"I don't suppose that door locks?" he asked, jerking his head toward the trailer.

Jolie bit her lip, hesitated for all of a second, then took his hand and led him inside, pulling the door shut behind her and flicking a latch.

"This will bring new meaning to the word *quickie*." She turned to him, her eyes widening in the dim light as he backed her against the wall.

"Don't care," Dylan muttered, pulling her shirt-tails out of her pants and unsnapping the shirt top to bottom with a quick flick.

Jolie returned the favor, slowed by the fact that his shirt had buttons. He considered it a blessing that his shirt still had buttons when she finally got it parted and ran her palms over his bare chest on her way down to his belt. Moments later his erection sprung free and Jolie was kicking off her boots, pushing down her pants and stepping out of them.

"I need you," she said. And even though he still had about a thousand questions crowding his brain, he shoved them aside and went with seizing the moment.

He wasn't certain how he got out of his boots or freed himself from one pant leg, but after he did, he lifted Jolie, who automatically hooked her legs around him as she grasped his shoulders. He wanted nothing more than to thrust into her, hard and deep, but instead he slowly lowered her.

Jolie gasped as he entered her. Her eyes closed and she sucked in air between her teeth as he slid home, inch by glorious inch. It wasn't until she made a small whimpering noise deep in her throat that his control broke and he thrust upward as far as he could go.

After that it was all a wild ride, Jolie clutching him with both arms and legs. Dylan made an effort to stay as quiet as possible, but the situation was getting away from him and before he finally emptied into her, he wouldn't have been surprised to learn that the wheels of the trailer were coming off the ground, despite the weight of the horse inside it.

Jolie shuddered and scraped her teeth over his shoulder then went limp against him.

His arms were shaking by the time he lowered her to the ground. "I, uh…"

Jolie laughed breathlessly, bringing a hand up around the back of his neck to pull his forehead to hers. "I needed that."

Enough said.

It took a few minutes to straighten their clothing.

Jolie's pants were inside out and now that sanity was once again the order of the day, Dylan was all about stepping out of the trailer looking as if they'd merely been escaping the rain instead of ripping each other's clothes off.

A good-looking woman with a reddish-brown ponytail pulled over one shoulder was leading a horse toward the trailer when Jolie opened the door and stepped to the damp ground.

"How'd you do?" Jolie called, the picture of nonchalance as she glanced up at Dylan, who decided that this must be Jolie's travel partner, Faith.

"Rotten run," Faith said. She nodded at Dylan as she walked by, then looked down quickly, a smile playing on her lips, making Dylan wonder if the trailer had indeed been rocking.

Jolie waited until Faith was busy with her horse before turning to him and running a hand over her hair. Her hat was still lying on the ground next to the truck and she bent to pick it up.

"Rodeo hat," she explained. "I never wear good ones in the rain." She bit her lip as her eyes came up to his. "Can't say I regret that."

He grinned at her, feeling more hopeful about… well…everything. And he wanted to kiss her again, but refrained. "I hate to hit and run, but I need to get on the road if I'm going to make Boise by midnight."

"Yeah."

Jolie smiled at him, looking as if she really was in favor of trying a relationship with him. All he had to do was to be patient. To wait for her to come to terms with a few things. Decide that loving him was worth the risk.

"Stop looking so damned pleased with yourself," she muttered, but she was looking pretty pleased with herself, too.

"Can't help it." He made a show of craning his neck to check Faith, whose back was to them, then leaned in to kiss her. "Gotta go."

"I know." Jolie smiled at him then when he turned to leave, she patted his ass.

MIKE CAME TO the store every day, drank coffee and watched his news, gossiped with his buddies, Karl and Cal, when they came by, which they did with increasing frequency—especially after he moved the desk against the office wall and brought in three comfortable chairs in which he and friends could watch the news.

Jolie wondered how Finn was going to take the new office arrangement. Personally she liked the warm, social feeling the store now had. Coming to work felt better than it had right after Dylan had left. Having Mike there all the time was in no way the same as having Dylan, but she loved having him around. She'd barely known her own grandfathers and her relationship with Mike was as close as she'd ever come to feeling like a granddaughter. And she loved how he'd cleverly drop hints about what a good guy Dylan was, and how, even though he'd chosen poorly the first time, that didn't mean he wasn't good partnership material.

Partnership. That was the word Mike always used, as if by avoiding the word *husband* he could prevent Jolie from seeing that he was indulging in a bit of matchmaking. She played along—although actually it wasn't playing because she agreed with him. Dylan would make a great partner.

The fear wasn't gone, but it was easing—to the point that when she found Dylan waiting for her as she walked out of the bar late Saturday night, fear was pretty much the last thing on her mind.

"You're back."

Indeed he was, leaning against her old GMC, all long legs and lean muscle, arms crossed over his chest, an I-want-you look in his eye. It was a wonder she didn't melt into a hot puddle right there in the parking lot. One corner of his mouth lifted as she moved closer and he reached out for her, drawing her to him, kissing her long and hard. She pushed her hands up into his hair, holding him as she answered his kiss.

"I kind of like the effect these trainings have on you," she murmured against his lips.

His hands slid down to her ass, pulling her against him. "I think it's you having the effect."

She laughed lowly. "No horse trailer here, buddy."

He pulled back a little, his hands moving to her waist as he made a show of looking around the almost empty parking lot. "Damn," he murmured softly.

"Follow me home?" Jolie suggested. "I have a horse trailer there."

A smile that bordered on wicked creased his cheeks. "Lead the way."

It wasn't until Jolie was driving home with Dylan's headlights in her rearview mirror that the concerns started edging in. It was so much easier when her hormones were more involved than her head, but that no longer defined her relationship with Dylan. Quickies in the horse trailer were all fine and good, but they weren't enough.

It shook her a little.

They parked side by side and made their way to the dark house where Gus greeted them effusively before dropping to his dog bed, exhausted from joy.

And then it was the two of them. Not in a horse trailer.

Dylan regarded her silently and Jolie knew she probably looked as uneasy as she felt. She was about to ask him if he wanted a drink when he gave his head a small shake, took her by the wrist and led her to the sofa.

Okay. This she could handle.

But he didn't try to kiss her. Instead he pulled

her onto his lap, pressed her head against his shoulder and wrapped his arms around her. "Stop thinking so much," he said gruffly, his breath feathering her hair.

Easier said than done.

But as his hands moved soothingly over her back and his heart beat beneath her cheek, Jolie felt her tense muscles begin to give. She exhaled softly and Dylan tipped her chin up.

"Better," he murmured. "Now maybe we should get some sleep."

She brought her head up. "Really?" she asked, making no effort to hide her disappointment.

"Unless you have a better idea."

She leaned in to kiss his gorgeous mouth. "Yeah… I do."

The next morning she woke to find herself spooned against him, his arm draped over her, as if protecting her. From what? The unknown future? Herself? She rolled in his arms so that her face was close to his, loving the feel of his breath on her skin.

He made noise low in his throat as his hand skimmed over the curve of her hip. "I like waking up with you."

The sun just coming up and she needed to get moving. Instead she slipped an arm over him. "I have a rodeo this afternoon."

"Where?"

"Twin Bridges. A couple hours drive."

"Any chance you can play hooky?"

"I was just asking myself that same thing."

"One time deal," he said, his voice still husky from sleep. "We'll turn off our phones, practice hanging out for the rest of the day."

"Practice?"

"Well, actually, I'm already pretty good at it."

"Wait a minute—I'm the one whose forte is looseness. I recall you being rather stiff."

He laughed low in his throat and then rolled, trapping her beneath him. She gave a choking laugh as his erection nudged against her.

"So are you in?" he murmured as he eased her thighs apart and slowly began to sink himself inside of her. "Hooky-playing, no-phones weekend?"

Her eyes drifted shut. Dylan nipped her lower lip, then softly kissed it as Jolie slowly exhaled and arched against him, even though it was impossible for him to go any deeper. "I'm in," she whispered.

THEY PARTED COMPANY on Monday morning, both feeling positive about their take-it-slow strategy. The less he talked about relationships, the more Jolie relaxed, and by the end of the week, it seemed almost normal for Dylan to show up at her place after having dinner with Mike. Jolie would fill him in on Marcel, who was fully recovered and even ate his medicine, which she hid in his food, and Mike and the not-so-exciting events at the store.

In turn he would tell her about his day and even though Jolie suspected that he was editing, she got a sense of just how mundane his daily shifts could be and came to the conclusion that she'd been over-thinking. Focusing on worst-case scenarios instead of seeing the reality of the job. Yes, Kyle had had some close calls, but he was also supremely macho and had brought some of them on himself accord-ing to Allie.

And so the days went. The only hard part was dealing with the news that now played constantly at the store. The television was in the office, but Mike's buddies were hard of hearing so the volume was louder than normal, which meant that every time there was an incident anywhere in the nation involving a police officer, Jolie heard about it. And her stomach knotted.

She'd talk herself down; tell herself that if Mike could handle this, so could she. Pretend that it wasn't scaring her. Bad things happened. But they lived in a quiet rural community. They'd be okay. Every now and again the unwelcome feel-ing that she was living in denial slipped through her defenses, but she squashed it instantly. She was refraining from thinking too much. That was dif-ferent than being in denial.

Besides, things were so damned good between

her and Dylan that she had to be doing something right, and that something was not jumping at every shadow. Granted, they skirted the serious issues of relationships and permanence and did exactly what he'd promised her they'd do…they focused on simply being. She loved it even though she knew that the situation couldn't go on indefinitely. At some point they were going to have to stop *being* and make some decisions.

That time came more quickly than she'd anticipated.

JOLIE STOPPED FOR doughnuts on the way to the store on a damp Tuesday morning, figuring that Mike would appreciate having some pastries for his friends, who had a tendency to show up on rainy days. She jumped a few puddles on her way across the graveled yard and pushed the door open. The bell jangled and she called hello to Mike who was standing in the office doorway, watching his television. He turned toward her and she could instantly see that something was very, very wrong.

Setting the doughnut box on the counter, she went to where he stood.

"There's been a shooting on the highway north of here."

Instantly the cold hit her; the same coldness she'd felt when her mother had told her she'd lost her father, weakening muscles as it spread through her body. "Is Dylan involved?"

"I don't know." He spoke grimly. "There are injuries. Maybe a death. The report was preliminary. I don't know."

Jolie blinked at him then turned blindly away. The next thing she knew, Mike was guiding her to a chair, sitting her down. She immediately stood up, but he pushed her down. "Sit."

"Then you sit, too," she snapped.

Obediently he sat as Jolie pulled out her cell phone, scrolling as fast as she could through various news sources.

"If it was Dylan, they would have contacted us."

Or they will. Her hands were shaking so badly she could barely operate the phone.

"I'll call Dispatch," Mike said, getting up and crossing the room to flip through the phone book. A moment later he was on the phone, identifying himself. "Yes. Give me Deputy Moody if he's there." The phone dropped into Jolie's lap as she sat staring at Mike's back, praying as hard as she could.

"Yeah. Jess. Mike—" He stopped abruptly and Jolie's heart almost stopped. For one long moment she was ten years old, not fully understanding that her father was dead. And once she'd understood what they were saying, she'd known they were wrong. Because that was impossible. Her father couldn't be dead. She needed him.

"I see." Mike's gravelly voice snapped her back to the present. "Right…no…no." The old man let out a breath that shook his entire body. "Thank you, Jess. Appreciate it. Yeah…anytime."

When Mike turned back, the rims of his eyes were red. "No deaths. The shooter was critically injured."

"Were any deputies involved?"

"A deputy made the initial stop. But it wasn't Dylan. He's on the other side of the county."

But he could have been there.

Jolie let her head fall back against the chair, fighting tears because she didn't want to upset Mike. Tears for the officers involved in the incident…tears for the ten-year-old girl who still lived inside her and was scared to death of losing someone else that she loved.

DYLAN WAS LATE getting home. He hadn't been involved in the shooting, but that hadn't lessened the impact. Life was short. He'd tried to call Jolie, but she'd only spoken to him for a few minutes, telling him that she was grateful he was all right and that she couldn't talk. So, instead of calling again, he waited until his shift was over then drove straight to the ranch.

It was nearly dark when he parked. The porch

light came on as he came up the walk and he realized that his pulse was pounding in his temples. He was nervous, damned nervous, because he had a feeling about what was coming after talking to Jolie for just those few minutes.

Sure enough, when she answered the door she looked distant, pale and not exactly welcoming. But after looking him up and down, she held the door open and allowed him to come in. Once the door was closed, they stood awkwardly and he fought to keep from stepping forward and pulling her into his arms, assuring her that everything was all right now and would continue to be all right in the future. It was pretty obvious from her closed-off expression and stance that Jolie would be having none of that. So he stood there, waiting, allowing her the first volley, his pulse pounding in his ears.

"I know now why I can't do this," she finally said.

"Jolie—"

"Your job. I can't be with you while you work in this job."

"Mike said you had a hard time."

She let out a choking sound. "Yeah. I had a hard time." She rubbed her forehead in a nervous movement. "Because I've been hiding from the truth, which is that I'm worried sick about your job. And I have these dreams where you die."

"I'm not going to die."

"You can't promise that. So don't. Because if people could promise that, I'm pretty sure my dad would have promised it."

"Jolie, I know it's rough."

"I won't go through that again. Okay? I won't sit in a hospital room and have some…nurse…tell me things I'm not ready to hear. Will. Not. Do. It."

"You're kind of going worst-case scenario here."

"And?"

"What happened today could have happened anywhere to anyone. A mall. A hospital. On the street." She folded her arms over her chest. "I worked for ten years as a cop—"

"And only got shot at once, right? And lost control of the car and hit a pole. And, sure, that could have happened anywhere to anyone. But it happened to *you*."

"I'm still here."

She blinked at him, as if holding back tears. He reached for her but she stepped back. "If you touch me," she said, "it'll only make this harder."

"Then what am I supposed to do?"

"I think…" She swallowed hard and looked at the opposite wall while she composed herself. "You need to leave. Give me time to figure a few things out."

"Will you figure them out?"

"I don't know." Her chin dipped down.

"I'm not leaving you like this."

She looked up at him. "Yes. You are."

"Jolie…this is killing me."

"It's not doing me any good, either, but I know what I can and cannot handle. So…maybe we can talk. Later."

"How much later?"

"A lot later."

"Jolie, there aren't any guarantees in life. You could marry a guy who worked in a shoe store—"

"Don't you think I know that?" Her lips curled slightly. "Have known it all along?" She touched her head. "Even though I may not have understood it. That's why I don't do relationships. And I don't see that changing any time soon."

THE DAYS DID not pass quickly. Instead they crept along as Jolie worked her way through the truth that she could no longer bury. She couldn't handle losing another person in her life the way she'd lost her father, and she wasn't going to increase the odds by tying herself to someone with an inherently dangerous job.

Pretending she could handle it had been nice for a few weeks, but her reaction to the highway incident, the crushing fear it reawakened, told her that she had to be realistic about her limitations. Maybe she was damaged, but if so she was damaged by circumstances beyond her control. Now all she could do was to mitigate damage by managing the circumstances she could control.

The shooting had opened up feelings and truths that she'd buried for so long, it was going to take her some time to get over them—but being impatient by nature, Jolie wanted the feelings dealt with now. It wasn't happening, so she did her best to fill her time and not think. Dylan helped by honoring her request and keeping his distance. She didn't hear from him. Didn't see him.

But she saw Mike every day at the store and that wasn't helping matters. She didn't want to be harsh with the old man, especially when she cared about him, but she also didn't want anyone interfering with her very sound decision to back off and live life the way she had before Dylan had come into the picture.

When she was at home, she spent her time running Jenabelle in the new arena, since the frequent rains had turned her outdoor practice area into a mini lake. The plank fences were all fixed and she'd managed to paint them during a week-long daytime dry spell, so now they shone white in the sun, or they did when it wasn't raining, making the ranch look more like its old self.

She'd hoped to mow the hay herself, but had hired a neighbor to do the job for her during the dry spell, because it was unrealistic to come home late from the bar then get up early to mow. A body

could only do so much. This body was trying
to do too much because she was trying so hard
not to think. She just wanted to do. Do. Do. Do.
Keep the second-guessing at a minimum. Having
finally confronted the truth, she knew her emotional capabilities…knew her lack of tolerance for
deep emotional pain.

Even though she missed Dylan, she told herself
it was getting better. Or maybe she was just getting numb, because she didn't seem to feel much of
anything anymore. Exactly as she'd felt after losing
her dad. As if she was wrapped in cotton, insulated
from the world, except when the grief broke forth
and she felt unbelievably raw and retreated once
more into her insulated world.

She was becoming a nutcase.

Mike left her alone at work, other than a pleasant good morning or the offer of coffee, therefore
she was surprised when he showed up out of the
blue one Sunday afternoon to visit Maisy, Daisy
and Karen. He fed his goats, stroked and patted
them, slipping them small treats from his pockets, and then they went to lean on the plank fence
to watch Karen graze with her herd.

"We'll find out if she's pregnant in a month,"
she said.

"If it's a boy, name it after me."

Jolie laughed and it felt kind of good. "Will do."

"Have you heard from Dylan?" he asked casually. Too casually.

"No." She did not expand on her answer, hoping Mike would take the hint.

He did not. Shades of Finn and Dylan and all of her sisters. She really needed to work on her conversation-stopping voice.

"He's doing well. He asked about you."

Jolie smiled without looking at him. "Well, tell him hi from me next time you talk to him."

"Why?"

The bald question startled her and when she met Mike's gaze, she could see that he knew exactly what was going on. Well, maybe not the nuts and bolts of the situation, but he knew there was unfinished and uncomfortable business there.

"It seemed the polite thing to say," Jolie replied honestly.

"Hmm." Mike looked out over the field where Karen was happily grazing. "Often all politeness does is hide true feelings."

Jolie's muscles tensed but her tone was casual as she said, "I think that's why it was invented."

"What are your true feelings?"

Another shock wave at the bald question and as Jolie turned toward him, her expression probably bordering on incredulous, he added, "I'm old. I don't have time to pussyfoot around."

"I think you have plenty of time left on this

earth," Jolie responded. When Mike showed no sign of being sidetracked, she said, "No offense intended, but that's between Dylan and me."

"You know he was betrayed pretty badly by that…woman…he married." He said the word in a way that told Jolie *woman* was not his first noun choice.

"Yes."

Another long silence, broken only by the sound of grass being rhythmically torn from the ground as the cattle grazed. Finally, Mike said, "You're right. This is none of my business."

"Thank you."

"My life kind of ended when Helen died."

Jolie pressed her lips together. "I imagine."

"I bet your life kind of ended when your dad died. You were pretty young."

"It wasn't a pleasant time."

"He wouldn't have wanted it to color your entire existence, you know."

It took her a moment to find her voice. "I know you mean well. I know you care for Dylan. But, Mike, I need you to drop this subject. I won't talk about it." She pulled a sharp breath in through her nose. "I can't talk about it."

Mike pushed off from the fence and before he started back toward his truck said darkly, "But maybe you can *think* about it."

Think about it she did. Jolie thought about it

as she worked and she thought about it when she trained. No matter how resolutely she pushed the thought aside, it rammed its way back into her brain.

Thank you, Mike.

It'd pass.

It had to pass. And in the meantime she continued to pour all her excess energies into the ranch. The garden, which had been Allie's pride and joy, was once again tilled and seedlings were popping up in the long rows, but the heavy rains that had started a few days ago were now threatening to drown them out and was also creating perpetually muddy areas in the barn where the water was pouring through. Ironically, just before the rain had started, she'd received an estimate for materials to reroof the barn and decided it would be a while before she could quit working at the bar at night.

But that was all right because it helped fill her time.

Sometimes she felt as if she was existing instead of living. But, try as she would, she couldn't come up with an answer to the problem except the one she'd been giving herself daily for the past month.

It'll pass.

Her question was…when?

CHAPTER EIGHTEEN

SINCE MIKE HAD made the feed store his second home and Gordy was hired on full-time for the rest of the summer to handle the warehouse, Jolie spent the month of July focused on rodeos, taking more days off than she probably should, given her need for a new barn roof. The rodeos gave her something to focus on, something positive that kept her from thinking about Dylan…or his job. She did enough of that during the night when she drifted off and no longer had iron control over her thoughts.

The dreams came, dark and vivid, and more than once she woke up reaching for Dylan, only to find an empty bed, which emphasized the shattering sense of loss the dreams brought to her.

She and Faith traveled together whenever possible, sharing the costs and talking about everything under the sun—even relationships, but that was a one-sided conversation because although she listened, she didn't contribute. Faith, of course, noticed, and Jolie was well aware, but the beauty of a close friend was that sometimes they let things like that lie. As Faith did. That allowed Jolie to continue to travel with her.

But after three weeks passed and despite refusing to talk about all the many things that her mind grabbed on to and tortured her with during the night, Jolie was beginning to wonder if she was ever going to settle. Ever going to feel normal again. She'd expected time to make things better, as it eventually had after her father had died. But time did not seem to be helping her issues with Dylan or his job. Breaking off with him wasn't even close to the trauma she felt after her dad's fatal heart attack, which left her wondering what the deal was. Why wasn't she feeling better? Was she pushing too much? Expecting too much?

Thinking too much?

Definitely the latter, but all the same…shouldn't something give?

The only positive was that she'd won enough money to cover her travel expenses and then some. She poured all of her energy and emotion into her runs and Jenabelle responded. They'd become unbeatable. At a price.

She and Faith went to dinner and drinks with a group of rodeo competitors in Havre after she'd won a particularly large purse, and for the first time in a long time, she felt a little like her old self. She didn't drink, because she was driving, but she laughed and danced and played a mean game of shuffleboard while wearing her opponent's hat. But even though she felt more lighthearted than she had in about a month, when Faith made a nod toward the door, Jolie handed the guy back his hat and gathered up her purse with no sense of regret.

"I didn't expect you to agree to leave so soon." And, indeed, there'd been many times in college when Faith would be ready to go home about the time Jolie was just warming up.

"I've changed," she said as they got into the truck. "Grown up, I guess."

"Or something is eating the hell out of you," Faith commented as she got into the passenger seat.

Or that. Jolie jammed the key in the ignition and they drove to the rodeo grounds, got into their sleeping bags and Jolie pretended to fall asleep because she didn't want to talk. Not even a little bit.

That night she came awake with a start, and even though she couldn't remember the dream, she knew it had to do with Dylan. Losing Dylan. It always did.

"You okay?"

"Yeah." Her standard answer. Of course she was okay. She was always okay. She'd survived one of life's biggest traumas and she was fine.

She rolled over in her bag, unable to settle after the disturbing dream.

She wasn't fine.

"I've got a lot on my mind," she finally said,

her voice low enough that if Faith had fallen back asleep, it probably wouldn't wake her.

"I've noticed."

"It's complicated." Faith shifted in her sleeping bag so she was facing Jolie, but she didn't say anything. She waited, just as Dylan had done, allowing Jolie to decide how much she wanted to spill. "It's got to do with Dylan and being afraid of his new job…being afraid of losing him."

"I thought you guys broke up."

"We did." Jolie's voice sounded small. "I'm still afraid of something happening to him."

"That's a reasonable fear, given his job."

"I care for him, Faith. And if something happens to him, then it's still going to tear me up, even if we aren't together. So why can't I just put on my big-girl panties and take this chance? Why am I so frozen up?"

"Have you talked to anyone about this?"

"You mean like a professional?"

"Or anyone? Are you just bottling this up? Taking the problem out and admiring it and then putting it away again?"

Jolie closed her eyes. "Maybe."

A long silence fell then Faith said, "You might want to do something about that."

"I might."

"You know that I'll listen any time you want to

talk." Jolie nodded even though Faith couldn't see her in the darkness. "No pressure."

"Thanks," Jolie said softly, feeling both relieved and self-conscious. She continued to lie on her back until her eyes drifted shut and the next thing she knew sunlight was filtering in through the gooseneck window and it was time to feed Jenabelle prior to starting the drive home.

She and Faith grabbed breakfast, laughed when they saw two of the guys they'd gone to dinner with slowly ambling toward the rodeo grounds, looking as if they'd just finished a very rough ride.

They kept the conversation light on the way home and when Jolie dropped Faith off in Dillon, she felt better. Stronger. And in need of a call to her mother. She had questions. Questions she'd never thought to ask. Questions she now needed answers to.

She waited until after she'd fed her animals and nuked a frozen dinner before settling in her chair and dialing her mother.

Anne answered on the first ring.

"Thank goodness one of my kids is checking in."

"We check in plenty," Jolie said with a smile. "How are you doing?"

"I'm well. As is Richard. What's up?"

Damn. This mother radar was something. Jolie found that it was just as hard to force the question out as she'd thought it would be, since it would no doubt cause her mother to ask deep, probing questions in return. So she danced around the issue a little.

"What made you decide to remarry?"

"I..." Jolie could almost see her mother's thoughtful frown as she ran through the possible reasons that Jolie might be asking this question. "There were a number of reasons."

"Were you in love?"

"Yes. Why?"

Jolie shrugged even though her mother couldn't see it. "People get married for a lot of reasons. Financial security. Companionship—"

"Love."

Jolie hated to admit it, but that wasn't the answer she wanted. "How did you...were you...able to take the chance again?"

There. The question was out and the silence that followed made Jolie's stomach tighten a little. "Chance? It wasn't like your father and I divorced."

"I know...but he died."

She heard her mother exhale softly into the phone. "What's going on, Jolie?"

"Nothing." The answer came so quickly that it sounded exactly like the lie that it was and thus perfectly represented her chosen strategy to deal with pain. Denial. "No. There's something. I'm having trouble getting over the fear of losing someone." There. She'd said it. And it was as hellish as she'd thought it would be saying the words out loud to her mother who was no doubt going to riddle her with questions.

Instead she got an, "Ah."

"I've never had this problem before."

"Are you sure?"

Jolie frowned. "Yes."

Another short silence then her mother said, "I think you have."

"How could I have when I've never felt this strongly about anyone before?"

Again she expected the "Who?" and instead got, "Why is this the first time?"

"I don't understand."

"After your dad died, you were the least reactive."

"Everyone grieves differently."

"That's what I told myself. But you were the baby. The one closest to Dave, the one who'd had the least amount of time with him."

Jolie blinked a little. "Yes."

"The other girls got angry at him for dying. They expressed."

"What did I do?" Because, honestly, she couldn't remember. That time in her life was oddly blank as far as memories went, except for that moment in the hospital when she'd gotten the news that her father wasn't walking out that door with them.

"Nothing. It scared me to death. You talked to

a grief counselor at school who told me that you'd grieve in your own time in your own way."

"I grieved." Her mother didn't reply and she said, "I think about him all the time."

"You didn't cry. You didn't let anything out. Sometimes you have to cry, Jolie. Sometimes you have to let yourself feel pain in order to get over it."

"I'm feeling pain," Jolie snapped. "Every single day."

"Feeling pain? Or focusing on the cause and avoiding the pain?"

"I don't know," Jolie said after a long pause. "I... need to think on this for a while."

"Promise me that this isn't the end of this matter. That you'll talk to me or your sisters. Or anyone."

"It's not the end, Mom. I fully plan to work through this." Because she couldn't continued living as she was now. "I need to go now. Think." Process.

"I love you," she said before hanging up the phone.

She'd grieved. She knew that she had... Hadn't she?

No, she hadn't gotten angry at her father for leaving her. And, no, she couldn't remember crying, but as the grief counselor had said, everyone grieves in their own way.

In their own time.

But when had her time been? She had a feeling

that it had either been in all the years between her father's death and now...or not at all. Because she now had this deep feeling that maybe she hadn't dealt with it. Maybe she'd shoved things down deep and left them there to fester.

AT SOME POINT Dylan was going to have to find his own place, but at the moment staying in Mike's guest room suited both of them. Mike had enough of a social life with his weekly poker game and the store that he didn't need Dylan there babysitting, but Dylan had a strong feeling that Mike thought he was taking care of him. So he stayed.

In the evenings when Dylan wasn't on shift they watched television and every now and again Mike would comment on Dylan's lack of social life. But he was very careful never to mention Jolie in conjunction with a social life. Mike knew something had happened between them. Something that had put Dylan in a distant mood that he had to fight to hide. Since it was ridiculously easy to put two and two together, Dylan said nothing about Jolie or a breakup and neither did Mike.

But that didn't stop Mike from studying him when he thought he wasn't looking, as if he was debating his next course of action. Dylan held his tongue, didn't tell his grandfather to stay out of it. If he did, then he was pretty certain Mike would get worried enough to actually try to interfere.

To preserve a feeling of normalcy in their lives, Dylan would ask about the store and Mike would answer in superficial terms. Then they would settle into their chairs and Dylan would wonder what the hell he was going to do about Jolie even though the inevitable conclusion was that there wasn't much he could do. She'd booted him out of her life and he couldn't exactly demand to be welcomed back in.

He did have a knack for choosing difficult women to love.

THE RAIN WAS causing havoc throughout the county and most of western Montana. The rivers were rising and a mudflow had damaged several houses built too close to a hillside denuded by a fire the previous summer. Dylan has spent a night helping people evacuate the area and keeping opportunists from coming in and looting the homes once they were abandoned.

Other than that, Dylan spent most of his patrol time on the roads near the rising river, gauging whether or not they needed to be closed and keeping an eye on the properties that would be most affected and most in need of emergency services. Some places were already sandbagging and as the rain continued, he was certain there'd be more.

"I'm worried about our place," Mike said when Dylan had told him that the Forty-nine Ranch was partially under water. "The creek is coming up fast."

And that it was. The usually placid Berry Creek that wound its way along the edge of town and then fed into the small lake near the center of the valley was lapping at the tops of its banks and flowing with alarming velocity. "Marion and Joe are going to start to fill sandbags tomorrow."

Dylan had wondered about the load of sand in the neighbors' driveway.

"I don't think the creek is going to prove that much of a threat."

"It's spilled over its banks before," Mike said and Dylan acknowledged that his grandfather would know better than he, who'd grown up on the opposite side of the valley.

"At least the store's okay."

"I have flood insurance for the store."

"It's not near a river," Dylan pointed out with a frown.

"Probably why the insurance was so cheap," Mike said, smiling a little. "Comprehensive package." He sighed and clicked off the television as Dylan got up and shrugged into his rain coat.

"You know," he said. "The rain was one reason I wasn't unhappy to leave Lanesburg."

"Into each life…" Mike stated.

"Yeah, yeah." Dylan felt as if he'd had enough rain of either kind for a while. He still missed Jolie too freaking much and there wasn't a lot he could do about it. She was scared of losing people she loved and he had no answers to comfort her. Just a frustrated knot in his gut whenever he thought about her, which was all the time.

He'd barely reached his SUV when a call came in that someone had tried to cross a flooded road and their car had been washed sideways into a tree. Cool. And he was certain that was just the beginning of his interesting day.

And so it was. He dealt with lost chickens, a couple of minor fender benders, two more aborted floodwater crossings and one long-ass argument with a citizen who thought that rising water gave him the right to park on his neighbor's lawn.

He ended up working a double shift due to various county-wide emergencies and came home exhausted. Jess Moody did him a favor and swung by the Lightning Creek to make certain everything was all right on that side of the valley. Jess reported back that all was well and that Jolie had come out of the house barefoot in the rain to see what he wanted.

"Did she look friendly?"

Jess gave him a look of male sympathy. "She looked...stressed. Probably worried about flooding."

Flooding, his ass. She'd been stressed about the possibility of having to deal with him.

When he got home, he found several half-filled sandbags near the garage. The pile of sand in Joe's driveway was gone and Dylan had to admit he was impressed that they'd managed to fill that many bags.

"Joe has more sand coming tomorrow," Mike said over coffee the next morning, which had arrived way too early. Dylan was due back on shift in an hour, and he planned to get as much caffeine into him as possible before he got into his truck.

"The creek is coming up higher than I thought it would," Dylan admitted.

"The last time it was this high I was in high school and this development was a cow pasture... an underwater cow pasture."

"You were right," Dylan said. He let out a long breath. "Can't wait to see what kind of craziness the floods bring out in our fellow man today."

But it turned out to be a fairly quiet day. He spent most of the day setting up hazard signs, assisting motorists that had to make detours and generally cruising the county. He was back at the station when his cell phone rang. Mike's number showed on the screen and he expected to be reminded to pick something up from the store when an unfamiliar voice said, "Dylan? Is that you?"

"Who's this?"

"J-Joe. Joe B-Bradford," the guy stuttered. "It's Mike. We have an ambulance coming."

"Ambulance?"

"Mike collapsed. Marion called the ambulance— wait. It just turned the corner."

"Is he conscious?" Dylan demanded as he pushed out the doors into the parking lot, his heart knocking against his ribs. "Joe! Answer me."

"I don't… I'm not sure. We were filling bags and he just keeled over. His eyes are closed…" Joe's voice became muffled as he called out, "Marion, wave so they see you."

Dylan jerked the truck door open. "I'll be there in ten minutes. Call me back when they transport."

Joe called Dylan back within a matter of minutes to tell him they were transporting. Dylan swung the SUV in a U and headed across town, arriving at the hospital just as his grandfather was being wheeled in through the emergency room doors. He'd seen his share of death and disaster, but Mike—he couldn't lose Mike. Not after he'd just moved home to spend more time with him.

A teary-eyed Marion Bradford came in through the double doors, her arms wrapped tightly around her middle as if she was cold.

"Are you all right?" Dylan asked, taking care to keep his tone patient even though he felt anything but patient.

"Yes. Fine. Mike was helping Joe fill sandbags and he collapsed."

"I know." Dylan shot a look toward the emergency room doors, then back at Marion. He put a comforting hand on her shoulder. "Where's Joe?"

"He went to talk to some Admissions people."

"I got this," he said. "You guys can go home. I really appreciate you helping him like this. I'll keep you posted."

"Please do that," Marion said as Joe came down the hall from Admissions. She stepped close to her husband who put an arm around her.

"Sorry this happened," Joe said. The man was pale. Shaken. "He insisted on helping."

"I know how he is," Dylan said. And if he survived this, he knew how he'd be in the future. A hell of a lot more careful.

If he survived this.

Dylan wasn't yet ready to face a world without his grandfather. He pushed through the door to the emergency area of the hospital and approached the desk, a grim look on his face.

THE PAST TWO weeks had not been easy for Jolie. Her mother had called twice and Jolie had been able to convince her that she was feeling better. That she was coming to terms with her issues, when really she had a feeling she was simply shoving them down deep again. If she wasn't, then she should have been able to call Dylan. Tell him she wanted to talk, to maybe see him again. She did want that, badly, but she wasn't making that call, which told her she was still too damned afraid to deal with losing him.

On the day of the Superior Rodeo, which she was traveling to alone, Jolie rose to a driving rain storm. She'd hooked up the trailer the night before and Jenabelle had had the good sense to hang out in the barn so she was relatively dry, but Jolie had a bad feeling about the rivulets of water running down the driveway.

She checked the weather and Gallatin was out of the storm path, which was swinging just south. She would not run Jenabelle in a slick arena and risk pulled tendons, but once she got the weather all-clear, she loaded her horse, put her lunch and her purse in the truck and headed down the road, windshield wipers doing their best to clear the sheets of water off the windshield.

Within an hour she'd driven out of the storm, but she could see it behind her, low, blue-gray clouds obliterating the horizon.

Jolie headed back early shortly after her run, loading up Jenabelle and hitting the road without waiting to hear how she placed. The Evans River was rising and there was talk of closing the road. The last thing she wanted was to be stranded, especially when she had hungry mouths waiting at home to be fed.

As she neared the Eagle Valley she simply hoped she'd make it home. Water lapped over the highway, closing one lane, but thankfully the state crews hadn't yet gotten there to shut the road. Half an hour later she rolled into her driveway and got out into a light rain. The storm was finally moving on and she hoped, truly hoped, that they'd seen the last of the rain for a while.

She unloaded Jenabelle and led her into the barn. Most of her horses were oblivious to the weather, but Jenabelle had always sought shelter during rain, so she was Jolie's barn princess. And even though it wasn't raining hard at the moment, she had a feeling there could be another deluge at any time.

After feeding and graining the mare and running fresh water for her, Jolie drew her hood up over her head and headed across the graveled drive.

Gus poked his head out of the dog house, then bounded across the sloppy yard to meet her. Jolie rubbed his damp head as she walked up the stairs, feeling ridiculously tired. The phone started ringing in the house and she hurried her steps. Only her mother called the landline and she didn't want Anne to worry. She'd made a mistake calling and tripping the mother-concern sensor, but at least she'd gotten some information to deal with.

She left the door open as she came inside, leaving wet tracks as she crossed the room. She picked up the phone, managed a breathy hello while the connection was still there, then nearly dropped the receiver when Dylan said her name.

"It's Mike," he said. "He's in the hospital having emergency surgery."

CHAPTER NINETEEN

JOLIE CLUTCHED THE phone as the nasty feeling of déjà vu swept over her. "Why?"

"Heart attack. He'd been helping the neighbors sandbag and had chest pains."

"I'll be right there." Jolie was already pulling keys out of her pocket.

"I don't think you can get there. The Evans River is across the road."

Then why are you calling me?

"I'll get there."

"Jolie… I called because you're a big part of Mike's life. Not so that you can risk your life getting to the hospital."

"I'll take the trestle road." And then she hung up. Moments later she'd unhitched her trailer and was in her truck.

She traveled across Dani and Gabe's place and followed the old county road almost fifteen miles to the trestle bridge that crossed high above the river. Even so, the water was roiling down below and Jolie half wondered if the ranch was going to be under water by the time she got back. At the moment she didn't care. She needed to get to Dylan and Mike. Before anything horrible happened.

I'm losing someone else...

Jolie shoved the thought out of her head and focused on driving. She had to get there. She had to at least have the chance to say goodbye, something she hadn't been able to do with her father.

As she left the county road and turned onto the almost-deserted highway leading into Eagle Valley she forced herself to relax her jaw before she cracked a couple of teeth. Finally she swung into the hospital parking lot and dashed across the ankle-deep puddles to the entrance.

Dylan was there, just inside the doors, his expression grim. He made no move to touch her and Jolie returned the favor even though she wanted to wrap her arms around him, assure him that she was there for him for as long as he needed her. "I was afraid you were going to get yourself into trouble."

"Me? Never." But the words sounded brittle and stressed.

"Mike's in the ICU."

Jolie knew the way to the waiting room, which hadn't changed much since she'd been there almost twenty years ago. Jolie stood awkwardly for a moment then sat on the edge of a paisley-cushioned sofa while Dylan sat opposite. His handsome face was pale beneath the growth of dark stubble that covered his cheeks and chin.

At that moment she would have given almost anything to prevent him from going through this again, because she knew all too well what this felt like. Her dad may have died two decades ago, but being here in this room, smelling those long-forgotten smells… She wrapped her arms around herself.

Finally, when she couldn't take the silence anymore, she said, "I've been here before."

"I know," Dylan said quietly.

"It kind of ended my world and I hope that doesn't happen to you."

"Me, too. At least not like this."

She understood his meaning. Everyone died. Loved ones had to deal, as Dylan had dealt with the lingering death of his father. But people shouldn't be ripped away from you when you least expected it.

And the next thing she knew she was moving, crossing the room and holding Dylan tight. She wasn't certain if she was comforting him or herself or both. She needed a connection. She needed to be connected to someone strong and steady and… there. Slowly, Dylan's arms closed around her and his hands moved over her back, up and down in a comforting motion as he held her against him. She pressed her check against his chest, squeezed her eyes shut and prayed for Mike.

She didn't how long they stood like that, but

she couldn't pull herself away. Finally she took a breath that made her body shake and he loosened his hold, pulling back so that he could look down into her face.

"No matter what happens," he said, "we have each other."

She opened her mouth but realized she had no idea what she was about to say so she closed it and mutely nodded. They did have each other. Here. Now. And she wasn't going to turn away from that comfort.

She cleared her throat and said, "I've really grown fond of Mike."

Dylan smiled a little, took her hand and led her to a chair. "Trust me, the feeling is mutual."

Great. That didn't make her want to cry or anything. Feeling her throat close, Jolie looked away as Dylan took the seat next to her. He laced his fingers through hers and set it on his hard thigh. And they sat. And sat.

Dylan's hold on her hand loosened but he didn't let go. Not even when he leaned his head back against the wall and fell sound asleep. He'd just come off a series of emergency shifts. She knew that from the call he'd made to Dispatch to fill them in on where he was and why. Two deputies stopped by to see him briefly, and shortly after they left, he fell asleep again.

Jolie stared at the wall, telling herself that she could do this. She could handle losing Mike.

No you can't.

She swallowed as tears spilled over and ran down her cheeks, but she made no move to wipe them away even as they ran down her neck and soaked into the edge of her shirt.

She closed her eyes but the silent tears continued.

"Jolie." Dylan's voice startled her.

"Sorry," she said, sitting straighter and wiping her cheeks with the backs of her hand. "I didn't realize you were awake."

"Why are you sorry?" He caught her hand in his, then reached to the side table and handed her tissues.

"All right, I'm not sorry," she admitted, "but… I think I'm losing it. Finally."

"Finally?"

She pulled in a shaky breath and focused on the opposite wall. "I talked to my mom about my dad's death."

It took Dylan a long moment to say, "Yeah?" Almost as if he was afraid that if he spoke, she'd clam up.

She felt like clamming up, but she'd started and now she'd finish. He deserved to know why she was the way she was.

She nodded because her throat felt thick. She

cleared it and said, "I didn't cry, I guess." She gave a small careless shrug. "Mom was afraid I hadn't grieved."

"Have you ever cried about it?"

She didn't look at him as she said, "People grieve in different ways."

"Agreed."

She pressed her lips together harder and stared down at the floor, feeling a little sick. "I think I was crying about it now. About him and Mike and...you."

"Me?"

"Don't ask me to analyze, but, yes. You."

"Come here." He took her hand and pulled her onto his lap, then he tucked her head so that it lay against his shoulder. He held her there.

Jolie didn't protest, because she realized that maybe he needed to hold her as much as she needed to be held. She was so damned tired of being abandoned.

DYLAN'S LEGS WERE going numb, but he didn't care. He shifted Jolie's weight slightly then pulled her back against him. He was glad she was there. People weren't meant to go through hard times alone and that was exactly what Jolie had done since the death of her father. And he was beginning to believe that she understood that now.

Finally.

They'd both lost a parent. But the difference between them, something he'd never appreciated, was that he *had* grieved. Hell, he'd grieved before he'd lost his father and after. It had sucked, but once it had been over, he'd moved forward.

"Sorry for the delay." The doctor all but burst into the room, startling Jolie, who jumped. Dylan stood, looking ready to face the worst.

"Double by-pass. He's resting comfortably, but he has a long road ahead of him."

Dylan felt the most amazing rush of gratitude as he stood staring at the guy who'd just saved his grandfather's life.

"He'll be all right?" Jolie asked cautiously.

"I think so, yes." He gestured at the sofa and Dylan and Jolie slowly sat as he took a seat on the chair opposite and discussed the surgery, emphasizing that it had been a close call, but that he fully expected Mike to pull through.

"You should go home," he said after answering all of Dylan's questions. "Get some sleep." When Dylan opened his mouth to speak, the doctor held up a hand. "If you want to stay, fine, but it won't help anyone. Be back here at nine and there's a good chance you'll be able to see him." The doctor nodded at Jolie. "Take him home. We'll call if there's any change at all. Your grandfather doesn't need you sleeping in a chair to prove that you love him."

"All right." Dylan took Jolie's hand and they walked to the nurses' station where he asked to be called if there was any change in his grandfather's condition.

It wasn't until the nurse said, "You bet, Dylan," that he realized he knew her. Three shifts and an emergency bypass had done a job on him. He patted the counter, feeling better about going home for a few hours.

"He made it," Jolie said in a quiet voice as they walked to where their vehicles were parked side by side.

"Thankfully."

Jolie stopped at her truck. He wanted nothing more than to ask her to come home with him, but one look at her face told him not to push matters, no matter how much he wanted to simply hold her.

"I expected the worst."

"The worst doesn't always happen," he said.

"Apparently." She looked away for a moment then when she met his eyes he once again saw the shimmer of tears. "I have to go home and feed. Check the water level."

"That's all right. I'll pass out as soon as I get home—unless my house is underwater." He waited until Jolie got into her truck and started the engine to start his own. He wanted her with him, but it wasn't time yet. She was still dealing, still figuring out how to grieve and how to take a chance.

He loved her, so he was going to give her the room she needed to figure it out.

CHAPTER TWENTY

MIKE HADN'T DIED.

Despite her certainty that he would, despite reliving the nightmare scenario she'd suffered through with her dad…Mike hadn't died.

Jolie was still working over the fact that the worst hadn't happened when she drove across the Staley property on her way back to the ranch. People you love could be snatched away in an instant, so therefore you had to be careful who you loved. How much you loved. That had been her mindset since she was ten years old.

Except the bad thing had only happened once to her. She loved her family, close friends, and hadn't lost them. In a way, she'd been blessed to have so many people to love.

And if Mike had died…would it have been easier to handle his passing had she never grown close to him?

Yes.

Would her life have been as rich?

No.

She wouldn't have given up getting to know him,

given up feeling as if she had a real grandfather for the first time in her life. It would have hurt like hell to lose him, but that was the trade-off for growing close and it was better to take a chance than to shut herself off due to fear.

And how long had it taken her to figure that out? Until she'd forced herself to actually think about the issues she had been ignoring.

It made her wonder how much more she had to learn. How much of the obvious was escaping her...and how she might clue in on that knowledge.

Jolie fed her animals, let Gus out of the house to do his business in the sodden yard, then let him back in to shake water all over the furniture. She barely noticed the canine shower as she headed for the stairs and bed. She fell into bed and even though she hadn't expected to sleep, she did. A deep, thankfully dreamless sleep that she woke from with a start.

Dylan needed her.

She needed him.

She reached for her phone and punched in his number, hoping she didn't wake him but sincerely doubting she would. He answered after the first ring.

"Where are you?"

"The hospital."

Her heartbeat stuttered. "Is everything—"

"Fine. I'm just waiting to see Mike."

She let out a breath. "Can I join you?"

There was the briefest of pauses before he simply said, "Yes."

DYLAN WAS IN the ICU when Jolie arrived and she waited for him in the same room where she'd sat the night before, certain that Mike was going to die. When Dylan came out of the ICU hall, she got to her feet and he smiled at her. An exhausted I-haven't-slept-in-days smile.

"He's doing okay," he said. "He recognized me. Squeezed my hand. I think he would have talked if there hadn't been a tube down his throat."

Jolie didn't want to think about Mike hooked up to tubes and monitors, but she was so glad to hear that he was making progress.

"Did you get any sleep last night?"

"Why do you ask?"

And that was her answer. "You look like hell." Or as close to it as he could come. No matter what, he looked good to Jolie.

"I didn't sleep," he confessed with a half smile.

"Do you want to go home? Try again now that you've seen Mike?"

He gave a slow nod then reached out to take her hand. "Yeah. I think I do."

Jolie walked with him as far as his truck, and when he went directly to the passenger side and opened the door, she got in without a word. He closed it, walked around to his door and joined her inside.

The drive to Mike's house was less than a mile, which he said had helped save his grandfather's life. As he pulled into the driveway, Jolie caught sight of the sandbags behind the house and the water creeping ever closer to the back fence.

Dylan didn't seem to notice or care. He met her at the hood, took her hand again and led her to the unlocked front door.

The interior of the house was pure Mike, only without him there. The news was still on and Speck was curled up in his chair. Dylan let the terrier out the back door and then came back in to pick up the remote and turn off the news.

"I left it on for her so that the house was as normal as it could be without Mike. She knows something's up."

"Are you going to be able to sleep?"

Dylan nodded and reached for her.

Jolie slid her arms around him, nuzzling his neck before bringing her lips up to his, kissing him deeply. He pulled her against him, kissing her back, helping her understand just how deeply he'd missed her.

He brought his forehead down to hers and she felt his breath fan over her cheeks as he said in a low voice that sent shivers through her, "I have missed you."

"Damn it, Dylan." She wrapped her arms tightly around his neck and hugged him tightly. "You make it so hard to live without you."

"Do you still want to do that?"

"No." The word came out so fast that Jolie half wondered if she'd really said it out loud.

But Dylan's reaction told her she had. He swung her up into his arms and headed down the hall to his bedroom.

Jolie needed him so badly, needed to let him know that she could be in this for the long haul. She wasn't miraculously better, but she was working on it. And she felt so right when she was with him. He did complete her, and if she lost him, she'd lose a part of herself, but that would happen whether they were together or not, because she realized now that she was never going to stop loving him.

Never. A very long time, but that was how she felt. Once they hit his room, they fell into his unmade bed, still half dressed. It didn't matter because this was not about long, slow, lovemaking. This was about reclaiming one another. Long and slow could come later.

Dylan managed to get his pants off and her pants off. Jolie gave up trying to help and just let him have his way with her, which he did. Afterward they fell asleep in a tangle of arms and legs. The last thing Jolie remembered was Dylan yanking a blanket up over them and then tucking her head under his chin. She'd breathed in his comforting scent and fallen asleep.

DYLAN WOKE WITH a start, disoriented in the semi-darkness, then slowly realized he was in his room at Mike's house, with Jolie in his arms. He stroked his hand over her hair. He'd find another job if the one he was in kept her from being able to commit to him. Sometimes you had to compromise, and he knew deep down that he'd get more satisfaction out of a life with Jolie than he was going to get out of law enforcement.

Damn, but he loved her. He pressed his lips to her temple, smiled as her eyes came open. "We should call about Mike," she said. "And then go visit him."

He reached for his shirt, feeling a sense of satisfaction that had eluded him for a long time. Jolie smiled at him as she slipped into her underwear; a tired smile with no hint of wariness or self-protection. His heart squeezed and he smiled back as she handed him his pants. He could spend every morning of his life like this, watching Jolie dress, having her hand him his pants, hopefully shed in the heat of the moment hours before. Yes. That was exactly what he wanted.

When they got to the hospital, they were greeted by the happy news that Mike's condition had improved significantly overnight.

"He'll be out of ICU before the end of the day," the attending nurse predicted.

Jolie squeezed Dylan's arm, but when he asked if she wanted to go into the ICU with him for a brief visit, she hung back. "Later. When Mike's feeling more himself." He frowned at her, wondering if her fears were kicking in, when she said, "Mike might not want to have me see him at his most vulnerable."

And she had a point. Mike was like that, and it touched him that Jolie understood. He squeezed her hand and went into Mike's room. When he came out, Jolie looked up from her phone and he gave her a thumbs-up. "You're right. He says he'll happily entertain visitors as soon as all the damned tubes are out of him and his hair is combed."

"I'm just glad he's all right," she said. But she didn't look at him and Dylan started to get an uneasy feeling. Too many times things had gotten out of hand because he and Jolie hadn't been up front with themselves or each other. He wasn't going to let that happen again.

They'd just stepped out onto the damp pavement when they turned to each other and said simultaneously, "I've been thinking—"

Instantly they both closed their mouths and then Dylan said, "You want to go first?"

"I'm looking into delayed grief counseling," she said simply. "I think I've sidestepped this matter for too long. My sisters handled matters differently than me, but that's okay."

"Totally okay," he agreed even though he had a hard time pushing the words past the lump in his throat. This was a big step. He reached out to take her hands and she laced her fingers through his.

"And you?" She lifted her chin and briefly he thought about losing himself in a long exploration of her lovely mouth.

"I won't work in law enforcement if it makes you unhappy."

She squeezed his hands but didn't jump on his offer as he'd expected. "I have this plan," she said slowly. "We take things one day at a time. We talk and love and deal. Even if I'm shaking in my boots, I'm not going to close you out."

"How could I pass up a deal like that?" He took her lips then and she melted into his kiss. When he finally raised his head as an elderly couple walked by, he said, "I'll be there for you. You be there for me. And you know what?"

She smiled against his mouth. "What?"

"I think we're going to make it."

And then he leaned in to kiss his cowgirl once more.

EPILOGUE

DYLAN SQUINTED OVER Jolie's shoulder at the computer screen. "I'm going to take your word for it that that's a kid."

"Wait." Jolie reached out and grabbed Dylan's hand before he got away and then pointed at the ultrasound photo of Dani's baby again. "See the nose? The little chin?" Her soon-to-be-born niece had the most adorable nose and chin.

"Oh, yeah," Dylan said. "I see now. Cute."

Jolie leaned back in her chair to smile up at him. "I can't wait to get my hands on her." Dylan gave a soft laugh and she tilted her head back farther, frowning at him. "What?"

He settled his hands on her shoulders, and bent to give her an upside-down kiss. "I kind of feel that way about you sometimes."

If it wasn't for the awkward position, Jolie would have pulled him in for a more serious kiss. As it was, she ran her hands up along the planes of his cheeks, gave him another quick kiss and then straightened in her chair as the video Skype call from Finn came in on her iPad.

"Hey, guys," he said once the connection was established, "have you finalized the plan yet?"

"Pretty much," Dylan said. "Are you sure they're going to let you out this time?" Finn's deployment had been extended from four months to six, and then, just as his six months were up, to an entire year. That had meant making adjustments at the store. Dylan had wanted to hire a manager, but instead Mike came back to work full time.

Finn laughed. "Twelve months is the max."

"Or so they tell you."

"Home in June. You can bank on it. So you're leaving for Colorado in early April... Jolie, are you sure you want to go with this guy?"

"What can I say? I'm smitten." Jolie smiled at the screen and reached up to run her hand over Dylan's arm as he stood behind her. She truly was smitten, but that didn't mean that the past few months were without their challenges. With the help of counseling, though, she'd learned strategies to deal with the fear, to stop expecting the worst and to enjoy the present. It was hellishly difficult at times, but Dylan was patient, and she was determined. And it wasn't as if he didn't have a few lessons to learn himself—like how to let go of a few words when things were bothering him. They were doing well together, and Jolie sometimes had a hard time believing she'd almost chosen a life alone over a life with Dylan.

"I won't be able to leave until May at the earliest," she said to Finn. "When Allie moves back." After sharing a few shots of Irish whiskey several nights ago, her older sister had agreed to babysit the ranch even though she hated the place. The next morning, Jolie had fully expected Allie to renege, but instead she'd murmured something about making peace and said she'd move home in May. Jolie didn't know what Allie was making peace with—the ranch or herself—but she didn't press. If her sister was willing to brave the ranch, then Jolie was going to Colorado with Dylan.

"So that leaves only one month or a month and a half, depending on my travel, et cetera, without you there calling the shots."

"Mike calls the shots as much as I do," Jolie said.

"Yeah. Strange how he was no help at all while I was managing the store and now he hangs out there full time." Finn made a comical face. "I must have been doing something wrong."

"You didn't have any doilies for sale," Dylan said.

"What?"

"Never mind," he replied on a laugh.

"Even though Mike is working full time now," Jolie said, "we don't want him to feel like he has to. He is pushing eighty, after all. We figure that if you're honestly going to be back in June—"

"Count on it."

"—We'll nix the idea of hiring an interim manager and instead just hire and train my replacement. I'll stay in the area until you get here."

"Sounds good," Finn said. He smiled a little.

"Homesick?" Jolie asked. Because there was something about him that she wasn't used to seeing. A touch of…loneliness, maybe? A hint of vulnerability in his expression instead of his usual full-on self confidence.

"Hard not to be. But all in all, I'm good. And I'm glad that not getting home until June doesn't screw things up too badly. Way to go, by the way," he said to Dylan, "getting accepted to that forensic biology program. I researched it. Looks like it's hard to get into."

"Studied my ass off."

Jolie could vouch for that. And she was also grateful that Dylan had managed to find a way to stay in law enforcement that didn't keep her awake at night.

The three of them talked for a few more minutes, then Finn had to sign off.

Jolie sighed and turned off the iPad. "I miss him."

"Me, too. But don't tell him."

She gave Dylan a serious look. "I don't know… he might need to hear that."

Dylan gave a small snort, but then he said, "Maybe so."

Jolie got up from her chair and crossed the room to where Dylan was shrugging into his heavy coat. It was February and still frigidly cold. "Maybe I'll come with you to see Mike."

She knew that Mike had wanted to discuss some ideas about the gift boutique, which he was preparing to take over during Jolie's absence. The gift section had grown and now covered almost half of the store, causing Mike to move some of the farm stock out to the warehouse to make room.

"I hope he plans to put in a lingerie section," Dylan said as he took Jolie's coat off the hook and held it for her.

"He has too many buddies hanging around as it is." But the store was definitely a friendlier place than it had been less than a year ago. Not quiet anymore. Jolie had to do a lot of her work in between snatches of conversation, but she liked it that way.

"Yep, geezer central," Dylan said as he opened the door. They stepped out into the frigid morning, only to stop at the edge of the porch. Jolie pointed at Dylan's truck.

"Flat tire."

"Looks like it."

"I could help you change that," she said, glancing up at him. "Or loan you money to buy new tires if you can't afford them."

He gave her a wry smile, obviously remembering saying those same words to her…just before he'd kissed her for the first time. "Or you could unhitch your truck from the horse trailer."

She shook her head. "I don't want to."

Their gazes locked for a moment before Dylan said, "It's too cold to change a tire. I say we abort mission until early afternoon. It is Sunday, after all."

"We can have Mike to dinner. Discuss matters then. I could put on a roast."

Dylan took Jolie into his arms, his breath warm on her face as he leaned in to touch his forehead against hers. "A roast in the oven. A long winter day…hmm. Whatever could we do to fill the time?"

Jolie raised her lips to his and smiled.

* * * * *